D1637908

SELECTED STORIES

books by the same author

Fiction
The Lipstick Circus
The Other McCoy
In A Dark Room With A Stranger
A Date With My Wife

Poetry
Spring's Witch
One Atom To Another
Body Parts

SELECTED STORIES

Brian McCabe

Argyll
publishing

First published in 2003 by
Argyll Publishing
Glendaruel
Argyll PA22 3AE
Scotland
www.skoobe.biz

The author has asserted his moral rights.

British Library Cataloguing-in-Publication Data.
A catalogue record for this book is available from
the British Library.

ISBN 1 902831 62 4

The short stories 'Shouting It Out', 'Losing It', 'The Host', 'Conversation Area One' and 'An Invisible Man' are from *A Date With My Wife* by Brian McCabe, first published in 2001 in Great Britain by Canongate Books Ltd, 14 High Street, Edinburgh EH1 1TE

 Scottish
Arts Council
The publisher acknowledges subsidy from the Scottish Arts Council towards the publication of this volume.

Origination: Cordfall Ltd, Glasgow

Printing: Mackays of Chatham Ltd

for Dilys, Sophie and Cleo

ACKNOWLEDGEMENTS

Acknowledgements and thanks are due to the editors and producers of the following publications and broadcasts: *Across the Water* (Argyll Publishing, 2000); *Best Short Stories* (Heinemann, 1992); *Breves* (Paris); *Damage Land* (Polygon); *Firebird 1* (Penguin); *The Glasgow Herald; The Glasgow Magazine; Identities* (Forlaget Futurum, Denmark); *I Can Sing, Dance, Rollerskate* (Harper Collins, 1988); *The Malahat Review* (Vancouver); *Marilynre varva* (Hungary); *Nerve; New Edinburgh Review; New Writing Scotland; The Panther Book of Scottish Short Stories; Pig Squealing* (A.S.L.S., 1992); *Product* (2000); *Radical Scotland; The Red Hog of Colima* (Harper Collins 1989); *Scotland Into the New Era* (Canongate, 2000); *Scotland on Sunday; The Scotsman; Scottish Short Stories* 1979,1980,1981,1982,1985 & 1993; *Sharp Edges; Shorts* (Polygon, 1998); *Shouting It Out* (Hodder & Stoughton, 1995); *Some Kind of Loving* (A.S.L.S., 1997); *Stand; Under Cover* (Mainstream); and for 'Shouting It Out', 'Losing It', 'The Host', 'Conversation Area One' and 'An Invisible Man' which are from *A Date With My Wife* (2001) to Canongate Books Ltd.

Several of these short stories have also been broadcast by BBC Radio 3, BBC Radio 4, BBC Radio Scotland and Radio Forth. 'Anima' was adapted for broadcast by BBC television. An earlier version of 'Conversation Area One' was adapted for the stage for the Traverse Theatre's series 'Sharp Shorts'. 'The Hunter of Dryburn' was adapted for the stage by the People's Theatre of Castlemilk. 'The Host' was adapted for film by Simon Hynd and was screened as part of the Edinburgh Film Festival 2003.

CONTENTS

Introduction

THERE ARE THREE questions I dread being asked after a reading. I dread them because almost always at least two of them are asked, and because although they are quite simple, even obvious questions, I have never been able to answer them to my own satisfaction, even if the questioners seem content with my answers.

I suppose the most frequently asked one is: where do you get your ideas for stories from? I sometimes feel like answering, as a character in one of my stories once did, 'What the hell does it matter where they come from, as long as they come?' I'm usually more polite, pointing out that in my experience, most stories don't begin from ideas – certainly not abstract ideas. Nor do they begin with a theme or a subject. When I wrote 'A Good Night's Sleep' I didn't sit down at my desk one day and say to myself, 'Right, let's write a story about the growing social problem of homelessness.' The story came from something much more concrete, as most stories do, in this case an actual encounter I'd had with someone who was homeless. So a story can begin from a snatch of overheard conversation, something witnessed, something experienced and then remembered, a place, a person, an object, something glimpsed from a window. . . This isn't to say that all stories are plucked directly from experience. In my experience, stories may draw things from experience – sometimes, but not always, personal experience – but always involve elements which are purely imaginative or fictional.

Even in stories firmly based on a memory of a personal experience, the very act of remembering is not as simple as we assume. We tend to think of our memories as accessible as snapshots in an album, books on a shelf, or videos we can simply take down and play, but memories don't come ready-made. We have to imaginatively recreate an experience as we remember it, so that fiction is already at work in the very act of remembering. Also, my memory is not particularly 'photographic' in the sense of being detailed, so when I come to write about an event I am remembering, I often have to make things up from the word go. Sometimes it is these invented elements and details which become crucial to the story and which transform the experience into fiction as opposed to a memoir.

I can think of numerous examples of this strange, complex process of things drawn from life and things made up mingling in my own stories. In 'The Lipstick Circus' I attempted to capture an experience I'd had as a very young boy, of being left alone in the house and feeling scared. Though based on a personal experience, and though I remembered certain details, I had to make up others in order to make the experience concrete enough for a reader to imagine. One of these details popped up during the first draft of the story. I had the father saying to the boy before he went out, 'Just watch the circus till your mother gets home.' Immediately I thought, why a circus? Why doesn't he just tell him to watch t.v.? But I've learnt to leave such things in during the first draft in case they go somewhere. It's almost as if my subconscious mind had slipped in that circus, as if it was saying to me: here's a circus if you want one, if you can use one. This detail did turn out to be crucial in the story: to counteract his fear, the boy uses his mother's make up to paint his face like a clown's, then ends up using the lipstick to draw a circus all over the walls of the house.

Similarly in 'Anima', though to begin with all I was trying to do was relate an experience I remembered – of feeling strangely upset about the idea of having to dress up for a fancy-dress party as a boy – in order to do this I had to invent things. Parquet-style linoleum might very well have been on the floor in the room where I sulked, I can't remember, but in any case that isn't why it's in the story. It's in the story because, as the boy is told by his sister, 'It was just like Mum to buy lino that pretended to be wood'. When I looked over the first draft, there were other such details which were basically examples of things trying to look like or impersonate other things, things pretending to be something else. Together, these details chimed in with what was happening in the story – the boy dressing up – and together, they made me think that here was a possibility of getting at something bigger than the trivial incident being related, to do with identity – how people define themselves and are defined by others. Half-way through that first draft, at the point where the boy's sister says she'd have to use make-up for his eyes, the story departed radically from the experience it was based on – my sister never dressed me up as a girl – and stepped fully into the realm of fiction, because by that point the story was making its own demands.

In other stories, in my experience, things move in the opposite direction: I begin with a premise which is completely fictional, one which seems to have floated into my mind from nowhere, and in developing this a fictional character begins to take shape, and a fictional event or action. . . In short, everything seems entirely fictional and removed from my own experience. Yet even such stories must be realised by drawing on life to some extent, and even such stories can lead to having to confront and relate an intensely personal moment from my own experience. This happened in the writing of 'An Invisible Man'. Unlike the main character, I have never attended a seminary or gone to confession, nor have I worked as a security guard in a department store. Yet what appeared to be a completely fictional affair led me to remember and write about my mother's death. I didn't see this coming at all as I was writing the story, until it was suddenly there in front of me, demanding to be addressed.

The second dreaded question is: 'Did that really happen?' My instinct is always to deny it, not for fear of litigation but because I know that what I've written is fiction, not history, certainly not fact. Yet in many stories, some of the events related did happen, and some of the people and places are people and places I've known. Some things in 'Shouting It Out', for example, are definitely drawn from my memories of childhood and of being a teenager. As a boy, I did go to the Saturday matinee at the local flea-pit, I did cheer and drum my feet with all the others, and I did see 'The Time Machine' and had nightmares about those 'Morlocks'. As a teenager, I did go to the same cinema with girlfriends, and although I don't remember shouting things out, I do remember this happening quite often. It was this idea which offered scope for fictional development – the notion of a teenager in a small town in Scotland taking it upon himself to be a kind of live film critic, poking fun at the romance and glamour and heroics of the movies. It gave me possibilities of exploring the question of how the media affect people's lives – in the story, the boy draws a distinction between two kinds of acting: the kind actors do in the movies and the kind he does himself with his girlfriend – and the 'shouting out' also offered a way to explore self-expression and how this is often discouraged and even suppressed. So it did really happen, but not the way I have written it in the story, because in the story I'm aiming at what Flannery O'Connor called 'fictional truth' rather than the literal truth, even supposing that such an objective version of the truth exists, which I doubt.

The third dreaded question is the one about influence. Norman MacCaig had a neat rejoinder – 'I prefer the word theft'. I've felt unwilling to cite my influences ever since I heard him say that, but of course influence does happen and sometimes it is important. However, it's always been a complicated issue for me. It's easy to reel off a few names of writers I have read and admired and even, as a young writer, tried to imitate, but that isn't necessarily telling the whole story, because at different periods in their development, writers come under different sorts of influence – not all of them necessarily good.

As a young writer I certainly came under the spell of some

great writers, and even learnt something from trying to write my own pastiche. With Chekhov, of course, this didn't work. I read and reread his short stories, and I realised they were great works, but they were impossible to imitate or parody. They appeared to have no discernible style, no linguistic quirks or flourishes to imitate. Later, I realised that what made them so great was something which is inimitable: his insight into human motivation and human relationships, which is something you have to acquire the hard way. Nevertheless, reading Chekhov made me see what a great thing the short story could be at its best, and so it made me want to write my own short stories.

Another kind of influence I have certainly felt, and which is definitely more like the kind MacCaig called 'theft', is something I believe all writers benefit from – simply learning practical things about the craft from reading other writers. I think there are so many writers I have learnt from in this way, but in terms of my short story writing, I have perhaps learnt most from Bernard Malamud. His stories taught me many things, but perhaps the most important thing was how to present a subjective point of view within an ostensibly neutral third-person narrative. I can see his influence in some stories quite clearly, though I was probably not aware of it at the time of their writing. 'A Good Night's Sleep' begins: 'Just as he was maybe beginning to fall asleep at last, George Lockhart, an insomniac, thought he heard something bumping softly against his door.' The character's point of view, his anxiety and frustration, are present in the texture of the narrative, and that is something I didn't know how to do until I read Malamud.

Those three questions are the ones I find most difficult

Selected Stories

to answer, but of course there are others. When it comes to more specific questions about the short story form, my answers are often just as convoluted, because I would hesitate to make any definitions of a form which encompasses a very diverse range of things and which is extremely versatile.

I've found that the short story form is often misunderstood, particularly in schools, by students but also by teachers. Sometimes it is completely misinterpreted as a peculiar branch of the essay, using the techniques of fiction but essentially a discourse in disguise, an illustrative way of presenting an argument and making a point. It is also sometimes discussed as if the different forms a story can take are entirely definable in technical terms. I've been asked more than once if a story has to have a twist in the tail. Many times I've been asked how I work out the plot for a short story, as if it is just a smaller version of a novel, when in reality most short stories don't have anything which could really be described as a plot. They have a narrative development – something happens, certainly – but 'plot' suggests a complex series of causally related events and in the short story there isn't room for that. Most stories I've enjoyed and admired as a reader are in fact fairly simple in that they tend to focus quite emphatically on one action, one event, one incident or even on something as small and fleeting as a moment in somebody's life.

I've always thought that the essential difference between the short story and the novel is not to do with length but approach. The novel is an accumulation of scenes, characters and events, whereas the art of the short story is the art of selection. It can be so selective that it ends before the 'action' has taken place, as in Hemingway's 'The Killers'. We know what must happen next, and we know what has gone before

– so in two brief scenes this short story suggests other scenes, and a whole society besides. At its best, this is what the short story does so well. By focusing intensely on something quite small, it suggests the lives of the characters beyond the reach of the story itself, and may even give a sense of the world beyond.

Brian McCabe
July 2003

Anima

'HURRY UP and make up yer mind,' said my father.

I went on staring at the dinette linoleum in silence. It wasn't yellow and it wasn't quite brown, but a sort of diarrhoea-colour in between. It was making me feel queasy, staring at it like this. I remembered my sister telling me that its pattern was called parquet and that it was just like Mum to buy lino that pretended to be wood. What had she meant by that? And what had she meant when she'd said that a dinette wasn't the same as a dining room? What was the difference? And why did we call it the dinette anyway? Nobody ate in here. Everybody ate in the living room, with the telly on and the fire. The only thing anyone ever did in the dinette was sulk. That was what it was for.

'Come *on*,' moaned my father, 'decide what to be and geez peace!'

What to be. How could I decide what to be? It had been

hard enough deciding to join the cubs. Now this: what to be? It was cold in the dinette, but I felt strangely hot inside – hot and shivery. I pretended to look out of the window at the garden, hoping my father would go away. Then I found myself looking out at it – at the weeds and the old gas cooker and the hut made of railway sleepers. It was getting dark, and the hut looked like a little animal cowering against the wall. I noticed the packet of seeds on the windowsill, picked it up and pretended to be reading the instructions. I'd bought the seeds weeks ago and my father had promised to show me how to plant them. He'd forgotten about it though. I heard him making the most of a yawn – why did he always do that? – and I knew that he was fed up with this father-and-son routine in the dinette. He wanted to be in the living room, watching the news and arguing with the Prime Minister. Instead he'd been sent in to talk to me because I was sulking.

I glanced up at him as he yawned again. He stood just inside the door, slouched forwards like a tired old bull. His belly hung over the sagging waistband of his trousers and his braces hung loose. His trousers and shirt were unbuttoned and his vest was a greyish colour. I started shaking the packet to hear the seeds. It sounded like they were whispering to each other in there.

'Come *on*. Ah've no got aa night!'

I looked at his face to see if the anger in his voice was real or just pretend. He stuck his head forward and glowered down at me in mockery, mimicking my own frown. Why wasn't he young, like other people's dads, and interested in hunting and fishing and camping and cars? Or at least in gardening? Why did my dad have to be old and tired, with thick tufts of hair sticking out of his nostrils and his ears? All he was interested in was politics and horse-racing and going to the pub. Why had my mother sent him in to talk to me? How could he help me to decide what to be? He didn't even know what it was like to be a cub.

'D'ye want to be a frogman, or what?'

That was typical. How could I be a frogman? I didn't have flippers. I didn't have goggles. Maybe the snorkel and the rubber suit could be pretended, but that wasn't enough.

I shook my head, stared at the lino and felt ill.

'How about an astronaut, then?' This time I shook my head even before I let myself begin to imagine the impossible silver suit, the helmet with the window in the front. . . 'Why no? Like Yuri Gagarin, eh?'

'How can I?' I heard my own voice whine, 'Astronauts've got silver suits and. . . and I don't!'

'Oh ho ho,' said my father, 'oh ho ho ho ho. . . ' He went on ho-hoing until it sounded almost like a real laugh, then he coughed and spluttered. 'Well, ye'll just have to be a wee monkey then, eh? That shouldnae be too hard!'

That was typical as well. All he could do was mock. He didn't understand how important it all was. As he opened the door to go out, he turned and made a face as if he was going to say something serious, which meant he was going to make a joke.

'Ach well,' he said, 'ye'll just have to go as yersel. One of the lumpen proletariat.'

What did that mean? What was the proletariat, and what had happened to its leg? As my father shut the door I threw the packet of seeds on the floor. It burst open and tiny seeds scattered over the linoleum. They looked like insects running away when their stone has been lifted. I saw my own shadow on the floor and suddenly it looked like a giant's shadow and the hot-shivery feeling swept over me again. No I wasn't going to be ill. If I admitted feeling ill, they wouldn't let me go at all.

I crossed the room and looked at myself in the mirror above the sideboard. Maybe I could be a pirate? But no, too many of the others would go as pirates, and the pirates would have eye-patches and cutlasses and bright, spotted neckerchiefs. My pirate would have a soot-blackened face and an old headscarf round his neck and that would be it. Too much like a real pirate, maybe. Or a cowboy? But no, somehow that was too obvious. I needed to think of something better to be, something original.

'What a fuss to make about a party,' said my sister as she came into the room. She came straight towards me then stood with her arms folded, staring at me. 'Right,' she said, 'you'll never get anywhere or be anybody if you can't even decide what to go as to a stupid fancy-dress party at the cubs. Turn round.'

I obeyed slowly, then stared at her elbows. This meant that I could avoid her eyes, which were too honest to look at for long without feeling guilty, and her breasts, which were too much a source of fascination and confusion.

'A pirate,' she said. I mumbled something about cutlasses and earrings. 'Chinaman,' she stated. I hesitated. Was it possible to be a Chinaman?

'But how could I make my eyes like a Chinaman's?' I whined, but my sister was already grasping me by both shoulders and turning me this way and that, looking me up and down, as if she could somehow tell whether or not I had the makings of a half-decent Chinaman in me.

'I'd have to use a curtain for the robe,' said my sister, 'a lampshade for your hat and. . . make-up for the eyes. . . '

Suddenly she stopped turning me and held me still and I felt the queasy feeling again – as if I'd jumped off a spinning roundabout. 'I know what you should be!' She took a step back and clapped her hands.

'What?' I said, beginning to feel wary.

'A girl.'

A girl! Was she out of her mind?

I opened my mouth to speak, but my sister got there first.

'You can wear one of my old skirts. The pink one with the zip at the back. . . We'll have to get you some stockings and high heels – I'll teach you how to walk in them, it isn't easy – and that blouse, that cream one with the frill at the neck. . .'

I searched her eyes – *The pink one with the zip at the back!* – for some sign that she was joking – Stockings? High-heels? – but there was nothing – *That cream one with the frill at the neck!* – except her wide-eyed, unflinching stare. Could she be as shocked by the idea as I was? *A girl!* My sister was out of her mind.

'They wanted a girl anyway.' She took another kirby-grip from between her teeth and pressed it into place above my ear. Her voice sounded strange because of the kirby-grips, like a ventriloquist's.

'What d'you mean, wanted a girl?'

'Instead of a boy, that's all.'

I stared into the mirror. She had stopped being me a long time ago, this creature with the thick coating of coloured grease on her cheeks, the bright red lips and darkened eyebrows. She wasn't me, but she was. Every time I spoke, her lips moved.

'Who?' I said, watching the bright lips moving in the mirror. *Who?* they seemed to be saying.

'Mum and dad,' said my sister, taking another kirby-grip from her mouth. She pressed it into place and added, 'I wish I had hair as thick as yours.'

'How d'you mean, wanted a girl instead of a boy?'

'Once they knew she was pregnant,' said my sister, standing back a moment to admire her handiwork in the mirror. 'I heard them saying they wanted it to be a girl. I wanted a sister too, you know. You came as a disappointment, I can tell you.'

'I couldn't choose what to be, could I?' I whined, staring in fascination at the bright lips. Had I said that, or had she? Was it my mouth, or hers?

'And you still can't,' said my sister. She picked up the hairbrush and began to brush the hair at the back of my head upwards. It felt all wrong.

'But that's different! Nobody can decide what to be before they get born!' I said doubtfully. But what if people could? What if I had, and what if I'd decided wrong?

'I'm not saying anybody can. All I'm saying is you weren't what we were expecting. You weren't expected at all, if you want to know the truth. You were a mistake.'

'What do you mean, *a mistake?*' The girl in the mirror raised her eyebrows, pouted her lips. And then the strangest thing happened – another mistake, maybe – and the girl in the mirror smiled at me. What did *she* have to smile about?'

'I don't know what you're smiling at,' said my sister, 'it's true. Mum got pregnant by accident.'

By accident? I had heard different versions of how It could happen, but this was a new one on me. By accident.

'How do you mean?'

'I'm your big sister, amn't I? I know things you don't, that's all. Mum and dad came up to me and they said, "How would you like to have a little sister?" Of course, I told them we couldn't afford it, but. . .'

'But why did they have one. . . I mean *me*. . . if you told them we. . . I mean *you*. . . couldn't afford. . . *it?*' My confusion as to what to call myself was made worse by the sight in the mirror. *It* seemed to be the best description.

'Because by that time it was *too late*. By that time she was pregnant, the damage was done.' She scattered the remaining kirby-grips on the glass-top of the dressing-table. The sound they made reminded me of the seeds scattering on the dinette linoleum and the hot, shivery feeling swept over me again. . . I imagined being a tiny insect when its stone is lifted, running away from the giant's shadow. . . Was I going to faint? (*Faint? Wasn't that what girls were supposed to do?*)

'What's the matter,' said my sister, 'don't you like it? Just the eyes to do now. Hold wide open.' She tilted my head back and began to attack my eyes with a little, evil-smelling, black brush. 'I wish I had lashes as long as yours,' she added.

'Wait till they see! Wait till they see!' My sister clapped her hands in delight and hurried out of the room. I heard her squeaks of laughter as she ran downstairs. It sounded like a balloon being rubbed the wrong way. I wanted to run and hide, but it was difficult enough to stand still in my sister's high-heels. I hobbled around the room, then something drew me back to the mirror. I sat down and looked into it the way I'd seen my mother and my sister doing it, tilting my face this way and that, touching my hair here and there with a hand.

The girl in the mirror smiled, but I felt more like screaming. (*Screaming? But wasn't that what girls. . . ?*) Now that I was alone with her, she seemed more monstrous than before. She swayed towards me and smiled her eerie smile again. And suddenly I knew what was so strange about her smile. It wasn't just that I didn't feel like smiling myself, though that was strange enough. No, the girl in the mirror was smiling at herself, pleased to see herself at last, smiling in triumph.

I stood up quickly and kicked off the shoes and ripped at the blouse, then the ill-feeling rose up inside me again as if I'd jumped off a roundabout. Then the world lurched and spun and all I knew was that I had to run, run because the stone had been lifted, run from the giant's shadow on the lino pretending to be wood in the dinette that wasn't the same thing as a dining room, run into the hallway where they stood at the top of the stairs, my mother with her hand flying up to her mouth letting out a whoop, my father forgetting to slouch because of what he saw with his eyes looking blue and amazed, run past them to the bathroom and the sink where I could let it all come up, hearing my father's rumbling laughter and my mother's whoops behind me and my sister's squeaking giggles like balloons, balloons with faces painted on them at the party, faces with faces painted on them at the party, faces of frogmen and astronauts and cowboys and pirates at the party, cakes and lemonade and sweets and games of musical chairs and blind-man's-buff and. . . I felt the cool hand on my burning forehead and I knew that I would never go now.

The Lipstick Circus

HE FELT IT THERE behind him when he turned round to
pick up the poker from the fender, felt its hot breath on his
neck. He turned round again as quick as he could, then stood
holding the heavy poker in both hands. Maybe the poker
would stop it coming out, maybe it would be scared of the
poker. And standing with your back to the fire meant it
couldn't get behind you the way it always tried to. But maybe
it could come out of the fireplace, out of the fire. He could
hear the fire behind him, hear the hiss of the coal. It sounded
like his father breathing, and sometimes it made another noise
that sounded like his father coughing. And when the fire
sparked, that was like his father when he was angry. Maybe it
couldn't come out of the fire, but it could come out of anything
else. It could come out of the television now that the circus
was finished and there was nothing on. It could come out of
the settee or the chair. Maybe it could even come out of the

china cabinet with the glass doors and the little golden key, where his mother kept the things he couldn't touch. There were cups and saucers with pink flowers on them and she kept them in the china cabinet because they came from China and they were too good. He didn't think it could come out of good things with pink flowers on them, but maybe it could even although it was bad.

It only tried to come out when he was on his own in the house like this. His mother wasn't back from her work yet, and his father had gone out to put on a horse. His father slept in the morning just now because he was on the night shift at the pit, and sometimes when he woke up he went out to put on a horse. He had cried for his father to take him out with him, but his father had told him to sit there and watch the circus until his mother came home. But now the circus was finished, and his mother wasn't home. He could feel the fire getting hotter on his back, and the poker felt heavier and heavier. Maybe it could come out of that picture of the blue lady on the wall above the sideboard, out of her big black eyes. And grab the poker out of his hands and. . . Suddenly the fire made a loud cracking noise, like the lion tamer's whip, and something sharp burned into the back of his leg. It was only a spark of hot coal, but he started crying anyway because it gave him a fright and he dropped the poker on the floor. He kept his back to the fire so that it couldn't slip behind him, and soon he couldn't feel the hurt place on his leg. But he kept on crying because maybe it would hear the crying and not come out, maybe it was scared of crying. But maybe it wasn't, maybe it would still come out. Out of the blue lady's eyes or maybe even out of the poker. Maybe it would even come out of the mirror with the wooden frame and the stand.

He looked over to where the mirror stood, on top of the sideboard under the picture of the blue lady. But he didn't think it could come out of the mirror, because he had heard his mother saying it was a good mirror. It might not come out of the good mirror or the good cups with the pink flowers, but it might come out of the poker. He stopped the crying a bit and looked at the poker on the floor. It had a long brass handle, and a thicker part at the end that was black from the fire. It might come out of that. He jumped over the poker and ran to the settee and jumped up on to the cushions. He turned round as quick as he could, in case it had come out of the clock on the mantelpiece and was behind him. It wasn't so he stopped crying now and ran round the settee to the big table. He pulled out one of the chairs by its back legs and dragged it over to the sideboard. One leg got caught in the carpet, and he saw the brown lino underneath. Could it come out of the cracks in the lino? He climbed up on the chair and stood looking into the good mirror.

At least now if it came out and tried to get behind him, he would see it coming. He could see nearly the whole room behind his own head, even the door into the hall. He would see it coming up behind him now unless it was smaller than him or the same size, but he knew it couldn't be. He knew that if it did come out it would be bigger than him, much bigger. He looked at his own face in the mirror. The tears were still dripping down his cheeks. He started crying again to see what it looked like, then watched himself wipe off the tears with his sleeve. Now his face was covered in snotters and dirty marks from the tears. It looked a bit like a clown's face and it made him start laughing. Maybe if he laughed it wouldn't come out at all, maybe it was scared of laughter. He laughed a bit more and watched the face in the mirror changing. The eyes were like little slits, and the cheeks swelled out like balloons, and he could see the teeth and the gums and even the tonsils. He laughed as long as he could, but after a while it started to sound like crying. It even started to hurt a bit, but that didn't matter if it stopped it coming out. Suddenly the chair wobbled and he had to grab the curved wooden back of it to stop himself falling. He didn't fall, but when he looked at the face in the mirror again it wasn't laughing anymore. And it didn't look much like a clown's face really.

On the sideboard in front of the good mirror, there were some of the things he couldn't touch. There was the golden case with the little round mirror in it and the pink powder his mother put on her face. And the pencils she drew her eyebrows on with, and the pink hairbrush with hundreds of black spikes like a hedgehog. Between the spikes there were some of his mother's dark hairs. He picked up the brush and started tugging out the hairs. When he had a clump of the hairs, he put the brush down and tried to mix the hairs with his own, but when he moved his head they fell to the floor. He picked up the brush again and started brushing his own hair up at the front and the sides. It was the kind of hair that stood up when you brushed at it that way, so he kept brushing it until it was all standing up on end like a clown's. This was even funnier to look at than the dirty marks, so he laughed for a long time at the face in the mirror, laughed until he could feel his eyes squeezing out two more tears. Then he picked up the little golden case he couldn't touch and opened it up and laughed even more because it looked even funnier in the little round mirror. He picked out the round piece of cloth with the powder on it and started dabbing his face with it the way he had seen his mother putting it on. He picked up some of the powder in his fingers. It felt soft, even softer than sand at the seaside, and it smelled like sweets. He took some on the tip of his tongue and tasted it, then coughed and spat the way his father sometimes did, because the powder tasted horrible. He shook the rest of it into his hair, then put the round piece of cloth back into the case and closed it.

It was good to touch the things he couldn't touch, the good things like this other golden case with the bright red lipstick inside. He pulled it open, then turned the part at the bottom that made the lipstick come out. He played at making it come out and then go in again. It was sort of like a tortoise sticking its head out and then pulling it in again. Then he saw an envelope on the sideboard with the red mark of his mother's mouth on it. It was very red, but parts of it weren't. There were thin white lines through the lips, and the two lips didn't join up at the sides. He started painting the lipstick on his own lips, looking at the mouth in the mirror. He smudged it over his chin, because he couldn't help laughing at his own face with the bright red lips and sticking-up, powdery hair. When he had finished painting his mouth, he pressed his lips against the back of the envelope, he saw the mark of his own mouth under his mother's. It looked very different. The lips were thin, and they did join up at the sides.

He threw away the envelope and looked at the face in the mirror. Now he really did look like a clown in the circus. He painted his nose with the lipstick too, then drew big black lines round his eyes with one of the pencils. There was a little jar of white cream, so he rubbed some of this on his face. He put some more lipstick on the lips, so that they bent up at the sides like a clown's He made a funny face at the mirror and laughed again. Maybe now that he looked like a clown it wouldn't come out, maybe it was scared of clowns. But maybe it wasn't, maybe it could still come out. Out of the blue lady's big black eyes, then pull the chair from under him the way clowns did in the circus, but this time not to make anybody laugh. He looked up at the picture of the blue lady. Her face was painted too, but not like a clown's and she was smiling but not the way a clown smiled. Her mouth sort of twisted up at one side and she had a purple flower in her hair. He had never seen anybody with a blue face, or a smile like that, or eyes as big and black as that, and he had never seen a purple flower. Maybe it could come out the purple flower.

He put the lipstick into his pocket and climbed down off the chair, then he pushed the chair back to where it was at the table. He tried to lift it and hold it up the way the lion tamer did in the circus, but it was too heavy. He could feel it there behind him again, feel its big black eyes. He turned round quick as he could. It wasn't there, but maybe it was faster than him, maybe it had jumped behind his back when he'd turned. He wedged himself between the table and the sideboard and stood with his back against the wall. He looked at everything in the room – the television, the fire, the settee, everything. Everything looked like it was going to move, and when he saw the clock out of the corner of his eye it seemed to jump off the mantelpiece towards him. When he looked at it again, it had jumped back on to the mantelpiece. Then the mirror did the same. Everything started jumping towards him, then jumping back into place. He made a dash for the settee and fell flat on the carpet behind it. He rolled over on his back and stared up at the lightbulb hanging from the ceiling.

Selected Stories

Maybe it could come out of the light, maybe its eyes were like lightbulbs so that when you looked at them you had to look away. He rolled over on his belly again and crawled along behind the settee feeling the lipstick in his pocket pressing against his leg. He crawled to the end of the settee and felt the draught coming under the door from the hall. Suddenly the fire made a loud cracking noise and he jumped to his feet and ran to the door. He could feel it there behind him as his fingers tightened round the handle and pulled and pulled.

It was cool in the hall and quiet without the fire. He sat on the bottom step of the stairs and looked at the coats hanging from the hooks. One of his father's jackets was lying on the floor, under a hook with nothing on it. His father was always throwing his jacket at the hooks and missing, and when if fell to the floor he didn't seem to mind. But his mother minded, because she was always picking up the jacket and hanging it on a hook. And sometimes she looked through the pockets of the jacket before she hung it up, and took out the little blue slips of paper with the horses on them. Then she took off her glasses and held them away from her eyes, to make the writing on the blue slips look bigger. And once when she had done this she had told him his father was a clown. He thought about this again, but still didn't understand it. How could his father be a clown? He didn't look like one. The only time he looked a bit like a clown was when he came home with his face black with the coal dust in the morning. But most mornings he washed it off before he came home. But if he came home with the coal dust on and smiled, then his lips looked very red – a bit like a clown's but not really. There was another thing his mother said that he didn't understand. She said she hoped he didn't grow up like his father. What did it mean? Did she want him to stay the same size? And how could he be like his father? Could he have blue slips with horses on them in his pockets, and the kind of comics his father had, with pictures in them that made his mother curse and spit? And how could he ever yawn the way his father yawned, as if he were playing a trombone?

He jumped off the stairs and started dancing round the hall and pretending to play a trombone. He imagined the big golden trombone sliding out and in, then he remembered the lipstick and stopped. He took it out of his pocket, opened it and dabbed some of it on his finger. Then he started dancing round the hall again like a clown in the circus, laughing and playing a trombone. If he laughed loud enough maybe it wouldn't come out, maybe it would stay in the living room. When he was tired he stopped and sat down on the bottom step again. He looked up the stairs to see if it was on the landing, but it wasn't so he moved up to a higher step. Then he looked round and saw all the red spots on the walls of the hall where his fingers had touched. He took the lipstick out again and played at making it come out and then go in again like a tortoise. Then he put his hand flat against the wall and drew round it the way his mother had shown him how to on a bit of paper. When he took his hand away there was a big red hand on the wall, bigger than his, nearly as big as his father's hand. He did the same with his other hand, then joined up the two hands with a lot of red lines. He drew in the body and legs and the head. He drew a pointed hat on the head, then a round red nose and little slits for eyes. When he had done the clown, he moved up a step and started doing a chair, and when he had done the chair he moved up again and started doing the horses.

When the lipstick circus was nearly finished he was right up in the upstairs hall, then he heard the door opening and closing and his mother coming into the hall. He heard her shouting his name and dropping her message bag on the floor. Then he heard her screaming. The scream scared him, but not as much as being in the house on his own with it coming up behind him. He started crying a bit, because somehow he knew that she wasn't going to like the lipstick circus. She ran up the stairs, but stopped on the landing halfway up and said some of the things she said about his father's comics. Then she ran up to the top of the stairs and screamed again when she saw him. She stood there with a hand over her mouth, staring at him. It scared him to see her staring like that. He had never seen her eyes looking so big and black behind her glasses. Suddenly the lipstick flew out of his hand and his feet were off the ground. She was pulling him into the air by his arm, and her hand was smacking his legs. It hurt and made him cry, but not the way he cried when he could feel it in the room with him making the clock jump off the mantelpiece. When he was dropped to the floor, he went on crying as hard as he could, but after a while he stopped because he could hear her crying too. She was sitting on the top step crying, with the fingers of both hands in between her eyes and her glasses. He had seen her crying before, but not sitting on the top step still with her coat on. He saw the golden case with the lipstick in it and he reached for it. Maybe if he gave it back to her she would stop.

He turned over one of the big coloured pages in his new book, then picked the red crayon out of the box and started to do a clown. It was strange how they shouted at you and hit you for making a lipstick circus, then bought you a big book with coloured pages and a box of crayons and told you do another circus. A crayon circus on a page of the book was good. When he had shown the first one to his father, he had put away his comic and looked at it and had given him a shilling and said he was a future Leonardo. He didn't ask his father what a Leonardo was, but it sounded like the name of a clown. And his mother had given him a biscuit and had said it was a good circus too. But a lipstick circus was bad, like the thing he felt when there was nobody else in the house. It could come out of anything. Out of the sideboard or the settee, out of the blue lady's eyes or the poker, the china cabinet or the mirror. Maybe it could even come out of him.

Interference

HELLO.

I'm outside the door again, I can talk to you. You're not like anybody else in the class. You're from Mars, you're a Martian. That's why I can talk to you, because I'm not like anybody else in the class either. Sometimes you sit beside me, don't you, when you want to ask me a question. Like what is one take away one on Earth. And I tell you the answer, nothing. Or when you want to tell me an answer, you materialise like in *Star Trek*. Just for a thousandth billionth of a second, then vanish back to Mars. Nobody sees you except me, nobody wants to. Nobody knows how to see you except me. See the dust in the air up there, where the sun's coming through the window? You're like the dust in the air – nobody notices you except me. And your voice is like interference on the radio – nobody wants to hear it except me. You can see everything. You can see through people, and you can see through walls.

You've got X-ray eyes, that's why. I wish I had X-ray eyes. Cheerio.

Hello, come in, are you receiving me? My situation is an emergency, I have lost all contact with the *Enterprise*. I've been put outside the door again, because of my abominable behaviour. I am on the brink of disaster, and the teacher says my behaviour is detrior-hating. It means getting worse. This is an SOS. I will continue until I am rescued or until my Oxygen runs out. I'll tell you what's been happening to me down here on the planet Earth. Last week she made me sit next to the Brains. The Brains is an Earthling, species girl. With red hair, freckles and specs. I had to sit next to the Brains. She was always too hot, always wheezing and sweating, and her legs were always sticking to the seat. It was the noise I hated, the noise her legs made when she unstuck them from the seat. And she wouldn't let me use her red pencil to colour in the sea. I know the sea's supposed to be blue *on Earth*, but on Mars it's red isn't it? And when I took that red pencil of hers out of her hand and broke it, the Brains started crying. It wasn't real crying, it was a special Earthling kind of crying. Sometimes they cry outside but not inside, it's more like watering eyes. And in the middle of the crying she said something about my clothes, because I've got a patch on the back of my trousers. I can't see it, but everybody else in the class can. So I got her back in the playground. I went into the Earthling boys' toilets and I drew up some of the water, the pisswater in the pan, into my new fountain pen. Then I squirted it into her face, and it went all over her specs. And that's how I got into trouble last week, all because I got a new fountain pen. I don't like using these Earthling fountain

Selected Stories

pens much, they make too much of a fucking mess. Yesterday the teacher held my writing up for everybody in the class to look at, so they wouldn't write like me. See I don't write like anybody else, see I write in a kind of Martian. Nobody can read it except me and you, it's in code that's why. See all the mistakes are secret for something, every blot is a secret wee message. But I got into the worst trouble for squirting piss into the Brain's face. The Mad Ringmaster got me, watch out for the Mad Ringmaster. Over and out, cheerio.

Hello, come in Mars, do you read me? My position is getting more abominable by the minute. So now she makes me sit on my own, so you can sit in the seat next to me. But you shouldn't materialise like that in the class, when everybody's listening to the radio. Everybody was listening to Rhyme Time, a programme of verse for Earthling children. Everybody thought it was interference, but I knew it was your voice talking to me. And I got put outside the door again because of you. Don't try and deny it, I did. It was that poem called Spring, all about the cuckoo and whatnot. And you were asking me what that poem is all about, because there aren't any birds on Mars, are there? And I saw you out of the corner of my eye, except you kept disappearing and coming back. Materialising. When I throw a stone in a puddle, everything disappears and comes back. That's what you're like, a reflection. So I had to tell you what Spring is and what a cuckoo is, so I started making the noise a cuckoo makes. *Kookoo, kookoo* – it sounds like its name. She thought I was taking the piss out of the programme, but I wasn't. I was talking to you in the secret wee voice, the one I'm talking in now. Billy Hope, she said, this is a classroom not a home for mental defectors.

Go and stand outside the door, come back in when the poetry programme's finished. But it isn't finished , because when I put my ear on the door I can hear it going on. She said it was bad enough having to put up with interference on the radio, without having to toler-hate interference from me.

I can't stand poetry anyway, it's worse than long division.

Maybe the next time you materialise, I'll use sign language to talk to you. I could scratch my nose for Hello. Everybody would think I was just scratching my nose. But then, if I had an itchy nose and I scratched it maybe you'd think I was saying Hello. And if I stuck my tongue out for Cheerio, I'd get put outside the door every time I said Cheerio to you because of my abominable behaviour. I just put my ear to the door again and I heard the interference. It was you asking me another question, asking me what behaviour means. The answer is, I don't know.

I'll tell you something though: my mother's got a screw loose, has yours?

Over and out cheerio.

Hello come in are you receiving me? Listen. You were born on the same day as I was, at exactly the same time, except *you* were born on Mars. You go to a primary school on Mars, and you're in 4B like me. You're last in the class on Mars, except it's great to be last on Mars. It's like being top of the class on Earth. And 4B is better than 4A there, isn't it, because everything's a reflection the other way round. You're like me the other way round. If I looked at you too much, I'd go cross-eyed like the Brains. See when you materialise in the seat that's empty, the seat next to mine – that's you doing your homework, isn't it? It's like Nature Study, except you're doing it on us, the Earthlings. I bet you're glad you're not at a school on Earth. With a voice that sounds like interference, you'd get put outside the door every day. I wish you'd take me to your Martian school with you. Then I'd be top of the class – I mean last – and then *I'd* be called the Brains. We'd be first – I mean last – equal. In the Martian primary school we'd be put outside the door for coming top of the class, because that's what the prize is on Mars. On Earth it isn't a prize, nobody likes it down here. And when you're put outside the door on Mars, you can travel through space and time. You can visit other planets. Down here there's nothing to do outside the door, there's nothing to look at. Nothing except the door. And the corridor, and the clock. Earthling clocks tell the time, every tick means a second. A second, a second, a second. No it doesn't say it, it tells the time with its hands. No it doesn't really have hands, it's a machine. No it doesn't have a mind, Earthling machines don't have minds. But cuckoo clocks say the time, they say koo-koo, koo-koo. But birds are different from clocks. See the birds on the windowsill up there, I think they're pecking for crumbs. You should do some Nature Study on them, because there aren't any birds on Mars, are there?

Or maybe there are some birds on Mars, but they look more like cuckoo clocks. But the clocks on Mars fly round and chirp the time.

Anyway I'll tell you what to say about Earthling birds. Put down that they've got wings, beaks, claws, feathers, tails and they fly. They eat worms and crumbs, and sometimes they migrate. It means go to Africa. See when they peck for crumbs they look like they're bowing, like actors at the end of a pantomime. Maybe they're all going to migrate to Mars, so they're bowing to say cheerio. I don't know if birds've got minds, but they must have minds to tell each other it's time to migrate. But they don't look like they've got minds, because they move about in wee jerks like clockwork. Clocks don't have minds. But birds fly, clocks don't. But aeroplanes and spaceships fly and they don't have any minds. Tell you what, put down that you don't know if birds've got minds or not, but put down that the Earthling people do have minds in their heads. Now I bet you're wondering what all this has to do with Nature Study. I bet you're saying to yourself, this sounds more like Martian poetry to me. But have you ever thought that the two subjects might be quite the very same? Especially when there's interference on the radio, the two subjects sort of blur with each other, don't they?

I'll tell you something else. My mother put her head in the gas oven and she lost her mind.

Cheerio.

Listen, if you don't pay attention, you'll never learn anything. Materialise *this instant*. That's better. If I catch you disappearing again or tuning out, I'm just going to have to make an example of you. Is that clear? Or else I will put you outside the door of your capsule and you will die. You're not stupid, you're lazy. You're a lazy, little *Martian*. You have opened my eyes more than once today and your behaviour is getting deterior-hating. Right, we're going to do some more Martian Nature Study. Any more interference out of you and I will give you long division or even poetry. Put this down:

Nature Study On The Planet Earth.

Under that, put this:

On the Planet Earth, everything is the other way
round. Most Earthling birds don't have names and
their mothers forget what to call them when they
go to visit the nest. The only ones with names are
crows, thrushes, blackbirds, sparrows, eagles,
vultures and cuckoos. The rest are just called birds.
Cuckoos are off their heads, they lay their eggs in
the gas oven. My mother can be heard on the first
day of Spring, and the noise she makes sounds like
her name. She is cuckoo so she lives in a home, her
home in another bird's nest. Behaviour means
going to Africa, or else abominable long division. A
bird is a flying machine, with a screw loose. Cuckoo
clocks have minds, as well as hands, faces and
speckled breasts. At dawn you can hear them tick,
and every tick means deterior-hating. Spring is the
time of the year when you scratch your nose for
Hello and stick out you tongue for Cheerio. Poetry
is people pecking for crumbs without minds in
their heads. After a pantomime, the actors migrate.
I am dust in the air, I am a reflection. I am the only
Earthling with a mind, and the mind is interference
from another programme. Koo-koo, koo-koo.
Cheerio.

Come in again, do you read me, hello. See that door along
there, behind that there's a wee room where you go to get
smallpox jags. On the wall there's this chart with letters on it.
On the top line the letters are huge, you'd have to be blind
not to read them. But they get tinier and tinier as they go
down, till you can hardly even see them. See this chart is for

testing Earthling eyes. If you don't get far enough down, you get specs. I got specs, but I smashed them on the way to school because everybody was calling me four-eyes.

Nobody's going to call me four-eyes.

The Brains wears specs, but nobody calls her four-eyes. Probably because she's always had specs, so nobody notices them. If you ask me, the Brains was probably *born* with specs on. And I had to get specs because of you. Don't try and deny it. It's with looking at you when you materialise, now my eyes are the wrong way round. I wish I had X-ray eyes, then I could see into all the classrooms, I could see what's happening inside them. The last time I was in that room with the chart on the wall, I got drops in my eyes that made me see a bit like a Martian. People didn't have edges, they sort of merged with each other. Blurred. But once when I was taken into that room, this nurse in a white coat gave me a book to look at. It was a Martian book. Every page was covered all over with hundreds of coloured dots. They looked like they were moving, sort of swarming like wasps. It was like what you see when you look at the sun too long, hundreds of coloured dots moving round. Then this nurse asked me if I could make out the shape or the number. Everybody in the class had to do it, it was a test. I'll tell you this, I was great at it. I was better than anybody else in 4B. If we got tests in making out the shape of the number instead of tests in long division, I'd be getting fucking gold stars every time.

The trouble is we didn't get marks for it. It was to find out if we were colourblind. I'm not colourblind, I *know* the sea's supposed to be blue. It isn't though is it, when you look at it up close? When my mother used to take me to the seaside, the sea always looked more sort of like the colour of piss.

And what about the Black Sea, what colour's that? I should ask the teacher: please Miss, is the Black Sea black? Miss, is the Read Sea red? What colour's the Dead Sea, Miss? Is that the one he walked on, or is that the one he parted? Miss how could he part a *sea?* Keep the noise down, it was a miracle. A miracle is something that doesn't happen every day on Earth. On Mars, everything that happens is called a miracle.

She put her head in the Dead Sea. Her mind got walked on, and parted. Keep the noise down, it was a miracle, miracle, miracle.

Over and out.

Hello. See it might be okay getting put outside the door, except everybody sees the patch. That's the deterior thing about it. See everybody knows I've got a patch in the back of my trousers, but when I'm walking out to the door everybody sees it at once. And I can feel this evil thing behind me, like an actor in a pantomime. Maybe people are like birds and don't have minds in their heads, maybe I'm the only Earthling with a mind. Everything else is a pantomime: everything everybody says, everything everybody does. Maybe even the Mad Ringmaster hasn't got a mind. I don't know if he has got a mind, because I can't be him. I've got to be me. But I know I've got a mind, but everything else could be a sort of colourblind pantomime. Like the Brains crying outside but not inside when I broke her fucking coloured pencil and squirted the piss on her specs. And the way my mother used to cry when she was losing her mind. She still does when I go to see her, but it's just like watering eyes. The tears drip out of her eyes like when a tap needs a new washer. She lost her mind, that's why. When you lose your mind on Earth, you go into a home for mental defectors. I've still got a mind, so I'm not going to be going into a home.

Hello mind, take me to Mars.

On Mars, everybody has a mind and you can *see it*. It looks like a page in that colourblind book. You look at all the swarming dots, you don't know what it is, then you make out the shape or the number. And that's what they're thinking, that's the thought. On Earth, people have to use words. They have to talk to each other, or write letters to each other, or phone each other up. If you want to talk to a lot of people at once, you have to be a teacher. Either that or you have to be on the radio or the t.v. Then you can talk to hundreds of people at once. Like the weatherman who was on before that Rhyme Time programme, except there was a lot of interference. Well, he was probably talking to about a million people at once. That's what I'm going to be when I grow up. I'm going to be the weatherman.

Cheerio.

Hello, come in, are you receiving me. In a few minutes there will be Clock Talk, a programme of verse for cuckoos. Before that we have a weather report from Mars.

This is the Martian weather forecast. Tonight it is
going to rain smallpox. The air will be full of
interference, and the sea will be going on fire later
on. Don't part it or walk on it, and don't go out
without getting your jags. Tomorrow morning, the
sun is going to be a shape or a number. If you can't
make it out, you're colourblind. The clouds are
going to start off huge and get tinier and tinier as

Selected Stories

they go down. If you can't read them, you'll get specs. There will be a lot of abominable behaviour later on, so don't get put outside the door. There will be no gold stars for anybody this week, or the next. Instead the sky is going to be covered in mistakes and blots. In the North, and South, and East, and West, there will be some scattered showers. You're bound to get drops in your eyes. The planet is changing shape. Watch out for meteors. Cheerio.

But if other people have minds, there isn't much point in talking to them, is there? Not even to one of them. Maybe you should score out the bit about Earthling people having minds, and put down that some do and some don't. And she doesn't talk to anybody else except herself. See she lost her mind, then went into a home, and now she's got two minds. And one mind talks to the other mind, I think. But I wonder if the other mind can hear it. Maybe it's more like interference. But what I can't understand is how one mind take away one mind equals two minds.

Over and out.

Hello this is an SOS. My Oxygen supply is running low and I have made no contact with the *Enterprise*. Beam me up before it's too late.

See down there over that balcony, that's the Assembly Hall. It means prayers. You put your hands together and you say, *Our Father Which Art in Heaven, Hallo'ed Be Thy Name.* Then the Mad Ringmaster stands up and everybody else sits down and listens. He makes a speech about the school. If you've squirted piss on somebody's specs, he reads out your name and you have to report to his study along the corridor there. Or if something's happened in the school, the Mad Ringmaster announces it. Like when one boy died, he announced it so that everybody would know. He said, *Today there is a shadow among us.* He's like you that boy, dematerialised. Nobody can see him. See he fell from a tree, and the blood ran over his brain. His soul went to Heaven, and his mind is a shadow among us. On Mars you probably have a different kind of assembly. You probably just sit in a big circle holding hands, passing messages to each other through your fingertips. Because hundreds of Martians can get together and think *one* thought, because you can sort of merge, can't you? Blur with each other.

I wish I was an alien being. Maybe the next time you materialise, if you touch me we'll maybe merge.

So I had to report to his study. I told everybody about it in the playground, I was the centre of attention. Attention is what you pay for somebody talking to you. It's like buying something with money, you have to pay it to hear what they say. I told them all your name for him, the Mad Ringmaster, but everybody just said his name's Williams. You call him that because that's sort of what he looks like, with his big black gown and curly moustache. And his belt instead of a whip. And I told everybody what he said to me in his study, when he was giving me the belt. You'd better start crying. See, he wanted me to cry on the outside, the way Brains did, the way my mother does. Like an actor in a pantomime. Then he could make an example of me. He could take me back into the class crying and then I'd be an example.

I am an example. But what am I an example of? I'm an

example of *you*, the other way round.

But if the Mad Ringmaster ever gets me again, I'm definitely going to go to Mars. He'll have to announce it at assembly, *There is a shadow*. . . no not a shadow. . . *there is a reflection among us. He got put outside the door, and the blood ran over his brain.* I wish you would exterminate the Mad Ringmaster, make him a shadow among us. Put him in a box and bury him, bury him in the Dead Sea. It's wrong to hope somebody dies, except on Mars. What's wrong here on Earth is right on Mars, or at least it's not wrong. Because not wrong isn't the same as right always is it? Like when you get a test, and you don't know some of the answers. So you don't put anything down, you just leave them blank. Well you're not wrong, are you? But you're not right either, or they'd give you a couple of marks for leaving it blank, but they don't except on Mars.

You know something, if they gave her a test she wouldn't be able to answer any of the questions. She'd get nothing out of a hundred. *Here comes the Mad Ringmaster.*

I'm inside the class again, I can't talk to you. He got me again, for getting put outside the door. He wanted me to cry on the outside again, to make me an example. But I didn't, I cried inside. My hands are on fire, they're Martian's hands. Touch my fingertips, touch. Send messages through my fire. Don't ask me any more questions, blur with me. My hands are full of a thousand stings, so are yours. It feels like a swarm of wasps, a thousand stings. You can feel the message, so can I. It's sore, that's the message. The teacher's reading a poem called Spring from a book. Pay attention, pay attention. Cheerio.

'Billy Hope, stop blowing on your hands. I'm going to read the first verse again, the one you missed because of interference. Perhaps you can tell us what it means, Billy. Listen to the words carefully:

> Pretty creatures which people the sky
> Are thousandfold this day,
> Feathered choristers, they that sing
> The livelong day away.

'Now, Billy, I want you. . .'

I am an alien being and I people the thousandfold sky.

'I want *you* to tell the class. . . what the feathered choristers are.'

My mother put her head in the sky and her mind flew away.

'Birds.'

The Full Moon

'WHAT IS IT?' asked the American lady. Unwittingly, she had voiced my thoughts – I was looking at her extravagant hairstyle and thinking exactly that: what *is* it? It looked like esparto grass trying to look like ice cream. But the enigma she was talking about was something of mine – a decoration I'd been making for the Halloween party in Ward One. I'd become so engrossed in the simple pleasure of making something that I'd scarcely noticed the visiting party. Besides, I had been working in the Therapy Unit for over a year and I'd come to regard the many visiting parties as something of an annoyance. I tended to ignore these processions of cheerful strangers – at times they made me think of sightseeing tourists – and get on with what I was doing while the psychiatrists showed them round. The Halloween decoration had been coming along nicely. I'd cut out a large disc shape from a sheet of card. One side I'd painted black, the other I'd adorned with golden paper, cut to size. To the bright side I'd added, with glue and glitter, the image of a smiling face. Then I'd attached a long line of thread, so that it could be suspended from the ceiling of Ward One.

'It's the full moon,' I said.

She picked up the moon by its thread, then held it out at arm's length the better to appreciate it – and avoid the glue.

'My, it's gorgeous,' she said.

This was praise, but it was praise from a woman with a frightening hairstyle, wearing a lime-green twin-set. Pinned to her lapel there was a rectangular identity badge, and under the name I made out words which told me that she had come from the Psychology Department of an illegible university. She turned to one of her colleagues, a young man in a brown velvet suit, also sporting a badge.

'Ain't it cute?' she said to him. In the vicinity of his nose there grew a sparse moustache, which resembled the dirty marks often left by elastoplasts. His vague brown eyes tried to focus on my makeshift planet. Dangling from the Twin-set's finger on its thread, it revolved of its own accord. . . now the dark side, now the bright.

'Yeah,' he said, 'what is it?' From the tone of his voice it was clear that he had been looking at people and their little achievements all day.

'It's the *moon!*' cooed the Twin-set. She gave me a slow, sly wink which made me think of a television programme I had once seen, to do with the habits of lizards.

'Mmm,' said Moustache, 'quite a moon. You gonna put that gold stuff on this side too?' He was pointing to the side I'd painted black. My moon did a quick about-turn, as if to invalidate the question.

'That's the dark side,' I said. Twin-set gave out a short squeak of delight.

'Did you hear that?' she whispered excitedly. 'He says that's the *dark* side. . . ain't that adorable?'

I noticed that my status had changed, somewhere along the line, from the second to the third person singular. She gave me a benign smile, and as she laid my cardboard satellite on the table, she enunciated her praise volubly, as if she thought I might be deaf.

'It's a bee-oo-tiful moon!' she said.

I was beginning to wonder why so much was being made of what was, after all, only a decoration, when I felt the lady's hand gently patting the crown of my head. I felt a curious tingling all over my scalp, which then ran down the back of my neck and swarmed up and down my spine – a sensation I would normally associate with moments of acute embarrassment, anger, pleasure, or seeing ghosts. I was forced to realise it – *they thought I was one of the patients*.

It was the first time I had been taken for a *bona-fide* mental defective, and for an instant I caught a glimpse of what it was to be treated as such and I panicked. I stood up abruptly, causing the chair I'd been sitting on to crash to the floor behind me. Immediately, Johnny threw his paintbrush to the floor and ran out of the room, slamming the door as he went. Johnny was a patient with many eccentricities, personality disorders, ontological anxieties or call them what you will, and sometimes he would take a loud noise or sudden movement to be an insult, directly aimed at his person. It had happened many times before, and I knew that he would run back to Ward One, then the nurses would calm him down and send him back to Therapy.

Moustache and Twin-set exchanged a meaningful glance, then I felt a hand on my shoulder.

'Sit down,' said Moustache, 'it's all right.' He righted my chair and pushed it into the backs of my legs. I looked around for another member of staff, but they had all gone into the Crafts Department with the other members of the visiting party.

'He's a bit jumpy,' said Twin-set, 'I think we should leave him alone.'

'We gotta be getting *along*,' said Moustache, unsure of how much of the message was getting through to me.

I raised my hand to detain them. I needed to explain. It was easy. All I had to say was, 'Actually, I'm not a patient at all; I'm a member of staff.' I might add, just for good measure, that I was in reality a Philosophy Graduate, working here in the Therapy Unit as a preventative expedient against unemployment. In my confusion I was able to utter three words. All three were monosyllabic, and I said them without much conviction,

'I. . . work. . . here,' I said.

'Sure you do,' said Moustache, 'siddown.'

'You should do some more work on that moon,' said Twin-set, 'I don't think it should have a dark side.'

She picked up the full moon and turned it over, so that it lay with the dark side up. Unaccountably, I did nothing to demonstrate my status as a sane, rational *employee*, but chose instead to reverse her action. I turned the moon over again, so that it lay with the bright side up. In its smiling golden face I saw my own features loom and distort.

'I figure he wants to keep one side of it black,' said Moustache.

I looked at his face, then Twin-set's, then his again. Both wore placatory smiles, but in their eyes I could read the vexation. It was as if I were a creature of a different species, one which might inhabit the dark side of the moon. I could not help myself – in a spasm of silent laughter, I sank weakly into the seat. I went on shuddering with laughter while, behind my back, they discussed me. What did I *have*? They spoke of Autism, Paranoia, Chronic Schizophrenia for all the world as if these were ailments people *had*, like measles! I wanted to correct them, I wanted to suggest that these were modes of being, that schizophrenia is something a person *is* . . . but I was giggling like a maniac and, after all, irrational laughter could be the symptom of anything. But now my IQ was the moot point. Was I low-grade, or high-grade?

'I don't know,' whispered Twin-set, 'but I'd sure like to look at his case notes. Did you see the way he looked at us just then? He's weird.' My diagnosis had come: weird. A terminal case of weirdness.

'Mmm,' said Moustache, 'it makes me wonder what's going on inside his head. You know, I'm sure some of these people are in touch with things which are uh. . . inaccessible to us, except maybe in dreams. . . '

As my fit of laughter subsided, I noticed that Billy, sitting at the far end of the room, was sniggering into his hand. All the other patients – apart from Johnny, of course – had continued with their work in an orderly, methodical way, but Billy had been observing the whole episode and now he was sniggering conspicuously. The sight made me shudder slightly, because Billy had forgotten how to snigger – he was a patient who seldom spoke, or did anything at all of his own volition. He waited until he was told what to do, then he made his gesture of obedience. His apathy was almost impenetrable. He slouched in his seat, appeared to stare into space for hours, and often his mouth hung open. He looked always disconsolate, bored. I watched with growing fascination as he made some pretence of looking at his drawing, while his features contorted into this unaccustomed thing which looked like pain but wasn't. It was laughter. I had known him for over a year and it was the first time I had seen him laugh.

'That moon's amazing,' said Twin-set to Moustache. They were making for the door into the Crafts Department. 'You know that old wives' tale about how the full moon affects them?'

'Oh sure, I've heard about that.' Moustache gave a little laugh.

'Well, you wouldn't *believe* what one of the nurses in the wards was telling me today. . . '

They waved their little bye-byes to me and closed the door behind them. My sanity was restored. On Billy's face there lingered an unmistakable smirk. Then less than a smirk, then nothing. I watched as his lower lip sagged, until his mouth hung open. He resumed his drawing, but his pencil scarcely touched the paper.

When I rang up Ward One, a nurse told me that Johnny had arrived in an agitated state.

'He said something about the full moon,' she said, 'but it isn't full just now, is it?'

'No, I'd been *making* a moon, out of card, and gold paper. It's a decoration, you see, for the Halloween party in your ward.'

She made a small, noncommittal noise.

'It's difficult to explain what happened,' I said. 'Is Johnny ready to come back over yet?'

'Oh, he's alright now. Mind you, some people say it does affect them.'

I mumbled something ungrammatical about people fearing madness more than death, then told her to send Johnny back to Therapy when he was ready.

I sat down at the table where I had been working. I turned the moon over and looked at the side I'd painted black. Perhaps it shouldn't have a dark side? I picked it up by its thread and held it out at arm's length. It turned, slowly. . . now the bright side, now the dark. Billy looked up from his drawing, but his pencil went on whispering against the paper.

'Hey Billy,' I said, 'ain't it cute?'

'Yeah,' he said quietly, 'what is it?'

Norman and the Man

NORMAN IS DRAWING a circle, and the man is watching him. It's a big circle, it wants to involve the whole page. Ominous, thinks the man. The way they grow, spreading like circles in water. Norman's mind is dark, wide water – who knows what's living in there? Standing over Norman, watching the line coil slowly around to meet itself, the man is mesmerised. It's as if, in a hopeless gesture, the man has thrown an idea into the darkness. And now he can stand back and watch, watch the disturbance it makes: one by one, and with a great deal of care he makes circle after circle. It has become Norman's work, his calling. They are only circles, thinks the man. Or not-quite-circles: each one is a little different.

The man has another idea. He goes away and comes back with a small round mirror. He gives the mirror to Norman. Norman grips it with both hands, looks at it. He reacts as a dog or a cat might react on seeing its own reflection: curious for a moment, troubled perhaps, then bored. But unlike a dog or a cat, Norman throws the mirror to the floor. By the time the man has picked up all the pieces, Norman has forgotten all about the mirror – he's getting his circle to touch, his empty circle. What was the man hoping for, some sign of recognition? It could be that at last, when he's done so many circles, Norman will look into one of them and recognise something there: his own reflection. In the meantime it's hard work for Norman, getting that line to bend, getting the circle to touch. Soon the man won't have a size of paper to contain it, this voluminous shape of Norman's. Then the man may have another idea: give Norman a piece of chalk, let him chalk his circle on the floor. Or outside, around the Therapy Unit, around the hospital and all its grounds, then around the city, the country. . . Ominous, thinks the man. Norman's circle could surround the world. Then everyone would have to live and die inside Norman's circle. . . but he's torn the paper again.

> *Start again, Norman, again. Hard work, making*
> *the circle. Let's do it one more time. Tea-time soon,*
> *biscuit.*

And with sticky-tape the man fixes a clean sheet of paper to the table, so that this time it won't be torn. And with one hand flat on the table, and with his face an inch from the page, Norman begins again: time after time, it's endless. The man walks around the room, looking at the pictures being done by all the others. All the others like Norman, but not quite: each case is a little different, as is each picture: that landscape with its mammoth black sun; the vermilion Christ on his cross; dark, unnamable beasts grazing in a violet pasture; one small Matisse of unlikely flowers; a self-portrait with lidless eyes. Everyone is doing a picture except the man. The man is the only one who can stand back and watch. Perhaps at one time the man could do pictures too, but now it seems that he can't. And perhaps that is why he is here: to show the others how to do what he can no longer do. He sits on a desk by the window, looking out at the hospital grounds: mosaic of yellows, reds and browns. Winter soon, thinks the man, then Spring.

> *Start again, Norman, again. We want to get here, here. Here's where the circle begins, and here's where it ends. No short cuts, or it won't be a circle. A circle, Norman, a circle. Or else the moon won't be full.*

Now the man is reading a report, a report about Norman. It says that he is twenty-five, mental age question mark. It says that he was admitted on a certain day more than twenty-four years ago. It says brain damage, severe motor difficulties. It says physiotherapy recommended, protective clothing and footwear. When he puts away the report, the man looks at Norman's clothes: a leather headguard, like a boxer's; elasticated trousers, grey; shoes with thick, wide soles which turn up at the toes. Walking is hard work for Norman, and very often he fails. Every step, thinks the man, must be deliberated. And for every action the effort must be grotesque. Norman's movements, thinks the man, so laboured, so wooden. . . they are more like guesses at motion. As if he is somewhere far above his body, too far above that crude puppet to know with any certainty which wire moves which jointed limb. Norman must jerk the wire and hope that the head will nod, that the hand is raised, that the foot will find the floor. That those dangling hands will parody a human gesture. Every day he walks from his ward to here, the place where he makes his circles. The man helps him off with his coat, because Norman can't do buttons.

At last, Norman has finished: his slow, slow circle is complete. Now he'll get his tea in the blue plastic cup with the lid – it's the kind of cup infants use. It's his, he knows it's his.

> *Tea-time Norman, biscuit. Hard work, Norman,*
> *hard work. Now, look at the circle: it's the moon,*
> *Norman, the moon. Is it good?*
> *Norman opens his mouth and utters: AAAH!*
> *It means yes, it is good. The circle has a certain*
> *AAAH. And when Norman has finished his tea, and*
> *when Norman has eaten his biscuit, he lets the cup*
> *fall to the floor and he rests: head down, his cheek*
> *on the table, one arm dangling loose by his side,*
> *with his legs splayed apart, with his twisted feet. . .*
> *Like a puppet, thinks the man, when the man who*
> *pulls the wires is away.*
> *Tomorrow a clean sheet of paper, and another*
> *circle by Norman. Does he get bored with it, day*
> *after day, making circle after circle? Yes he gets*
> *bored, and the man gets bored: wishing the day*
> *were done, the season over, the year. Winter soon,*
> *then Spring.*

Selected Stories

He can stand at the window and watch it: like a brief, accidental mark on a blank page, there is a tiny figure against the snow. It moves, it grows. Such excruciating progress it makes, the man wonders why it doesn't give up. He sees it falling and getting up again, resuming the pilgrimage. The gait is like a metronome, thinks the man, head swerving wildly to right and to left. When he loses the rhythm he falls, then the page looks blank. Perhaps this time he'll stay down, but no.

The snow on the path has been compressed by many feet, and even the man must tread carefully. When Norman sees the man he stops, one foot in the air, and raises a hand to greet him. The foot comes down missing the ground, and Norman throws both arms up in consternation. He falls, it is the only thing he does quickly, flat on his back. The man covers his mouth with his hand, laughing because he can't help laughing, as at a fallen clown. And even as he approaches, even as he extends his hand to him and hears his animal cry of outrage, and even when he sees that the clown's mouth is not a smile after all but a deep stripe of despair, even then the man can't help. . . But everything is reversed and it is the man who bellows his outrage, the man who is being laughed at, the man who has slipped and fallen on his back, and now who is the clown with the mouth of despair? And after a moment Norman and the man are both laughing at each other. If someone were to pass by now, what would they see but two grown men sitting down in the snow, laughing at each other?

Okay Norman, it was the moon but today it's going to be the sun. No sun in the sky, Norman,

Norman and the Man   61

until you put one there. Today, a clean sheet of
paper.

But as the man tries to help him to his feet, Norman resists. He shakes his head from side to side. He doesn't want to get up, apparently. Apparently he wants to sit there in the snow. Then, reaching out as if to retrieve something he has lost, Norman begins to dig up the snow with the fingers of one hand. Where he furrows it up, the black of the path begins to show through.

Get up, Norman, get up.

But now the black begins to grow into a line, and the line begins to bend and yes it is indisputable: with his hand he is digging a circle. The man joins in, digging up the snow on his side, disclosing a black arc. And soon they will touch, making a circle to end all circles – it's bound to surround them both. And if someone were to pass by now, what would they see?

Walking up the slippery path, it's like two drunk men going home: hard to say who is taking whom. Both swerve, stagger, collide. When they are inside, the man begins to help Norman off with his coat, but Norman wants to play his little game with the man. He grabs the man's arms and holds on to it tightly, gets his other hand around his neck and pulls him forward. When they are face to face, Norman looks into the man's eyes – who know what's living in there?

Let go, Norman, let go.

But he has a vicelike grip, and will let the man go when

he pleases. That's the little game Norman plays with the man, but the man doesn't like the little game of looking into each other's eyes. And when he is free the man makes Norman work again: gets his paper taped to the table, his paint brush in his hand, his chair pushed in and he's ready. Norman gets into the mood, gets a grip of the situation, his mind into gear, then:

> *The sun, Norman, the sun. Without it, no light,*
> *none. Everything dark, cold.*

Holding the brush as if it were a dagger, Norman makes a slow stab at the water-pot, then grinds the brush into the paint. He begins the thick black outline, and later he'll fill it in. The man stands back, watching. What moves upon the face of the waters? What light from a black, black sun?

Does he see that they are good? Sun, moon, planets: it's Norman's universe. Now he goes through his portfolio, examining each, one by one. It takes an age to look at them, to review and appreciate each. Every so often Norman grabs the man's arm and shows him one, pointing a finger at its empty centre.

Norman opens his mouth and utters, AAAH!

> *Let go, Norman, let go.*

The man collects together Norman's circles and puts them away in a drawer, because now he has another idea. He gets a clean sheet of paper, sits down beside Norman, signals to him to pay attention. Norman yawns, looks bored. The man takes a pencil and begins, with a great deal of care, to draw.

A circle, Norman, a circle.

Norman nods his head, yawns. A circle, of course it is, what else could it be. Then, inside the circle, the man draws another circle. It is much smaller than the first. Next to it, another small circle. Norman laughs, yawns. It doesn't take the man long to make a circle touch.

Two little circles inside a big circle. Eyes, Norman,
eyes.

The man touches the circles, then points to his eyes. He makes a circle with his finer and thumb and holds it in front of his eye. Then he adds to the drawing.

And this is the nose, and the mouth.

And to the head is added a body, to the body arms and legs. Circles for hands and feet, circles for the buttons of his coat. It's simple, it's rudimentary.

A man, Norman, a man. It's you, Norman, look.

The man points to the drawing of the man, then points to Norman. Norman looks at the drawing. Curious for a moment, troubled perhaps, then he shakes his head from side to side and throws the pencil to the floor. He grabs the man's arm, wants to play his little game, but the man doesn't want to play. He pushes Norman away, then repeats the process:

two small circles inside of a big one. Nose, mouth, ears. And to the head a body, to the body arms and legs. He hands the pencil to Norman, and Norman throws it to the floor. Norman rests his cheek on the table, lets his arms dangle down by his sides. The man stands up, walks around the room looking at the pictures: a smiling face with the legend 'GOOD BOY' written above it; a thickly crayoned dinosaur confronts the words 'THE STONEAGE'; inside a dark tunnel, a figure carrying a torch; the tree with its green, mysterious fruit; tiny swastika-ed aeroplanes, on fire in a rain of bullets. The man sits down by the window, looks out at the sunlight, the trees. There is a faint green haze around the branches, and the buds are beginning to appear. The effort begins again, the colossal effort of things. The man looks at Norman's face and sees an empty circle.

Everyone is sitting out in the garden. The tables and the chairs have been brought outside, and now everyone is sitting in the sunshine drawing or painting a picture. Everyone except Norman and the man. Norman is oblivious to the heat, the insects, the birdsong, because he has fallen asleep. His head has drooped on to the table, covering the drawing he's done. His hands are dangling down by the sides of his wheelchair and his pencil is lying in the grass nearby. The man is indoors, writing a report on Norman. It says that Norman has a broken ankle and will require a wheelchair until he is able to walk again.

The man comes out into the garden and walks around looking at the pictures. When he comes to Norman, he shakes him by the shoulder.

And slowly he comes to life. The hand fumbles at his eyes,

his nose and his mouth, as if trying to pluck the sleep from his face. Norman sits up slowly, moving like a man underwater. He screws up his eyes, looks up at the sun. He opens his mouth and utters, AAAH!

The man retrieves the pencil from the grass. Norman laughs, startled. It's a trick the man has done, a conjuring trick. Everything is a conjuring trick. The man offers Norman his pencil, but he shakes his head from side to side and yawns. He doesn't want to draw, apparently. He's finished his drawing. The man looks at it: a mess of heavy black lines and circles. It makes the man look away.

What is it, Norman, what is it?

Norman laughs, nods his head slowly, stabs at the picture with his finger. The man sees a muddle of misshapen curves, overlapping and smudged hopelessly. Curious for a moment, troubled perhaps, then he looks away. Norman grabs at the man's arm, gets his other hand behind his neck, pulls him down until they're face to face. The man sees a tiny version of himself in the pupil of Norman's eye.

Let go, Norman, let go!

The man loosens Norman's fingers from his neck and pulls away. He goes indoors, to his reports.

Norman looks at the drawing on the table in front of him. It's his, he knows it's his. He points to a tangle of circles, then slowly lifts a hand to his eyes. He stabs with his finger at the heavy scribble above, then claps a hand on his headguard. He goes on, although the man is no longer beside him,

Selected Stories

pointing to the drawing, then pointing to himself. To those buttons all sizes and shapes, to the multitude of twisted arms and hands. To the feet more monstrous than the face, to the wheels overlapping the legs. He opens his mouth to utter, but the man can't hear. And at last it is Norman who must wait for the man. It could be that at last, when he has looked at so many of the drawings, the man will look into one of them and recognise something there: that although it is laboured and grotesque, and although it makes him want to look away, it is the image of a man nonetheless and he is recognisable.

Killing Time

ARCHIE NEWTON held his feet out to the sides and watched the pedals go round on their own – round and round dementedly, because of the fixed wheel. That was the only thing he didn't like about the bike – that, and the dynamo he couldn't get going. His dad would've fixed it in a flash. The man was a genius when it came to bicycle repairs. Handy with clocks he was too, got them going again in no time. Archie had got the bike when he'd died, and his watch, and the old-fashioned lighter with the flip-open lid. The watch had stopped working already – stuck just before noon, or midnight – and now the dynamo. . . but he wouldn't need lights until the winter. By that time he might have a job, he might have a *motorbike*.

'Wrrrummm, *wrrrumm!*' said Archie, the way he had done when he was younger.

He waited till it slowed down, slipped his feet back on to the pedals, then started going as hard as he could. When he got to the path between the swingpark and bowling green, he held his feet out to the sides again and closes his eyes and waited for the Feeling. He had discovered the Feeling years ago, during the summer holidays between primary and secondary school. And he still got the Feeling when he rode fast enough over the ridged concrete of the path. The bike shook so violently that he could feel the shudders coming up through his body, till his head began to feel fuzzy and. . . and then he fell off, unless he opened his eyes in time.

It was worth falling off for the Feeling.

He picked up the bike and cursed. Two kids who were playing on the merry-go-round jumped off and jeered at him. They doubled up, held their sides and cried *Oh-ho-ho, ee-hee-hee* in a parody of laughter. Archie spat at them, a dry little spit of contempt, but they went on jeering. He watched their antics and frowned. There was something serious in their ridicule, something joyless. He turned away and surveyed the bike for damage. The chain had come off again.

'Bastard,' said Archie to the bike.

The strident voices behind his back redoubled their laughter. A forced, false laughter, but contagious for all that. Suddenly he couldn't help joining in with it. After a few minutes of trying to keep it in, he sat down on the path beside the bike and let it out. There was triumph in ridicule, but in madness there was release: his body rocked back and forwards until at last it lay on the warm concrete, twitching with laughter. When he stood up again he saw that the kids had stopped. They stared at him in silence, horrified, *appalled*.

'What are you lookin at ya bastartn fuckin wee shites?' said Archie. 'Fuck off or Ah'll come owre there an gie yez a punch in the mooth!'

He heard his own voice going on like that, heaping threat on threat, curse on curse. It was his voice all right, but it didn't sound like his own. It sounded more like his dad's. He'd caught himself doing things too, just the way he moved a hand or found himself sitting in a chair, that reminded him of the old man.

He put the chain back on, then wiped his fingers on the knees of his jeans – already black with oily smears. He looked through the bowling green railings to where a sprinkler was spinning a fine whirl of spray. On the other side of it, some old men were laying out the rubber mats and practising their throws – about to start their game. Archie noticed that among them there was a young girl – she couldn't be much older than him. She was walking to the far end of the green, carrying the jack in her hand. He shaded his eyes with a hand, like a Red Indian, the way he had done when he was younger. She had long brown hair and from here she looked. . . okay. He could see no sign of Starky, the greenkeeper. He'd probably be in the pavilion, not listening to his transistor. Starky always did that when he had nothing to do. Sat there not hearing the music, staring out at the green. Once, Archie had asked him why he never switched it off, and Starky had said that it made the time go quicker. That was like something his dad had sometimes said about work – when you're busy, the time goes quicker. But time was Time, wasn't it? So how could it go quicker?

Archie looked at the watch his dad had worn and smiled. The time was the same as always: a minute to twelve. The watch didn't work but he still wore it because, well, it was still a watch.

He ran over to the roundabout, grabbed hold of the iron handrails and started to make it go. The kids jumped clear, screeching and yelling in a mockery of panic and outrage. They stood back and watched as he made the wooden hexagon spin. He put one foot up on the footboard and pounded the concrete with the other. When it was going round and round dementedly he brought his other foot up.

He bent over the seat and peered through the wooden slats at what was underneath: a kaleidoscope of whirring litter and dirt, with long stripes of light where the sun came through the slats. He tried to read some of the names on the sweet-wrappers as the light swung over them: *Milk Choc. . . Tobler . . . smrts. . . Wagwheee. . .*

When he looked up again he saw the kids flash past. Swings, the pavilion, blur of railings, bike, more railings, concrete, the kids. The two of them stood side by side, engrossed in this spectacle of endless motion. . . round and round. He scudded the heel of his gymshoe on the concrete to slow down, then bent over the seat and peered again between the slats, moving the roundabout round a little at a time. Once he'd seen a fifty pence piece underneath. Charlie had lain down on his back and stretched his arm in beneath the footboard, while Archie had held the roundabout still and given him directions from above: 'Left a bit, along a bit, back. . . ' It would be harder to get the money out on his own, and anyway he couldn't see any. Just old lollipop sticks, sweetwrappers and dirt.

He staggered a little when he jumped off the roundabout, so the kids started holding their sides again and doing their pantomime of laughter. Strange the way they weren't really amused, but went through these motions like actors rehearsing a scene. Everything was a bit like that in the park, like a piece of make-believe. The painted wooden pavilion, like a stage prop from a Western. Starky the parky, trying to make the time go quicker. The shaved and levelled lawn of the green . . . it didn't look like grass. And the people strolling up and down the paths, and these kids.

Archie made to kick them and they made as if to run away. Then he did kick one of them and he squealed with real fright. The other one shouted, 'We'll tell oan you, ya big bastard, you're too big to play oan the swings!'

Archie felt the voice rising up inside him again, but stopped it before it started.

'Nyaa', he said, turning away.

As soon as his back was turned the kid who'd been kicked stopped squealing. It hadn't been much of a kick anyway, more of a soft thump on the behind, but from it Archie had taken some small satisfaction. It had worked too, because now the kids went back to the roundabout and let him be.

He walked to the chute and hoisted himself up in big strides, taking six or seven of the tiny steps at a time. At the top there was a kind of cage of iron bars. He climbed up on top of the cage and dangled his feet over the sides, the way he had done when he was younger. He took out the cigarette he'd pinched from his mum's packet and put it between his lips. He lit up, closed the lighter and turned it over in his palm. Somehow he knew that when the wick turned or the flint ran out, or when it ran out of petrol, he wouldn't do anything about it. He'd just let it stop working, like the watch and the dynamo. Everything was going that way anyway, winding down, running out of whatever kept it going. It was the way things wanted to go.

He looked over the park to where he lived, but couldn't tell which house was his, or even which street. He knew it was empty anyway. His mum would still be at work, the kids at school. Since his dad had died, everything in the house had been breaking down. The lights in the hall and the upstairs landing had stopped working, fused. It was up to him to fix them, but he'd always found an excuse. It had happened gradually, but it had happened – everybody had stopped bothering. Even about getting a job, making a start in life and all that, Archie had not only stopped caring but had stopped pretending to care. When his mum made some suggestion now – her latest idea was night school – he just shrugged and got on with what he was doing. What he was doing was usually nothing.

Beyond the brown roofs he could see the Forth, and the fire-topped chimneys of Grangemouth. Charlie was some-where over there right now, playing with one of the biggest chemistry sets in the world. Hard to believe that Charlie, mad Charlie who'd do absolutely anything for a laugh, who'd done no more work than Archie had at school, had found a job in a *laboratory*. How was it possible? Archie tried to imagine him at work, wearing a white lab-coat and a collar and tie, arranging the test-tubes in long wooden racks, labelling pyrex beakers full of strangely coloured liquids, writing down the enigmatic formulae. And going to the canteen for his lunch, and sitting at a table with *scientists*. And all the other experts – chemists, engineers, computer people, time and motion men. . . and Charlie! How could it be?

Archie looked over the bowling green and noticed that Starky had come out of the pavilion and was fiddling with the sprinkler. He'd turned the water off, and now he was moving it to another part of the green. It was strange to watch him at his slow labour, oblivious of everything except his little task: to move it from here to there, then from there to somewhere else. That was work, it was what Starky had to do. He had to do it because he was the greenkeeper and green had to be kept green. That was what all work was like: keeping the green green green. Because when they couldn't work any more, the old men needed to play. But they couldn't remember how to, so they needed a game to play at, a game with rules and scorecards and balls of wood and a nice green green with a pavilion to put on their overshoes in, so as not to mark the green. And that was why Starky was so engrossed in moving the sprinkler, because he was the greenkeeper keeping the green.

Archie watched Starky marching back into the pavilion, and a moment later the water was spinning from the sprinkler again. Charlie had always made fun of Starky, imitating his slow gestures and his doleful, let's-take-one-thing-at-a-time way of talking. One night they'd sprayed their nicknames, Chic and Titch, on the back wall of the pavilion:

'Ah wish Ah could see his face when he sees it!'

'He prob'ly wilnae even notice it. . .'

'He's *bound* to see it. Imagine what he'll say!'

'He'll say. . . he'll say: What. Have. They. Buggers. Done tae ma PAVILION!'

Archie smiled at the memory of it, but without Charlie it wasn't so much fun hanging round in the park. Charlie was moving on to other things – learning to drive, getting a girlfriend. Archie was still riding around on his bike, and he'd even got into the habit of calling in on Starky just to pass the time.

The two kids had come over to the chute, and one of them was already half-way up the steps.

'We'll tell oan you,' he shouted, you're too *wee* tae smoke!'

Archie flicked the smouldering end in his direction and watched it do a tiny somersault through the air. The kids made faces and blew raspberries. Instead of going down the chute, Archie caught hold of the support poles and swung down between them. Something made him hang there as long as he could, dangling between the poles and being jeered at by the kids, his feet some two yards above the ground. He saw his tall shadow on the concrete and closed his eyes and waited for the Pain.

From the pavilion came the hysterical sound of an accordion playing a reel. He leaned the bike up against the wooden balustrade and looked at the dancing spray of water. Round and round and round, as if bedevilled by the music. He looked again at the old men – there were three of them – and the young girl. One of their daughters maybe, or a granddaughter? He shaded his eyes again to look at her, but she was too far away to see in detail. He could smell the heady smell of mown grass, and the sweet fragrant smell of sunwarmed wood. Good smells, but he didn't feel good. Not bad either, but some peculiar feeling of longing he hadn't felt before.

He imagined walking over to the young girl, telling her that there were other things to do, taking her away from those old men. But then where would he take her? He watched as one of the old men threw the jack to start the next round. The girl stood behind the jack and began clapping her hands

– why was she doing that? The next old man stooped and almost knelt down on one knee as he threw the first bowl. It curved in the wrong direction, then disappeared over the edge of the green. Archie laughed briefly, without humour, then turned and stepped into the shaded cool of the pavilion.

'Hi Starky.'

Starky's sandwich paused on the way to his mouth.

'Oho,' said Starky, 'so it's you, is it.' The hand with the sandwich raised its index finger. 'Well if Ah've telt ye once Archie, Ah've telt ye a hundred . . . ' Starky bit into the soft white bread, swallowed with a muffled gulp. 'Ah've telt ye a *hunder* times: *Mister* Stark's ma name, an that's what ye'll call me!' He stared at Archie from his watery eyes as he spoke. The mouth opened slowly and went for the sandwich.

'Been busy today, Mister Stark?'

'Mmmuh?'

Archie waited while the mouth filled up with tea, chewed loosely at solid and liquid alike, then swallowed all of it with a *glump*.

'Ho Ah've been busy aaright!' The thick finger prodded the air.

'It's aaright for some o us, eh? Yooz young yins on the dole! But some o us huff tae *work!*' Starky's eyes looked forgetfully at the sandwich. He hadn't said that very well. He took the last bite, drained his cup and smacked his lips. After a moment, he cleared his gullet softly and uttered, 'Ah've mowed that whole green, there's how busy Ah've been!'

'Any tea in the pot?' said Archie.

Starky ran a fat palm over his bald crown and declared, 'Oho, so now we know! Now we know what ye're efter!' Archie smiled and sat down on the edge of the table. From there he could look out of the little window and see the girl. She was flicking back her hair and clapping her hands again. 'An ye can take yer arse off o there,' said Starky, 'there's a seat, if ye want a chair'

Archie pulled up a chair and sat down. Starky poured out two cups of thick dark tea, humming absently along with the accordion music. Suddenly the music stopped, and both looked at the radio. There was no sound apart from a faint crackle, then from outside the young girl's voice calling,

'*Five feet. . . one o'clock.*'

'What's she. . . ?' Archie began, but the radio announcer's voice interrupted him, apologising for the fault in transmission. The accordion music resumed, more demented than ever.

'Dead time,' said Archie.

'Ye what?'

Dead time. It's what they call it, when there's nothing on the air.'

Starky raised his eyebrows and farted briefly.

'O I beg your. . . ' He farted and chuckled simultaneously, then put a hand to his mouth to suppress an abrupt belch. 'Dead time is it now, well Ah've never in aa ma born days heard o that, it's a new yin oan me Archie.' He ran a palm over his baldness again and bit his lip. 'Ah've heard o *killing* time, mind you, but no this *deid* time ye're telling me.'

'Killing time,' said Archie, sipping at the bitter, tepid brew, 'what does that mean Starky? Ah mean Mister Stark.'

Archie knew what it meant, but asking him a question was a way of keeping the conversation from seizing up. Starky's face had gone blank with doleful consternation.

'Ye dinnae mean tae tell me you've never heard o *killing*

time,' he said. He sucked up a mouthful of tea and grimaced as he swallowed it because it had gone cold.

'I've never heard of it,' said Archie. He tried to peer over the window ledge from where he sat, but it was too high.

'Well, it *means*. . . ' Starky's eyelids fluttered slightly as he looked around the pavilion for a definition. This business of having to define the phrase seemed to make him lose all patience. 'Ach, it's an *expression* Archie, ye must ken it. It *means*. . . well *you* should ken what it means, ye *dae* it every bloody day – buggerin aboot oan that bike o yours, *that's* killin time! When ye could be employin yer time usefully lookin for *work!*'

As he spoke the accordion music became faster and faster, until Starky's patience ran out and he switched the radio off as he shouted the word *work*.

They heard the young girl's voice calling again, '*Two feet, at three o'clock.*'

'Which reminds me,' Starky resumed, 'ye can gie me a hand wi they edges. They edges are still to be done.'

As Archie followed him out of the pavilion, Starky shook his head slowly from side to side and said, 'Aye, so ye never heard o killin time. . . Ah wonder what they've been teaching ye at school aa these years, eh?'

'Killing time,' said Archie, 'that's what they taught me.'

Starky chuckled laboriously and vented a series of high-pitched farts. 'O I big your par. . . Ah dinnae ken. What's causin. Aa this flagellance. Ho Ah think ye're right there Archie, that's aa they dae teach yez nowadays.' Starky stopped outside the door. The thick finger prodded Archie's arm, then pointed towards the old men at the far side of the green. 'Did ye ever hear o anything like that?'

Archie shrugged. 'Like what?'

Starky bent down slightly and brought his face so close to Archie's that Archie could smell the breath. There was amusement in his pale eyes as he spoke.

'Blind,' he said, 'every man jack o them, blind as bloody bats.' Archie turned his face away from the breath and looked over at the young girl. She was standing behind the jack and clapping her hands, waiting for the next old man to bowl.

'But she can't be. . . ' Archie began, but Starky leaned closer and poked him softly on the shoulder and said,

'Partially sighted.' He went on, pleased that his revelation was having so much effect on Archie. 'They're frae the Blind Asylum. You watch.'

Archie watched one of the old men. He was saying something to his companions, and when he spoke he revealed a black gap between his eye-teeth, and when his face turned upwards Archie saw the shadowed, sunken eyelids. It looked as if his head were leaking darkness.

'You watch this,' said Starky, as the old man stooped and swung his arm back, throwing to the sound of the clapping. The bowl rolled slowly along the green, swung inwards and came to rest a long way in front of the jack. The girl stepped forward and bent down, seeming to guage the distance between bowl and jack.

Starky nudged Archie gently in the ribs and said, 'Ye'd like tae get her in the buses, eh? Whether she can see or no. That widnae make ony difference in the dark, hmmm?'

'*Seven feet, at six o'clock!*' cried the girl to the old men, then she took up her position behind the jack again and clapped her hands.

His dirty talk having failed, Starky chuckled and said,

'*Dead* time, ye're telling me aboot. Well. . . ' he motioned loosely with a hand towards the girl, '. . . there's *blind* time for ye!' He ran his hand over his head and chuckled slowly. When he had finished and his humour had failed, he turned his watery gaze on Archie and said, 'Ye see, Archie, when she says seven feet at six o'clock like that, it's nothing tae dae wi time, really, it's aa tae dae wi the position o the *bowl*. A mean six o'clock means. . . well, if ye picture a clock, Archie, wi the jack in the middle. . .'

'Ah ken what it means,' said Archie. He was watching the next bowl traveling along the green. It swung inwards and slowed. It came closer than any of the others, close enough to enter her shadow. When it kissed against the jack, it made a small 'cloc'. The old men smiled and congratulated one another. Suddenly Starky began clapping his hands together loudly.

'Good bowl, marvellous!' he shouted.

At the sound of the loud clapping from another direction, all three of the men became confused and cocked their ears enquiringly. The girl peered over towards the pavilion.

Archie stepped down from the pavilion and climbed on his bike. Somehow the thought of the young girl, partially sighted herself, helping the blind old men to play bowls. . . it filled him with a strange disgust. He pushed down on the pedals and started cycling towards the gate.

'Hoi!' cried Starky, 'What aboot they edges?'

'Ah've got better things tae dae wi ma time!' Archie shouted without turning round.

'O ye have, have ye. Such as *what*?' cried Starky.

As he looked over his shoulder to glimpse the reddened, infuriated face of Starky, Archie stopped pedalling and felt the fixed wheel forcing his feet to go round and round.

'Nothing!' he shouted, then he picked up speed and swerved through the gate and rode away to do the Nothing.

The Shoes

ARCHIE NEWTON lifted out the inner bag, then undid the packet and flattened it out on the kitchen table. He laid one of his shoes on top, then drew a line around its sole with a biro. He did this twice on one side of the packet, then he turned it over and did the same with the other shoe. He sat down and started cutting out the foot-shaped pieces of cardboard.

'Ma, what time is it?' he shouted through to the living room. The television was on, and his mother did not hear him. He tried to fit the first piece of cornflake packet into his shoe, but it was too big. As he trimmed it with the scissors, he shouted again to his mother, but she didn't hear. He looked at the clock on the kitchen window sill, but he wasn't sure if the time it told was the right time. It was the same little square blue clock his mother once tried to 'brain' him with. He'd been out with Jane, and hadn't come home till two in the morning.

He stopped what he was doing to laugh, remembering her with that clock in her hand, raising it high above her head and swearing she would *brain* him with it. She'd picked up the clock because it had been the nearest thing to hand, but now the picture in Archie's memory made him think she was blaming him for the passing of time itself. He shouted again, and when she didn't hear he felt annoyed and shouted louder,

'Ma, what time is it?'

His mother hurried into the kitchen and began to bang things around on the cooker.

'There's a clock there, isn't there,' said his mother.

'Is it slow or fast?'

'It's right as far as Ah know.'

'It's always wrong,' said Archie. He fitted the first foot-sized piece of cardboard into his shoe, then picked up the second piece and started trimming it with the scissors.

'Ah'm gonnae miss this bus,' said Archie.

'Ye will if ye dinnae hurry,' said his mother. 'Where is it you're goin' anyway my lad?'

'Nowhere,' said Archie, 'just out.'

'Well mind and watch yersel,' said his mother, 'and don't be late.'

'Aye ma,' said Archie in a bored voice. He concentrated on fitting the second piece of cardboard into the shoe.

'What a mess in here,' said his mother, as she stepped between the foot-shaped pieces of cardboard on the floor. She poured hot water from the kettle over the dirty dishes in the sink and went on, 'Reminds me of the time we went ballroom dancing, me and yer faither.'

Selected Stories

'Before ma time,' said Archie. He struggled to fit the third piece into his other shoes, then took it out and trimmed it with the scissors. 'Ma, Ah need a new pair of shoes!'

'There's a perfectly good pair in the hall,' said his mother. 'He'd only worn them twice before he died.'

'Ah cannae wear them,' said Archie, 'Ah need a new pair!'

'We'll just have to see,' said his mother. She laid the cups to drain on the steel draining board.

Archie stood up and stamped his feet on the kitchen floor. He pulled on his jacket.

'Would ye look at this mess,' said his mother, picking up a few pieces of cardboard and the bag with the cornflakes in it.

'Ah'll have to run for that bus,' said Archie. Out in the hall and with a hand on the front door, he heard her calling,

'You mind and watch yersel now, and don't be late!'

He shaded his eyes with a hand because of the sun coming through the window. He looked at the way her arm curved at the wrist when she poured the water. He'd never been alone with her in the house like this before. There had always been her mother, or her sister, or her big brother in another room. Usually she took him into the front room, the one the family never used. He wasn't used to being with her in the kitchen like this, and that was making it harder to tell her.

He sat and watched her face as she chattered and made tea and smiled at him, as if tonight was like any other night. Was she beautiful? He couldn't tell, her face kept moving. All he could tell was that her skin looked dark against the light from the window, dark but sort of glowing, and when she looked at him her eyes were very alive. The other thing he could tell was that he would never sit here and watch her like this again as she moved around the room talking and smiling, because even if he did it would be different. She was changing into a very beautiful person all the time, and if she was beautiful it was all to do with this changing thing. She was smiling at him a lot, and that was making it harder.

He looked out of the window and tried to concentrate on a little cloud above the rooftops. It didn't seem to be going anywhere or doing anything. It was that kind of evening, as if time wasn't passing.

'You take sugar?' she said, and she laughed because she'd never made tea for him in her house like this before and it was ridiculous.

'Two,' said Archie, then he laughed too because he had never had tea in her house like this before and it was ridiculous. It was all a bit like they were married, and that was making it harder.

'My mum used to make tea for my dad, before he died,' said Archie. He liked saying things to her which were dead obvious as if they were dead interesting.

'It would be strange if she did after,' she said, laughing loudly.

'She does sometimes,' said Archie, 'sometimes she pours out an extra cup.'

'Really?'

He liked making her laugh like that, then saying something that made the laugh change into really. And he wanted to kiss her because she was interested in the cup laid out for the dead, and because of the way her eyebrows went when she said really. But kissing her would only make things harder.

She came over to him and handed him a cup of tea. He

put it on the floor beside his foot, then felt uncomfortable because of the shoes. It was a nice kitchen, nicer than his house – it even had chairs a bit like armchairs, as well as the ones round the table – and every so often he remembered about the shoes. The big holes in the soles, the heels worn down almost to the uppers. The cardboard insoles he'd put in before leaving the house had worn through already, and now he could feel the new holes – holes in the holes. The last time he'd taken her out – to the pictures to see a D.H.Lawrence film – she'd noticed the shoes. He'd turned from the ticket-booth and seen her looking down at his worn heels, then she'd looked up at him and tried to hide it, but he'd seen the pity in her eyes. He'd felt angry about the pity, and hadn't started kissing her till halfway through the film. They'd gone on kissing for most of the second half, and he'd got his hand up inside her blouse, then down inside her jeans. She'd told him she loved him, but wanted to see how it ended.

Archie stared at his shoes. The heels were worn down even more now. He looked out of the window. The cloud had moved. He looked at her face: changing. Soon her mother would be back from work. He would have to tell her soon.

She curled up in a chair opposite him and eyed him and licked at her tea.

'You look like a cat when you do that,' said Archie.

'Do what?' she said. She licked at the tea again and grinned.

'That,' said Archie.

She yawned and stretched out an arm.

'Did you go to your nightclass last night?'

'Yeah.'

'What was it like?'

'Great. The teacher says I'll get an 'A'.'

'Then you'll go to Art College. D'you think you'll be a famous artist?'

Archie thought for a moment.

'Probably,' he said.

He was just about to cross his legs the way he had seen a famous artist doing it on t.v. with one ankle resting on the other knee, then he remembered about the shoes.

'I wouldn't talk to you if you were a famous artist,' she said. She came over to him and sat on the floor in front of him, leaning her elbows on his knees. He drew his feet as far under the chair as they would go. 'I wouldn't even come to the phone if it was you.' Her eyes had that look in them that said *so there*.

'How come?' said Archie, although he knew she wasn't really serious. They were never really serious when they talked about anything, they just talked and let the words take them somewhere.

'I'd chuck you,' she said.

'What for?' said Archie, playing along. But he knew that all this would only make it harder.

'I'd be too embarrassed. It would be like going out with *Eamonn Andrews*.' She laughed loudly about this, but stopped halfway when Archie didn't join in. And he knew that he would be laughing too if not for the shoes and the pity.

'But you'd say hello to me in the street!' said Archie, as if he was really serious.

'Well, I suppose I'd say hello in the *street!*' She laughed again, but stopped this time as soon as she'd started. 'What's wrong with you?' she said, frowning. She pulled away from him and frowned at him as if she were his mother. And he wanted to kiss her again because she was trying to frown and she didn't have the kind of face which could frown really. He said nothing, but leaned forward and stared at his cup of tea. She tugged at his sleeve. 'Hey, what's the matter with you tonight?'

'Nothing.'

'There is. What's wrong? You're not here.'

'How d'you mean?'

'You're not *here*,' she repeated, tugging at both his sleeves and trying to pull him into here. When that failed, she sat back and looked at him with narrowed eyes. It was one of those things Archie liked about her, all the crazy things she could do with her face. 'Look,' she said, in the tones of an offended auntie, 'ye havnae even *touched* yer tea!'

Archie looked at the undrunk cup of tea at his foot and suddenly felt like laughing out loud because it was ridiculous. Suddenly everything was ridiculous: this being in the kitchen together as if they were married; his mother telling him to 'mid and watch yersel' before he'd come out; the extra cup poured out for the dead; her saying it would be like going out with Eamonn Andrews. Everything made him want to laugh, everything was ridiculous. Everything except the shoes and the pity. He concentrated on the holes in his soles as a way of stifling the laughter. He waited for a minute, then he said it.

'I want to finish it.'

He'd wondered how it would sound when he said it. Now he'd said it, and he knew how it sounded. There was no beauty in it, and no pity. It sounded ordinary and ridiculous. He didn't look up, but heard her gasp.

'Why?'

When he did look up, he saw the first tear dripping from her eyelashes. She leaned forwards to put her arms round his neck, and the tear fell into his cup of tea. Then he could feel her mouth up against his ear and she was asking him why again. When she pulled away, her cheeks were wet with the tears.

'Are you fed up with me?'

'It's not that.'

'Why then?'

'It's just. . . time to finish it, that's all.'

'Time?'

She looked at the clock on the wall, as if the real explanation might be found there. Archie looked at it. It was the kind of clock his mother would have liked to possess.

'Who's that?' said Archie, as they heard the front door opening and someone came into the hall.

It was getting dark when Archie opened the door of the Boulevard Cafe in the High Street. He went in and saw Charlie there, sitting at the corner table they always sat at.

'Well,' said Charlie, 'How d'it go?'

Archie said nothing, but hung his head. He waited for the waitress to come, then ordered a tea.

'Did ye tell her?' said Charlie. Archie nodded and stared at the table. Charlie gave a long, low whistle. He was good at long, low whistles. 'Did ye pick the right time, the right moment?'

'There isn't a right time for it,' said Archie.

'Right enough,' said Charlie, 'But tell me what happened, eh? What did ye say? How did she take it?'

Archie shook his head and stared at the table.

'Okay,' said Charlie, 'tell me later.'

Both sat staring at the table until Charlie thought of something else to talk about.

'Hey,' he said, 'what d'ye think of these then?' He raised one leg above the level of the table, then pointed the toe of his shoe first one way, then another. He swung round in the seat and raised the other leg, so that both shoes were visible. 'Just got them the day. What d'ye thinka them? They're magic, eh?'

'Magic,' said Archie, without looking at the shoes. Then he did glance at them. They had Cuban heels and chiselled toes and elasticated gussets down the insides, they were black and shiny and new, and he saw that they really were magic.

A Breakdown

PETEY YAWNED and watched the machine pick up another batch of tin cans, rotate, then put them down on the chute. They fell between one another as they rolled away, until they were rolling in single file, then disappeared through a narrow hole in the wall. On the other side of the wall, a mechanical finger would turn them upright and prod them onto a conveyor belt, which took them then to be filled, sealed and labelled. Before one batch had rolled away, the can-loading machine had picked up another in its rotating claw, and was already holding it in position above the chute. Petey blinked his eyes and yawned again. You had to admit it, that machine was fast. It could do the work of two men, and as Wilson, the production manager, had said the day it was installed, it *never* had to go to the toilet. He'd looked at Petey and Bill with that chilling look of his and added: it doesn't smoke. After that Bill had been put on inspection at the other end of the line, and now Pete's job was to operate the can-loading machine, which amounted to switching it off and on, and to watch out for damaged cans. If a bent can got into the sealing machine it could cause it to jam, then the whole line would be held up.

Petey rubbed his eyes with his knuckles. It wasn't so easy to do nothing after all, and the noise of the machine and the endless watching had given him a dull pain behind the eyes. He'd had headaches at work before, but this was a different kind of pain, dull, persistent. He'd had it for a few days now, just behind the eyes. He'd have preferred a real headache to this not-quite-a-headache which never seemed to go away completely. Sometimes he thought it wasn't a pain at all, that it was all in the mind, but then he would feel it again – dull, a feeling of deadness, as if something had seized up. Before the machine had been installed, he'd found the work hard on the back – he was an old man, after all – but at least he'd had Bill to talk to. Now the only people he saw were Wilson, who came round to check up on him every so often, and the forklift driver every time he brought round a new stack of cans. But neither of these men were willing to stop and have a bit of a conversation. That's what happened to you when you got old. You weren't worth talking to any more, your words didn't count.

Petey got down off the stool and walked over to the stack of empty cans. Each stack had a dozen layers, and between each layer there was a sheet of card. Petey had to discard the card, so that the machine could move on to the next layer. He waited until it had picked up the last batch of cans, and when he pulled away the card the silver rims of the next layer gleamed like a steel honeycomb. He picked out one of the shining cells and looked at his elongated reflection in its surface. Like a face on t.v. when the vertical hold has gone. . . or was it the horizontal hold? One of the holds, anyway. Petey squeezed the tin between the palms of his hands, until he felt it give and crumple. When he looked at himself again, part of his face was missing. He walked around the chute and watched them rolling down. They seemed to be grinning at him, like a row of teeth. He took the one he'd crushed, a bad tooth, and slipped it between the others. It didn't roll too well, but the momentum of the others carried it down until it disappeared through the hole in the wall.

Wilson came around the wall and swiped the air with his hand, meaning cut the power. Other people would've tried to shout above the noise of the machine, but not Wilson. Petey pushed the STOP button and a red light showed. The machine stopped, a clutch of hollow cans held high above the stack. In the sudden silence there was the rapid click of Wilson's heels as he approached. Something about that sound made Petey want to shiver. The way the man looked at you too, and talked to you, it was eerie.

'There's been a breakdown,' said Wilson.

'What?'

'The line has been held up. You may take a break.'

'Is the line held up?'

'Yes.'

'Can I go to the canteen?'

Wilson smiled. It was a patient little smile, the kind of smile you might use with a child who asks for something he can't have.

'I'm afraid it isn't open yet.'

Petey appeared to think this over, conscious of Wilson's

even gaze on him. You couldn't look at the eyes like that, you had to let them look at you. Why didn't the man say something?

'What's up anyway?' said Petey.

'The sealing machine jammed. We think a damaged can. . .'

'I didn't see any,' Petey declared, averting his eyes. After a long moment of silence, Wilson turned and went back around the wall. The efficient click of those heels. When he was gone, Petey got down off the stool and began stamping some life into his feet. He leaned his elbow on the stool and looked at the control box. Apart from the STOP button with the red light, there was the GO button with the green light and, underneath them, a black switch with the word PAUSE printed above it. Below that there was the dial which set the speed. For the moment it looked like a rudimentary face, with two different coloured eyes and an open mouth. Petey smiled and shook his head, then he felt it again, that dead feeling. He took out his tobacco and his matches, then furtively rolled a thin cigarette between his fingers.

'Hear that?' said Petey to the machine. 'There has been a breakdown. You may take a break!' He smiled to himself. It was four in the morning, the line was held up and here he was, the saboteur – an old man with a pain in the head, talking to a machine. 'I must be going crazy,' he said, then put the cigarette between his lips and struck a match. He found himself blinking, startled, when the flame appeared, as if it were the last thing he expected. As he smoked he rolled another cigarette, and he noticed that his hands were trembling. Sometimes they did shake a little, but not as badly as this – as if something had given him a bad fright. 'Maybe I *am* going crazy,' he said, laying the badly-rolled cigarette on top of the control box. He saw the face again, laughed a little and said, 'That one's for you.' He chuckled at the idea of it – a man talking to a machine – but still, it was better than not talking at all. 'Go on,' he said to it, 'have a smoke before Wilson comes back.' After a moment he added, 'Course, I forgot. You don't smoke, do you?'

He looked behind him to see if anyone was around. If someone heard him offering the machine a cigarette. . . 'They'd think I was talking to myself,' said Petey to the machine, 'but I'll tell you something. I may be old, but I'm not senile. I just. . . think aloud sometimes. It's different.' The machine, as if attempting a rejoinder, let fall one of the cans from its hooked and gleaming fingers. It fell on top of the stack, and the tin against the tin made an argumentative noise. Petey was startled by the noise, then he laughed. He walked over to the stack and picked up the fallen can, then came back and dangled it in front of the red and green eyes.

'You dropped one,' said Petey, 'you're not so hot.' He chuckled a little as he walked back to the stack, shaking his head from side to side and repeating, 'You're not so hot.' The honeycomb pattern made by the shining rims spun around suddenly, and the inside of one can seemed to swell up, as if a tin had decided to open its mouth and speak. But it didn't want to speak, it wanted to eat. Petey felt himself falling into the shining mouth, but he stopped himself in time, putting a hand in front of his eyes.

'Jesus, what's wrong with me tonight?' said Petey, squinting up to where the claw of the machine waited above the stack. He backed away, climbed up on the stool, then lit the second cigarette. His hands were shaking badly now, and as he looked around him his lips were moving slightly, as if he were trying to recall something, a word or a phrase which would let him know where he was and what he was meant to do there.

'Maybe you are fast,' he said, 'but listen, if you work your guts out one night, they expect it of you the next. And the next, and every night. You wouldn't catch me and Bill. . . we went at out own pace. Sent a man round, a work-study man. Listen, what we did was. . . we picked up eight, eight at a time, instead of. . . ' Petey held out his hands and spread the fingers. You could get one on each finger and trap another two between the handfuls. '. . . instead of twelve, how about that? Said we were as fast as what was it. . . humanly possible.' He went on, his voice growing quiet, speaking absently to the machine, 'It's okay for you, you never had a childhood. . . you don't know what it's like to. . . *play*.' The word sounded odd as he said it, slightly ridiculous. He repeated it a few times, quietly, to himself, until he no longer knew what it meant. He thought of the playground at the school he'd gone to so many years ago, with its tall iron railings and the windowless shelter for when it rained. He could see them all, as if from above, all the children playing in the playground, but none of them had a face, and what were they playing at?

Petey shook his head and rubbed his eyes with his knuckles. When he looked up he saw the row of cans on the steel chute, waiting to roll away. They looked like teeth, bared in a grin. When they came towards him and made to bite, Petey jumped down from the stool and, shuddering violently, held out a warning finger and began uttering threats and curses in a voice that wasn't like his voice. But suddenly he was aware that he was standing there and threatening what was, after all, only a row of tin cans on a chute. As he lowered his arm and looked up at the claw of the machine and saw

Selected Stories

that it was just a mechanical device for picking up cans. . . and how could a few buttons on a control box resemble a face? Petey pressed his temples with his hands. 'Take a walk,' he said quietly, 'you need to get out, get some air.'

Wilson pushed open the rubber flap of the factory door and saw the huddled figure by the factory wall.

'There you are.'

'Yes, I'm here.'

'I've been all over the factory, looking for you.'

'I thought I'd get a breath of air.'

'The line's been going for almost an hour.'

'Listen, is it playtime yet?'

'Pardon?'

'Is it playtime? Don't get me wrong, I've worked all my life, I'm a good worker, but that machine tried to attack me. I had to come out into the playground, but nobody else came out. I didn't see any, on my oath. You wouldn't catch me and Bill. Mister Wilson, is it playtime yet?'

Wilson took the old man's arm and began to guide him towards the door.

'Yes,' he said, 'it's playtime now.'

The Hunter of Dryburn

YEZ'LL HAVE a drink.

Whit izzit, a pinta heavy izzit? A pinta heavy. N whitzzat yer young lady's drinkin? Hullo darllin, aaright? Aaright. Gin an tonic izzit? Gin an tonic it is. No problem friend, Ah insist. Pinta heavy na gin an tonic. On me.

Yez dinnae mind me talkin tae yez, dae yez? Mean dinnae get me wrong, ken whit Ah mean, mean Ah'm no meanin anythin or anythin. Mean Ah'm no tryin tae chat ye up or nuthn sweetheart. No tryin tae chat up yer burd or nothn son, aaright son? Aaright. No me, naw.

Naw but is soon is yez walked through that door Ah could tell. Ah could tell yez were in love and that, the paira yez. Stauns oot a mile so it diz. Na could tell yez were educatit people ken. Na could tell yez wernae frae roon aboot here, that wiz obvious. See it's no very often Ah get the chance, mean tae talk tae folk like youz in here ken. Ah enjoy a bitty intelligent conversation ken. So Ah sez tae masel, whit wid the Auld Man adone? He's deid ken, death by misadventure. Yez probably read aboot it in the Evenin News. So Ah sez tae masel, the Auld Man widda bought these young people a drink, had a bitty conversaion ken. See the Auld Man wis like that ken. Friendly. Hospitable pal, you've said it. Unless he didnae like the look o somebody, then he wisnae quite sae hospitable.

So yez took the wrong road frae the motorway, ended up in sunny Dryburn? Jist thought yez might as well pop in for a quick wan, fair enough. Is soon is yez walked through that door Ah sez tae masel Aye, they've probly took the wrong road frae the motorway. Quite frankly like, if a thought for wan minute yez had come in here deliberately like, Adda tellt yez tae get yer heids looked. See Dryburn? Sa dump.

Tell ye this hen, you're beautiful so ye are. Naw seriously. Nae offence son, aaright? But Ah mean how diz a boy like you get a beautiful wummin like that? It beats me, so it diz. Nae offence son, aaright?

Aye Dryburn's a dump aaright. Mean yez can see that for yersels. Mean it's no whit ye'd caa a village even. Mean, whit is there? Thirz haufadizzen shoaps. Thirz a chip shoap. Thirz the church and thirz the chapel. An thirz four pubs. Five, if ye count the hotel up by the motorway. See folk used tae pass through here a loat before thon motorway. Nen there used tae be a station up by the steelworks. That's where he worked, the Auld Man, afore he deed. Shut doon noo though, the steelworks. Yez widda liked tae meet the Auld Man, no that he went tae Uni or nuthn but. But he wis an educatit man ken, ayewis wi a book in haund. Edgar Allan Poe, Ernest Hemingway, you name it. Ah've been readin a bitty this Ernest

Hemingway masel ken, story boot shootna lion. Ken the wan Ah mean darlin? That's it son, that's the wan.

Aye, he's a great writer right enuff. An thirz a helluva loata good advice aboot huntin an that in this story. Course it's aa about a place in Africa or somewhere like that, jungle an aa that ken, no a place like Dryburn. Whit's that yer sayin sweetheart? Aye it looks aaright frae the train right enuff, but sa dump. See the trains used tae stoap in Dryburn afore they shut doon the station ken. It used tae be mair o a community ken. A mean, no a community exactly but. But at least ye could get a train oot o the bliddy place. See the Auld Man wis a repectit person in Dryburn. Yez probly read aboot him gettin killt, in the Evenin News it wis. Aye. Mean he wisnae like a doakter or a lawyer like, but folk looked up tae him ken cause he wis educatit. Educatit hissel so he did. Used tae sit in that coarner there, in his wheelchair ken, and poke folk wi his stick and tell them tae mind their fuckin lagwitch. An folk pyed attention tae him tae. See everybiddy went tae him wi their payslips, Ah mean if they couldnae work oot their tax or their superan. Or like if somebody had tae go up tae court, they ayewis went tae him tae find oot their rights, ken. It wis like they consultit him aboot anything like that. That's right sweetheart, you've said it. He wis a walkin Citizins' Advice Bureau. Except he couldnae walk much ken, cause o his legs.

He had it up here see, the Auld Man, he could work things oot for folk. Take numbers for instance, he wis a wizard wi numbers. Mean if somebody had a win on the horses ken, the Auld Man could tell them exactly, doon tae the last haepenny, exactly how much they'd get back, minus the tax an everythin. Naebody could touch him at poker. Or dominoes. A wizard, he wis a wizard aaright. See noo that

The Hunter of Dryburn   103

he's deid there's naebody else like him left in Dryburn, naebody who can tell folk how much o a tax rebate tae expect ken. Except mibbe me. See that's why Ah'm talkin tae youz educatit folk like, so Ah can mibbe learn somethin frae yez.

Tell ye something son, ye're bloody lucky so ye are. Beautiful wummin like her, don't try an deny it.

So Ah'm readin this Ernest Hemingway tae try and educate masel a bit ken. See me and the Auld Man used tae go in for a bit o huntin wirsels, up by the Union Canal. Course, there's no very much tae hunt roon aboot here. Nae lions an tigers, ken? But there's a heluuva loata rats up there at the canal. Hundredsa big dirty great rats. Ah wonder if Ernest Hemingway widda done the same, Ah mean if he lived in this area. No much else tae dae in Dryburn except hunt rats, take ma word for it. Mibbe he'da enjoyed it, ken, then he'da come in here wi me an the Auld Man efter a guid night's huntin an had a few pints wi us. Aye, right enuff son, it wid be Absinthe if he wis buying. Here that wid gie Louis, the barman owre there, that wid gie him somethin tae think aboot. Absinthe by Christ. See Louis used tae take a rise ootae us when we came in here wi the guns ken. 'Here come the big game hunters!' he'd say, or 'Bag any tigers the night boys?' He wis ayewis at us aboot it ken, then wan night the Auld Man shot him. Yez shooda seen Louis' face. Yez shooda heard the langwitch in here that night! Ah mean he wisnae hurt or nuthn, the pellet jist nicked his airm. Course, the Auld Man said it wis an accident ken, said he wis jist pretending tae take aim ken an the thing went oaf in his haund. Yez shooda heard Louis, talk aboot wild! He wis gonnae bar the baith o us, but he needed the custom ken. Louis stoapd pullin oor leg aboot it efter that, Ah can tell ye.

Selected Stories

Ever shot anything son? Naw? Ye dinnae agree wi it? So how come ye like readin Ernest Hemingway, eh?

Skip it son.

Ah gave it up anyway, efter the Auld Man deed. See that's how he goat killt in the end. Yez musta seen it in the News, quite a scandal so it wis. Well, we were up there oan the canal bank wan night, ken, jist sittin watchin the ither bank. It wis near the railway bridge up there, ken? Yez've probly seen the canal frae the train. That's where ye get the rats. So there we were, me an the Auld Man, jist waitin, when who should come along but two well-known members of the local constabulary, ken?

Mean Ah ken it's no nice, shootin rats, it's no very nice, but if ye've read Ernest Hemingway ye'll ken aa aboot the waitin bit. It wis the waitin bit that wis guid – like fishin, ken? Nuthn in the canal tae fish for though, that's why we got the guns in the first place. We didnae talk much, me an the Auld Man, when we were waitin for the rats. Naw, we jist liked sittin there oan a nice night, wi the sun oan the water an aa that, waitin. So along came this pair and startit asking us questions an aa that. The Auld Man jist sat there sayin nuthin, so Ah did the same. See, he wisnae a very talkative person unless he felt like talkin, an he never really liked talkin tae the polis. He widnae say somethin unless he had somethin tae say, see whit Ah mean? Aye, You've said it son, laconic. The Auld Man was laconic as hell sometimes. An this was gettin up the polis's nose, the wan who wis askin aboot the guns and what not. Nen the ither wan says, An what exactly is it ye're plannin tae shoot in any case? Nen the Auld Man says Vermin. Just like that, Vermin. Oh, so it's vermin, is it? says the first wan, the wan askin aa the questions, an then he says somethin aboot us bein vermin wirsels. Nen it transpires they want us tae haund owre the guns there an then. See it wis when wan o them tried tae take ma gun that it startit. A fight.

Now, can Ah ask ye tae tell me, honestly, do Ah look like a violent person? Do Ah, tell me straight? Naw, Ah'm no violent. Well, hardly ever. But it wis like when ye're wee, in the playground at schuil, an somebody bigger than ye tries tae take away yer luck-bag ken? That's whit it wis like – Ah jist saw red. So there wis a bitty a scuffle oan the canal bank, ma gun went oaf an wan of them got a pellet in the neck. Then the coshes, ken? Ah wis strugglin wi baith o them when Ah realised the Auld Man wis in the canal. He'd went right under. Probly he tried tae get in among us wi his stick, ken? An he musta got pushed intae the water. Ye can imagine whit it wis like. Ah couldnae swim tae save masel, neither could the Auld man. So the wan without the pellet in his neck had tae strip oaf an dive in. Ah remember the ither wan sayin, Let the auld bastard droun! By the time we got him back up oan the bank, he wis deed. So that wis that.

A tragedy, the paper called it. Course, Ah wis up in court for resistin arrest, assault an aa the rest o it, but the judge wis lenient cause o the Auld Man an that. Whitzat hen? Ring a bell, does it? Think ye mibbe saw it in the News? Aye, it's likely.

Sorry tae be sae morbid an that.

Thing is, Dryburn's no the same place without the Auld Man. Ah blame masel for whit happened. Ah shoulda had mair sense than tae start a scrap wi the polis. So Ah'm tryin tae educate masel, see, so Ah'll be able tae help folk decode their pyeslips an that.

Tell me something before ye go, friend. What's yer honest

opinion o Ernest Hemingway as a writer? A ken he's a great writer an aa that, but earlier the night Ah wis readin that story aboot shootn the lion, and Ah donno. Ah couldnae be bothert feenishin it. Ah came doon here for a coupla pints insteed. It's no Hemingway's fault ken, it's ma fault. Ah wis enjoyin the story an everythin, till it gets tae the bit aboot the kill ken. Cause the trouble is ye see, Ah jist cannae imagine the lion. Ah jist cannae picture the lion in my mind, know whit Ah mean? Aa Ah can imagine's a rat, a dirty hairy great rat. A rat's no the same as a lion, somehow.

Yez'll be on yer way, then. See, it's no very often Ah get the chance tae talk tae educatit people like youz. Ah wisnae tryin tae chat ye up or nuthn seeetheart, aaright? Aaright son? Ah wisnae trying tae get aff wi yer burd or nuthin son. See Hemingway? See if he did live in this area, in Dryburn like, he'da probly left years ago an got hissel a joab as a journalist.

Ah'll tell ye somethin else while yer lady friend goes tae the toilet, son. It's no very often we get wummin like her in here. Nae offence, but she's quite a catch. Quite a catch, Ah'm sayin. If ye want ma advice, haud ontae her. Or somebody else might, believe you me.

Ah'm no meanin anythin or anythin, but ye're a jammy wee swine so ye are and don't you try an deny it.

Selected Stories

The Sunbather

HE HAD SEEN HER there every day, in the same place beyond the rocks, a little away from the main stretch of beach. Clearly she had chosen the spot with care – it allowed her enough privacy to discard the lower half of her black bikini as well as the top. To get to it she had to pick her way over the high, jagged rocks, then follow a winding goat-track through bushes and down to the little cove. Already she had an allover suntan as deep and as rich as anyone could wish for, but every day she was back again: stretched out on a long white towel with a red stripe, stuck to her shadow like a slim brown lizard. He'd guessed that she must be an American girl – even from a distance he could see that her heavy blonde hair was obsessively well-groomed. Every time she changed her position, which she did with monotonous regularity, she would brush the hair over and over, then arrange it so that it was perfect. On the few occasions when he had actually seen her going into the water – not to swim, of course, but simply to cool down – he'd noticed that she always tied the hair up first and took great care to avoid getting it wet. The thick blonde hair, the black bikini, the suntan, the narrow waist, the languid walk – it was all cliché, of course. He had seen it so many times before in holiday brochures, films and colour supplements. Once, squatting among the rocks high above her and wishing he had brought his binoculars, he'd watched her shaking out that golden hair as she walked from the shallow water up to her little crescent of sand, and for a moment it had seemed as if he were watching an advertisement. There was nothing original about her then, yet he found himself scaling the rocks each day to watch from above, and though he didn't actually try to conceal his presence, he didn't make a point of being conspicuous either, but moved silently to his vantage point as an atheist might tiptoe into the rear of a church.

He didn't enjoy sunbathing himself. His fair skin burned and blistered too easily, and he had that underdeveloped kind of body which looks so awkward and vulnerable in beachwear. He had come to the island with a different purpose in mind, bringing with him a bag heavy with paints, drawing materials and even a foldout easel. He was after all a trained painter, and had just finished his first year of teaching in a comprehensive in Surrey, but so far he had done nothing apart from one or two stylised sketches, unworthy of an 'O' level, of the lemon trees outside his hotel window. He tended to spend the afternoons in the tavernas, stunned by the heat and unable to order his thoughts, drinking beer after beer until it was time to think about dinner. Though he hated to admit it to himself, and had given no indication of it in the one postcard he'd managed to write but not send, he was bored with being on holiday. Perhaps this was why he took an idle interest in the sunbather – far from bored, she seemed perfectly at ease, in her element. The fact that she was always alone on that little fingernail of sand somehow enhanced this. As he watched her change position, or bow her head to tie up the hair, or apply more oil to her long brown thighs, the word which always came to his mind was devout. Perhaps he was also intrigued to find that the illusion, this creature of the brochure and the screen, really did exist in life. In any case his idle interest soon grew into a fascination, and he found himself longing to go down to the cove and lie there on the sand beside her. He found if difficult to foresee any kind of conversation – what do you talk about to a completely naked stranger? – but imagined it pictorially: the gently undulating horizon of that long brown body against the luminous blue sky. Perhaps a single cumulus cloud suspended above her, its shadow falling on her breast. Surrealism, in his experience, could be all right if the subject was suitable for that kind of treatment. He wished he had brought his oils.

He became so preoccupied with the sunbather that one afternoon, even though the sky was completely overcast, he struggled over the rocks as usual in the hope of finding her there in the cove. When it was clear that she wasn't there, he sat down and waited hopelessly, telling himself that if she came by he wouldn't hesitate to speak to her. Certainly he'd introduce himself, strike up a conversation, maybe invite her to go for a beer. He imagined her blue eyes – he hadn't actually seen them, of course, but felt sure that they would be as blue and immaculate as the sky had been until today – gazing into his over a candlelit dinner. The elegant brown Modigliani of her shape against the white walls of his hotel room. His hand following the contour of her neck and shoulder, feeling the texture of that brushed blonde hair. The fact that she wasn't there and, he knew deep down, wasn't liable to appear on such a cloudy day, allowed his fantasy to accelerate as he waited, sweating and itching in his thick cotton shirt and cutoff jeans. The air was heavy and humid – surely it must rain or thunder soon, surely something must transpire. When the images crowding into his mind began to insult even his own sense of what was credible – surrealism was surrealism, but life was life – he picked up his bag and sketch-pad and made his way back to the beach. There were a few people sitting on the beach in groups of three or more. Half a dozen men were playing with a Frisbee, and as he walked past them he eyed their tanned, well-proportioned bodies – would she even consider being seen alongside a pinkish, freckled, narrow body such as his? As he turned to walk up the beach, the Frisbee whirred past his head, so close that it made his ear tingle. One or two of the men laughed, and a dark-haired girl who lay on the sand nearby reading a book looked up at him over the rims of her glasses. He felt himself flush as he passed her.

He hurried on to the village, where he stepped into the dark cool of the first taverna he came to. The waiter was a boy of eleven or twelve who looked, in his white shirt and black waistcoat, like a miniature adult. He came over to the table and wiped it and said yes. Feeling the need to get a little drunk, he ordered a metaxa with his beer. He watched as the little waiter – perhaps he was older than he seemed? – poured the drinks and brought them to the table, carrying the tray on one hand just as if he had been doing the job for decades.

Already he had that air of deliberated boredom of the professional waiter. He thanked him and gulped noisily at the beer, then laid the sketch-pad on the table and opened it. He had taken it out with him in the hope of doing something – a sketch of the sunbather, even from a distance, would be better than nothing – and now he doodled on the blank pages as he drank. He found himself trying to draw her from memory, but with each attempt it became clearer that he hadn't seen her closely enough. The figurines which resulted were imaginative in the worst sense. The first attempts were crude versions of a brochure photograph, with the blonde goddess stepping out of a badly-scribbled sea. The drawings degenerated as he drank, the last being little better than dirty drawings.

He was staring at the doorway when a girl stepped through it, tossed her rolled-up towel on to his table and collapsed into a seat opposite him.

'Mind if I join you?' she said. She leaned back in the seat and yawned, but her brown eyes magnified by the glasses looked wide open and eager for contact.

Recognising her as the girl who had witnessed the Frisbee incident, he flushed and stammered that of course he didn't. The waiter came over and said yes, with that look which said I've seen it all before. As she ordered a beer, some bread and feta, black olives, he looked at her closely for the first time. She had straight black hair, still wet from the sea, which clung to either side of her head like treacle, dividing to expose two large pink ears. She had a wide, straight mouth which opened into a grin as she spoke to the little waiter. Her body wasn't exactly ideal, being more like two bodies joined at the waist – the top half small and thin despite the wide hips and heavy thighs – but she was not unattractive. And there was the wide-eyed eagerness about her despite the slovenly way she sat – as if she saw her own body as an encumbrance, so much unnecessary luggage. The voice too was a curious mixture of laziness and impatience as she asked him where he was from, and what he did, how long he had been on the island, as if she wanted to get these boring preliminaries out of the way as soon as possible so that they could talk about something important.

'I teach too,' she said, 'in the heart of darkest Manchester. As you can imagine it isn't quite the Prime of Miss Jean Brodie. More like the breakdown of civilization as we know it. On a daily basis, that is. Still, I won't bore you with my repertoire of anecdotes, all that classroom violence and staffroom intrigue and exam futility, all those little things sent to try us in our struggle to spread the word. We're on holiday after all, although in my case it's more a convalescence, but still. . .'

She spoke in a flat, bored tone, but the words came quickly to her. He listened to her and smiled and said nothing, moving around restlessly in his seat. 'Mind if I have a look?' she said, her hand already on the sketch-pad. He did not want her to open it, but felt unable to say no.

'They're doodles,' he said, 'a waste of paper.' She opened the pad and began turning it this way and that. The waiter brought her beer and the food she had ordered. She popped an olive into her mouth, cut a slice of the feta and laid it on a piece of bread. She jammed this between her teeth and, taking a wide bite, began chewing energetically. After a moment she gulped at her beer and flicked a page of the sketch-pad over.

'Who's this,' she said, 'Miss World?' She stabbed at the darkly pencilled buttocks with a finger. 'I wish I had muscle-tone like that! Not likely with my figure. Not at this rate anyway

– they smother everything in olive oil here.' She held up the bread and cheese to show him that it had indeed been dressed with olive oil, then pointed to the sketch. 'Who's the centre-page spread?'

'It's nobody,' he said, 'no one I know, just a doodle.'

'Quite a shapely doodle,' she said, taking another olive and spitting the stone into her hand. 'If you did know her you'd be lying there beside her I'll bet.' She was pointing to another of the drawings, in which the impossible long-legged sunbather lay stretched out on the sand.

'Maybe I would,' he said, forcing a smile.

She poured more beer from the bottle into her glass and said, 'Along with a few hundred others.' She went on to talk between mouthfuls as she flicked through the sketch-pad – he could tell she found the drawings amusing and pitiful – about how overcrowded the beach was, how she'd never believe another brochure-blurb in her life, how she'd come to the island for peace and quiet. Of course she'd wanted to meet one or two interesting people, but so far had come across only the usual 'loud men without brains' like the ones playing frisbee on the beach. Those, and then the hateful middle-aged British couples intent on having chips with their moussaka. With a kind of bored indignation she told him that in three days she hadn't met a single person she could have an intelligent conversation with. He pretended disbelief – he'd been on the island three weeks and hadn't had any convers-ations, intelligent or otherwise. He nodded and smiled as she talked, but his three weeks of silence and solitude felt like a heavy weight inside him, dragging him down. He had to force the words out one by one – it was an effort even to ask her where she was staying.

'Alexandros,' she said, making the name into a yawn, 'same as you. I'm on the ground floor at the back, room nine. Come down one evening if you like. I've got a bottle of duty-free cognac. I could show you some of *my* drawings.'

'How did you know I'm staying there?' he asked.

'I saw you at dinner the other night. You're in the upstairs part, are you? Which room is it?'

'Eighteen.' He said, at the same time wondering why he felt so reluctant to tell her his room number. 'So you've been doing some drawing here too?'

She told him about the drawings she had been doing. Nothing serious really, just quick things of the old women in their black shawls, the men leading their donkeys, the children playing in the village square, and then the one or two abstract things in which she wanted to capture something of the island's atmosphere. . . She began to talk more generally about art in relation to experience, and he sensed that a long discussion on aesthetics would soon be underway if he didn't interrupt.

'Maybe I'll come down then, see what you've been doing.' He drank the last of his metaxa quickly and stood up.

'Are you off now?' she said. For the first time there was a note of surprise in her voice.

'I think I'll get back to the hotel now,' he said, 'have a siesta.' She shrugged and popped another olive into her mouth. As she chewed on it she looked at him steadily, and the look in her large eyes seemed to be saying, why are you running away just when we're getting started? Before he left she asked him his name and told him that hers was Barbara. And it was with a feeling of escape that he stepped out of the taverna into the bright glare of the street, though when he asked himself why this should be so, why he hadn't at least suggested that they meet for dinner, he couldn't say.

Later that night in his hotel room, after eating a congealed slab of moussaka in a dreary little taverna at the far end of the village, he fell on the bed and thought of going down to room nine. What was wrong with her, after all? She was intelligent, friendly and even attractive in an individual sort of way – so why not? Even if they didn't actually have what is called a holiday romance – and wasn't that, watercolours or not, what he'd really come looking for? – they might spend some time together usefully, even enjoyably. All he had to do was get up, shower and change, then go down to room nine. Instead he drowsed and dreamt of the sunbather: blonde, suntanned, perfect, she was stepping from behind a screen – one of those screens the models had undressed behind at art college – and she was wearing that black bikini, so brief that it merely emphasised the features it concealed. There was sand all over the studio floor, and among the many easels and deck-chairs the students were sitting talking and smoking cigarettes, or lying in attitudes of catatonic collapse. All were dressed in shorts or swimsuits because of the heat. He was determined to find a good space of sand in this overcrowded studio and set himself up before the model was posed – but where was the model? He caught a glimpse of her towel with the stripe disappearing through the studio door. He hoisted the easel – unfortunately it was the cumbersome art college kind, not his little foldout one – and staggered through the studio with it on his back. A Frisbee whirred past his ear and somebody laughed derisively. Someone else jeered behind his back, shouting something about Christ on his way to Calvary, and then he was through the door and in a long corridor of light. He picked his way precariously over the rocks, past the college cafeteria and down to the cove. He could see her down there, spreading out the towel and kneeling down – could she be praying? – and already she was unfastening the top of her bikini. In his hurry to get down to her, he slipped on a loose rock and the easel swung from his grip. In wonder he watched it bounce and leap and tumble over the rocks, at last plummeting down to land upside-down in the sand. There it stood, the image of a primitive gallows. He ran down the goat-track, shouting to the sunbather and waving a hog's-hair square-headed brush in his hand, and at last he was approaching that slender brown back. When she turned around, he woke up with a gasp.

The days became less clearly defined, ran into each other as the sky ran into the sea. It had rained often and the sky had become more or less permanently overcast. There had been no sign of the sunbather anywhere. What did she do when it rained? The question intrigued him more than it should have. Every day he made his little pilgrimage to the cove, and every day he was disappointed. Every day, too, he had seen the treacle-haired Barbara in and around the hotel. His own reaction to her puzzled him. Though she had more than once come over to him and begun a conversation, he had responded as stiffly as a Presbyterian minister to her suggestions and invitations. But then this was of no real importance. What mattered was that he was in love – he felt sure that this was no delusion – with the stranger he'd seen enacting her daily ritual, communing with the sun down in the cove. One thing which had continued to trouble him, however, was the climax to that dream. When she had turned

Selected Stories

to face him, why had his subconscious seen fit to substitute
Barbara's bespectacled eyes, her wide grinning mouth and
even the black roots of her hair showing through the blonde?

One morning he awoke to find that outside his window the
birds were singing in the lemon trees, and above them the
sky was a cloudless blue vault. Thanking God aloud, though
he was no believer, he swore to himself that this time, if given
the chance, he would not hesitate. He would use every trick
and tactic he knew to make his fantasy real. In the intervening
days he had planned it. When she arrived at the cove he'd
already be there, in a little place he'd found under an
overhang. That way she wouldn't be able to see him from
above and be put off by the presence of a stranger in her little
sanctuary. She'd catch sight of him only when she reached
the foot of the goat-track, and then he'd look up and say hello.
He'd be sitting there working on a drawing, of course – he'd
already done one or two stylish things of the rocks around
there and Barbara had found them quite impressive – and if
his prayers were answered she'd be intrigued enough to come
and have a look. He knew from tiresome experience how far
people were sometimes prepared to go out of their way just
to peer over his shoulder when he worked outside. If that
failed, he could always ask her if she might be interested in
posing for a few sketches. He was a trained artist, after all,
and if he knew anything about figure-conscious American girls,
he knew that she would be flattered. Even if she didn't agree
to pose, such an invitation would surely be less obvious, less
crude than the usual conversational gambits. He felt confident
that he could take it from there.

Going over his plan in his mind, he showered quickly

and packed the drawing things in his bag. Deciding to skip breakfast – he could always take her for lunch somewhere – he hurried downstairs and stepped into the bright glare of the street. As he came to the end of the village, he entered a small tourist shop on impulse. If he was going to be sunbathing with her, he should have a tasteful pair of shades and some Ambre Solaire. He chose a pair of sunglasses from the display rack, walked up to the counter and then saw her: the white towel with the red stripe hung from her shoulder-bag.

Over the black bikini she wore a full-length transparent beach-gown. The blonde hair had been tied up in a pony tail with a scarf, and he noticed that the roots were dark. For a moment she had her back to him as she paid for whatever she was buying and waited for her change, but even so he felt with sudden certainty that he had made some great mistake.

When she turned round he almost laughed – not at her, but at his own foolishness. She was fifty, over fifty, probably approaching sixty. The loose skin of her neck was creased and gnarled and furrowed. To make things worse, when she turned she bumped into him, apologised in a hard, tense American voice – he'd been right about something – then smiled at him enticingly. Had she seen him there, high above her in the rocks, the distant admirer? The grimly smiling, heavily made-up face was a taut mask of distress and anxiety. He stepped back in fright, stuttering apologies. Devout was not the word – she was fanatical. It was etched into the deep lines at the corners of her mouth, around the eyes, across the brow. . . the desperation of a woman to stay young, attractive, fashionable. It shone in her hard blue eyes like a mirage. When she had gone, he paid for the sunglasses and dropped them into his bag, thinking vaguely that the purchase was appropriate give his blindness.

It was late in the afternoon when he locked his room door and went down to room nine. He knocked quietly, but no one answered. He tried again later that night and again the next morning. When he made enquiries to the old man behind the hotel desk about an English girl called Barbara – black hair and brown eyes, wears glasses, staying in room nine – the old man grinned and with his hands made the shape of a buxom woman in the air. Then he told him that she had left the previous morning, to visit one of the other islands before going home. When he asked the old man which island, the old man scratched his armpit, sighed, stuck out his lower lip and said, 'To Crete maybe, maybe to Rhodes.' He could not, of course, say which.

The Fight

HE WAS GOING to see a fight.

'Shut your ears,' said his father.

He didn't think he really meant him to put his hands over his ears, he meant don't listen to the language. He tried not to, but the more you tried not to hear the language, the more you couldn't help hearing it. Even if you covered your ears with your hands, like he'd done once when he'd heard his mother screaming and shouting about something his father had done in Gorebridge, even with your ears covered you still heard things – your breathing in and breathing out, your heart beating, your throat swallowing. It was incredible if you did it when you were eating crisps. It sounded like an avalanche.

An avalanche was something he liked to think about. He liked the idea of it starting with one wee stone rolling down a mountain, then it bumped into another wee stone and it started rolling down the mountain as well. The two wee stones rolled faster and faster, then bumped into another two stones a bit bigger, then they started rolling down the mountain as well. So four stones bumped into another four, making eight, then they bumped into another eight, then the sixteen became thirty-two, then sixty-four, then a hundred-and-something and then it was an avalanche.

Even if he did cover his ears, he knew he'd still hear the voices coming nearer in the night, the men's voices cursing and swearing and singing, only they'd sound like they were inside him, like the cursing and swearing and singing was coming from him and not from not-him.

He tried shutting his eyes instead, but that just made the voices sound nearer, and the cheesy smell of the brewery and the rain smelled stronger, and the muddy path felt squelchier. And shutting your eyes didn't stop you seeing things, just the same as covering your ears didn't stop you hearing things. Even when you were sleeping, you kept seeing things. The only way to stop hearing things and seeing things and smelling things was to be dead. He tried to imagine what it would be like to be dead, to be not-him. It might be like being a stone.

He bent down and picked up one that was lying on the path. It looked dark but shiny in his hand. He put it in his pocket and felt it. It felt wet and slippy and jaggy. It had a sharp corner and a secret rounded part and a flat bit. It was just a thing, but maybe things were really alive inside of themselves, maybe the stone in his pocket was really glad that he'd picked it up. Maybe it had been lying on the path for ages just hoping to be picked up by somebody and taken somewhere else. When he clenched it tight in his hand it cut into his palm and hurt him. How could a thing that could hurt you like that be dead? Maybe being dead wouldn't be like being a stone after all, maybe you just floated around in space not hearing or seeing or smelling or touching or tasting anything, because how could you without ears and eyes and a nose and hands and a mouth? But maybe you just floated around above the clouds having memories and dreams. Maybe you could still have memories and dreams even without a brain to have them in, but he couldn't really imagine that – but maybe the only reason he couldn't really imagine it was that he was an atheist.

The sky looked orange, not like the sky where he lived. There were no fields in Edinburgh, just houses and streets and the orange light from the streetlamps. They were walking over a muddy stretch of wasteground where there were no street lights. Somebody, one of his dad's friends, knew the way, and everybody was walking behind him in single file.

He wished he'd stayed at home with his mum and his sisters. At this very moment he'd be sitting of the floor beside his mum's chair in front of the fire, watching Harry Worth doing the thing on the corner of the shop window, raising one arm and one leg and making it look like both. Before he'd left, he'd eaten a bowl of broth with barley and golden bubbles in it. He'd supped up the golden bubbles and left the barley at the bottom of the bowl. Now he felt hungry and wished he'd eaten the barley as well. She'd made him wear his Burberry. He hadn't wanted to wear it, but now he was glad of it.

The voices were coming nearer all the time. There were too many of them. It was a song. They weren't singing it though, they were shouting it.

'*Hullo, hullo,* we are the Billy boys! *Hullo, hullo. . .*'

So that was who they were. They were Protestants and they went to an Orange lodge every Tuesday night. His big brother had gone along to join the Orange band to learn to play the drums, then his dad had given him hell about it, so his big brother hadn't been able to go back. But then his big brother had saved up for a drum kit and had joined a band called The Trailblazers and had run away from home to start a new life in Doncaster.

His big sisters had told him about a Catholic school they'd gone to before his dad had an argument with the priest and told him never to darken his doorway with his mendacious propaganda again, and that was why he'd got sent to a Protestant school and his big sisters had got moved from the Catholic school to the Protestant school.

It was OK being an atheist except his dad always gave him a note to stop him going to the church at the end of term. He'd asked his dad why he couldn't go and he said it was because he was an atheist who didn't believe in God and he only sent him to the Protestant school because it wasn't as bad as the Catholic school, because there wasn't a school for atheists.

So when all the other kids went to the church he had to go to the sickroom. That was OK except everybody took the piss out of him and called him a heathen. Sometimes just being in the sickroom made him feel sick. Once he'd really been sick into the sink and the nurse had put her hand on his forehead while he was being sick. He could still remember how cool her hand had felt on his forehead and how he'd wondered why she was being so kind. Maybe she didn't believe in God either, maybe atheists helped each other to be sick and had cool hands to hold each other's hot foreheads.

There was a burn in the middle of the wasteground. He could hear it trickling in the dark but it was too dark to see. Now that it was happening he knew it was the way it had to happen: they reached the burn at the same time as the shouting men. Maybe there was going to be a fight on the way to see the fight. He held the stone tighter in his pocket, so that he could feel its hardness cutting into his fingers and his palm. It was alive, and if there was a fight he'd send the stone flying through the air at one of the other men. The stone would enjoy that, because if you were a stone probably the only excitement you got was when somebody threw you. He could just imagine how it would feel, to be stuck in one place for years and years, then somebody notices you and picks you up and sends you flying through the air or rolling down a mountain.

Across the burn somebody had put planks of wood for a bridge. His father's friends were silent as they crossed the plank bridge and came face to face with the other men. It was like they were going to a funeral. Then he heard his father say, 'Awright boys? Mind the wean, eh?'

Then he knew everything was under control. The men who were shouting made a great thing about standing aside and letting him past. One of them smiled at him before drinking out of a bottle. One or two hands patted his head. It felt good to see all these men standing aside for him, but it didn't feel so good to be called the wean. He was glad he was with the men who were silent, not the shouting men. He knew they were strong, as strong as any men could be, strong inside as well as with their hands, because they were miners. If a fight did start, they would win. And even if they didn't win, they would fight as well as they could, they would stand by each other, and so even if they lost the losing would be almost like winning.

Now that he was passing the other men he could see they were younger. One or two of them had Elvis haircuts and white shirts and thin black ties, like his big brother. Some of them weren't really men yet, they were still just big boys.

He took his father's hand and they walked on across the wet, dark wasteground. He was glad when they came to a lane that led up to a street and there were streetlights again and pavements.

'Da, are we nearly there?'

'Aye, we're here.'

It was good to see the bright light on the boxing ring and to drink his Bovril and eat his hot pie. The men around him kept smiling and winking at him and pretending to punch him on the jaw. One of them nodded at him and said to his father, 'Get him in the ring, get the gloves on him.'

His father gave him the programme and pointed out which boxers were from the Rosewell gym. He pointed to a name and said, 'Les. He's our new boy.'

He knew Les. Les had done a paper round before he'd left school to go down the pit and sometimes he'd tagged along helping him to deliver the papers.

He could smell beer, wet coats, Brylcreem and a vinegary smell that made his stomach shrink.

The first fight was fast. The two boxers didn't dance around like he'd seen boxers doing on t.v. They just wheeled round in the middle of the ring and battered each other. At the same time they kept hanging on to each other as if they wanted to have a cuddle.

He looked round at all the men watching the fight. That was worse to see than the fight. They were all shouting and snarling and punching the air with their fists. Then he look along the row at the miners. They were laughing. And now that he looked at the boxers, they were throwing punches at each other so fast that it did look quite funny, like a cartoon. His father had a big grin on his face and said to the man next to him, 'Need tae get that pair on the march!'

Sometimes all the miners got together and went on a march. It meant they all walked along the road together from one town to another town. Sometimes they had these big banners with words written on them in golden letters. They all sang songs as they walked along the road together, but it was really another kind of fight. He had heard about a march some miners had gone on to see a prime minister, who lived in a house in London with a policeman outside the door. He had seen the policeman once on the news. He felt sorry for him. Imagine having to stand outside somebody's door all day not doing anything. He imagined the policeman standing there all day wishing it was lousing time so that he could get home and get his tea. Then he would sit down by the fire with a big plate of steak pie and chips on his knee and maybe he'd see himself standing outside the door on the news and he'd say to his wife and his kids, 'Look, that's me.'

The last march his father had gone on had been to Hawick and he'd brought him back a pair of boxing gloves. He'd woken up in the morning and they'd been hanging on the headboard of the bed. He'd put them on right away, jumped out of bed and started boxing his reflection in the mirror.

It was Les's first fight. When he climbed between the ropes and stood in the glaring light he looked dazed, like an animal kept in a cage underground for a long time, then let out in the sunshine. He had curly black hair and the kind of eyebrows that slanted up in the middle. He looked around at the crowd and blinked his eyes. Then the trainer put his gumshield in his mouth and started shouting into his ear. Les kept nodding at what the trainer was shouting in his ear and sniffing his gloves and blinking his eyes.

The bell rang and Les went out to meet the other boxer, who was from Gorebridge. The boxer from Gorebridge had a ginger crew-cut and as soon as the bell rang and the fight started, he punched Les on the head and knocked him down. All the miners were shouting to Les to get up. Les lay on the floor of the ring while the referee counted. He started to get up, but it was too late. He was out. The fight was finished.

As Les climbed out of the ring, the miners shouted to him, 'Never mind, son!'

'Ye'll be awright next time!'

One or two of them stood up and went over to Les to pat his shoulder. Les kept shaking his head and blinking his eyes and asking what had happened.

There were other bouts and some of them had boxers who were from the Rosewell gym. The miners were up on their feet, shouting and punching the air like the other men. All except for two men who were wearing black suits and bow-ties. They were the judges and nobody knew where they came from. He wondered if they always wore the black suits and the bow-ties, even when they were sitting in their living rooms having their teas.

He was put in the snug and his father got him some lemonade and a packet of crisps and left him there. It was good to be on his own at last, just to see the shadows of the men on the frosted glass without having to see them and listen to them. The walls of the snug didn't go up to the ceiling and he could hear all their voices, talking and laughing. When he had finished his crisps and lemonade, he started pretending to be a boxer, to be Les, to be knocked out with the first punch. He played at losing, like in the game of best deaths they sometimes played on the railway embankment. What happened was that one of you went up to the top, everybody else shot you, then you fell off your horse and rolled down to the bottom and died. Everybody got a shot of getting shot, then everybody voted to choose the best death. You couldn't choose your own death, of course, you had to vote for somebody else's. He liked being shot, he liked falling, then rolling down the embankment and lying completely still. When he'd played at cowboys and Indians, it had always been more fun to be an Indian, a bareback rider, wearing warpaint and feathers, firing arrows and spears and yelling wallawalla-wooska, shot from your horse to roll over and over in the dust and die – that was better than blowing a bugle and firing a gun.

He danced around, pretending to be in the ring and to be knocked out, to fall on the floor then start to get up, to be counted out, to lose. To be led out of the ring with your head hung down and everybody patting you on the back and telling you it was all right.

He had to stop when two other boys were brought into the snug. They'd been at the fight as well, but they were from Gorebridge. The older boy was wearing a Burberry exactly like his, except that it was dark blue rather than dark green. He had a freckly face, and his black hair hung over one eye at the front. He had big nose with a bump in the middle of it. The younger boy had sticking-out ears and hunched shoulders like he was trying to hide his neck, and he was waiting to see what the older boy would do.

'Where d'you come frae?' said the older boy.

'Rosewell.'

The older boy looked at the younger one and sneered. The younger boy grinned.

'Ye a Proddy?'

He shook his head.

'So ye're a Pape, eh?'

He shook his head again.

'What are ye then, a fuckin Mormon?'

He thought about pretending he was a Mormon, but he knew this boy wouldn't let him away with it, he'd find out he was lying.

'Ah'm a atheist.'

'A what?'

'A atheist. I don't believe in God.'

'Aw aye, a atheist, eh? But are ye a Prodestant atheist or a Catholic atheist? Eh?'

The boy started poking him in the chest with his finger and repeating, 'Eh? Eh?'

He could feel his heart hammering, like somebody running, and the dizzy feeling in his head. There was a heavy feeling in his belly like he was going to be sick, then he smelled the vinegary smell and knew what it reminded him of. It reminded him of other fights he'd had, of how he'd felt before the fight, scared and excited.

The older boy was pushing him against the wall. Already something had come loose inside him, he could feel it moving, growing. And everything had been leading up to this, this was what the whole night was really about. It was alright losing when you were playing at losing, but not when it was real. The boy pushed him harder against the wall and he could feel the thing inside moving faster, like stones rolling in his head. They held each other and wheeled round and fell, then the boy was on the floor and he was on top of him and his hard fists drummed against the boy's hard head as the stones and boulders rolled and bounced and collided out of control in his head, and his heart hammered faster and his fists drummed harder and the boy's bloodied face blurred with the tears because he couldn't stop, because it wasn't him, it came from not-him, rolling and crashing through him like an avalanche.

The door of the snug opened and his father stood there shouting, 'What in hell's fire is going on in here?'

He stood up. The other boy stood up as well and started crying loudly, then the younger boy joined in.

He had been crying too, but now he stopped. He hung his head, afraid of what his father would do. Even although the other boy had started it, he knew that because he'd won, he'd get the blame.

The Face

HE DIDN'T want to see the face.

It was like a railway tunnel, except this tunnel sloped down the way, down through the dripping darkness, down into the deep, dark ground. He could see the dark shine of the rails and he could feel the ridges of the wooden sleepers through the soles of his gymshoes. It was very dark. He was glad his father was there with him.

It would be good to go back up to the daylight now, where the miners were sitting round a brazier, eating their pieces and drinking hot tea from big tins with wire handles. One of them had given him a piece and let him drink some tea from his tin and had pointed to different birds and told him their names, while the other miners talked about the pit and how it was closing. One of them had said he'd be quite happy never to see the face again.

He remembered the first time he'd heard about it. His father came in late from the pit and walked into the kitchen very slowly and sat down still with his coat on. Then he took off his bunnet and looked at it and put it on the kitchen table and talked to his mother in the quiet voice not like his usual voice. Like he couldn't say what he had to say, like when some of the words get swallowed. Because somebody had got killed at the face, John Ireland had got killed at the face, so he'd had to go to Rosewell to tell his wife. That was why he was late. Then his mother took a hanky from her apron pocket and sat down and started crying and his father put his hands on her shoulders and kissed her like it was Christmas except this was a different kind of kiss. Then his father looked up at him and nodded to him to tell him to go through to the other room, so he went through and watched t.v. and wondered how the face had killed John Ireland, the man who ran the boxing gym for boys, and how something terrible could make people need to kiss each other.

He could hear the water dripping from the roof of the tunnel and trickling down the walls and the scrape and crunch of his father's boots on the ground. They sounded too loud, but in the dark you had to hold on to sounds. Like when you shut your eyes and pretended to be blind, hold on to them to stop yourself hearing what was behind them, where it was like the darkness was listening.

Every few steps he could see the wooden props against the walls, but they were nearly as dark as the walls. And he could just make out the shapes of the wooden sleepers and the rails, but he didn't like the darkness between the sleepers and between the props. If you looked at darkness like that too long you started seeing things in it – patterns, shapes, faces. . .

He listened to his father's voice. It sounded too loud, and crackly like a fire, but you could hold on to it. He was telling him about the bogies that used to run up and down on the rails in the old days, taking the coal up to the pithead. It was good to hear his father's voice talking about the old days, but he didn't like the sound of the bogies. He asked what a bogie was and listened as his father told him it was sort of like a railway carriage on a goods train. He knew that anyway, but he wanted to hear his father telling him again, just in case.

There were other bogeys – bogeymen. He asked if there were bogeymen down the pit. His father laughed and said that there weren't. But he knew different, he knew that it was dark enough down here for bogeymen, especially now the word had been said out loud.

Sometimes if you said a word over and over again it started to sound different. It started to mean something else, to mean what it sounded like it meant. Then, if you kept saying it over and over again, it started to not mean anything, the word started to be a thing. And the thing didn't mean anything except what it was.

He tried it now, saying it under his breath over and over again. . . but before the word could lose its meaning, his father had stopped walking. He stopped too and turned, glad that they were going to go back up to the light, to the ordinary world.

'You go on.'

At first he wondered what his father meant, then he knew. He wanted him to keep on walking down into the dark. Alone. He pretended not to have heard and took a step towards the start of the tunnel, then he felt his father's hand on his shoulder and his heart pounding in his chest.

'Down ye go.'

He didn't move. He didn't say anything, hoping his father would lose his patience with him and change his mind.

'Are ye feart?'

'Naw, but. . . '

But what? He turned to the darkness. He could still see the rails and the props and the sleepers, but only just. He didn't want to see the face.

'Go on.'

He started walking down into the darkness. He had sometimes seen it in his dreams, after his father had come home late and spoken in the quiet voice to his mother about John Ireland. At first there was just the dark, the pitch-black dark that was blacker than coal, because even coal wasn't always black, because sometimes it was blue or grey, and sometimes it had a dark shine to it, like the cover of the Bible, and sometimes the coal had seams – of fool's gold, or the thin, brittle, silvery seams of mica – but the darkness in the dream had no shine to it, no seams, it was pure black. Then you felt it there like a shadow in the dark, a shadow that went long and went wide, went thick like a wall and went thin like a thread, then the shadow had the shape of a man and the man had a face and the face was the face of John Ireland.

He stopped walking, turned around and looked back at his father. He called to him and asked if he'd gone far enough.

'Further.'

It was good to hear his father's voice behind him, but it didn't last long enough to hold on to. Why didn't his father walk down further too? Why did he have to walk down on his own? Sometimes his father liked him to walk in front of him along the street. 'Walk in front,' he'd say, 'where I can see you.' Like the time he'd taken him to the gym to see John Ireland and he'd seen John Ireland's face. It looked like a bulldog's, with a flattened nose and a crushed ear and big, bloodshot eyes. In the dream it looked worse. In the dream, somehow you forgot it was the face of an old boxer. John Ireland had given him a pair of boxing gloves. He'd tied them together and put them round his neck on the way home. And his father had told him to walk in front, where he could see him. But that wasn't the reason, not the real reason he wanted him to walk in front. It was because he wanted to dream about his son being a champion boxer. He hadn't gone back to the gym because his mother had put her foot down, but he still put the gloves on sometimes and pretended to be a champion boxer. Now there wasn't the gym because of what had happened at the face.

Maybe it wouldn't be like the face in his dream, but he still didn't want to see it. He stopped and turned around. He could still see the dark shape of his father against the light from the start of the tunnel. He shouted to him and waited.

'Go on.'

His father's voice faded to an echo.

He turned and walked further down into the dark, the pitch-black dark even blacker than coal, then he felt it there, a shadow in the dark. . . He stopped, turned and shouted to his father. He could still see the dim greyish light from the start of the tunnel, but now he couldn't see his father.

He shouted out again. His own voice echoed and he heard the fear in it, then all there was was the listening darkness all around and the pounding of his heart. The shadow had the

The Face   139

shape of a man and the man had a face. . .

As he turned to run away he was lifted in the air and his father's laughter filled his ear. He was laughing and saying he was proud of him because he'd walked down on his own, proud because now he was a man.

He rubbed the bus window with his hand and looked out at the big black wheel of the pit. He watched it getting smaller as the bus pulled away, till it was out of sight.

'Da? Why are they gonnae shut the pit? Is there nae coal left in it?'

'There's plenty of coal.'

'How then?'

'The government wants it shut.'

'Where'll ye go tae work then?'

'Mibbe in Bilston Glen.'

'Is that another pit?'

His father nodded. He waited a minute, then he asked,

'Da? Has it got a face as well?'

'Aye, it's got a face.'

'Is it like the face in your pit?'

His father shrugged.

'Much the same.'

'Da. . . Ah *saw* it.'

'What?'

'The face.'

His father shook his head and smiled at him, the way he did when he thought he was too young to understand something.

'Ah did see it!'

'Oh ye did, did ye? What did it look like then, eh?'

'It looked like the man who ran the gym.'

And he knew he'd said something very important when his father stopped smiling, turned pale, opened his mouth to say something but didn't say anything, then stared and stared at him – as if he couldn't see him at all, but only the face of the dead man.

Shouting It Out

HE COULD do it in the dark, with Christine there beside him, surrounded by everybody just sitting there watching the film, when the only sound was the soundtrack, so loud it was like somebody whispering in your ear. He knew how to wait for that moment when everyone was totally into the film, when nobody was coughing or giggling or whispering or eating popcorn. A moment like now, when there was just the eerie music and David Bowie taking his first step on the planet earth. Without having to think about it, he shouted it out: 'Step we gaily, on we go, heel for heel and toe for toe! '

Christine thumped him on the chest and told him to shut up, but it had worked. Although she was embarrassed, she was laughing. Everybody was laughing – or it seemed like everybody. Really it was probably just a few folk here and there across the cinema, but in the darkness it felt like the whole cinema was laughing. Now it would be good to get them on the tail-end of the laugh with something else, but already the usher's torch was looking for him among the seats and Christine was telling him to keep quiet. He huddled down in the seat as the beam of the usher's torch tried to find him.

'Keep it quiet along there!'

Christine punched him lightly on the arm. He liked it when she hit him. It felt so different from being punched by one of his pals. There was something very light and playful about it – it made him feel bigger and stronger than he was. He liked it when she touched him in any way at all. Even if she just touched his sleeve, it was like he could feel the touch on his skin. And although his friends said she was hackit, a dog, he liked her big brown eyes, her thick dark hair, her wide mouth with the deep corners that twisted up so quickly when she smiled – everything, really, except the nose. She didn't like her own nose either, and sometimes covered it a bit with her hand. At first her nose, and what his pals said about her, had really bothered him, but now he was getting to like being with her – they'd been going out together for nine weeks – and in a funny way he'd started to think her nose wasn't so bad. It made her look foreign – Greek, Spanish, or Italian. He liked the way sometimes a little crease wrinkled the side of her nose when she laughed. It suited her.

He watched the film for a while, but then, just as David Bowie was arriving in the small town in the middle of nowhere in the desert, he couldn't help himself. He had to shout it out: 'Excuse me. Ah'm lookin for Mairi's weddin!'

Laughter. But this time the usher's torch trapped him in its beam and Christine hid her head behind his shoulder. He could feel her shaking, shuddering against him as she held in her laughter.

'Right you – out!'

'Who? Me?'

He went through the routine of protesting his innocence until the usher gave up and went away, with the warning that if there was any more of it he'd be out.

Christine hissed into his ear, 'What a red face! Can you no just watch the film, like everybody else?'

'Okay.'

Like everybody else. He slumped forward in the chair, made his mouth hang open and stared like a zombie at the screen.

Christine shook her head, thumped him on the arm and laughed. That was one of the things he liked about her – he could make her laugh.

He'd been coming to the same cinema since he was seven or eight years old. He could remember a whole gang of them coming to the Saturday matinee, sometimes bringing their roller skates to skate down the aisle until they were thrown out. Buying cinnamon sticks at the chemist's and smoking them behind the cinema before they went in. The old man with the cap hanging over one eye who sold the Kia-ora. He was so old and bent and wrinkled, they were scared to buy his juice. Climbing over the seats, drumming your feet on the floor when the film broke down, cheering when the cavalry arrived. . . Then there was that really scary film called The Time Machine with the monsters called Morlocks. They were big and blue and hairy, a bit like gorillas except they lived under the ground. Above the ground was a kind of paradise. The people just played around all day and wore futuristic clothes and ate exotic fruits, till they heard the siren. When the siren sounded, they all froze and became like zombies, the zombies of paradise. They had this glazed look in their eyes as they walked, hypnotised, to the caves that led down into the underworld where the Morlocks waited for them, stirring the cauldrons – and guess what was for dinner? Although it seemed like a hoot now, the film had given him nightmares for weeks as a kid. He could remember checking in the wardrobe and under the bed at night, checking for Morlocks. And after his dad had come and put his light out and told him to get to sleep, he had sometimes shouted it out into the darkness of the room, 'Go away, Morlocks!'

But in his dreams the darkness of the cinema had blurred with the underworld the Morlocks lived in, and the Morlocks were coming down the aisle like wild ushers with flaming torches in their paws, and the old man who sold the Kia-ora had turned into a Morlock although he still had his own face and the cap hanging over his eye, and when the siren sounded he was stirring the Kia-ora in the Kia-ora machine and all the kids were queuing up to buy it.

For a while the nightmares had bothered him so much that he'd stopped going with the gang to the matinee. He could still remember those Saturday afternoons without the gang, kicking a puckered ball against the wall of the house, playing at Patience, throwing stones at nothing in particular. Then one Saturday he'd plucked up the courage to go back to the cinema, although he was still scared of the Morlocks and the darkness that would happen when the lights went down and the golden curtains opened. And it had been all right, the film had made him forget all about the Morlocks – until now.

He looked along the row at all the faces bathed in the bluish light from the screen, staring up at the film. They looked so stupid, so dumb and stupid and hypnotised. They were like the zombies of paradise, their mouths hanging open, their eyes staring up at the screen. When the film finished, when the siren sounded, they'd have to go and meet the Morlocks who waited for them at home, stirring the cauldrons. . .

He started laughing silently to himself at the idea of it. Christine felt his chest shaking, turned to look at him and said, 'What is it?'

He shook his head and said, 'Nothing.'

But she could always tell when he was keeping something to himself. She persisted, 'What is it? Tell me!'

When he still wouldn't tell her – it was too long and complicated and anyway she wouldn't find it funny – she pretended to be annoyed. It looked like she was acting. Acting was something they did together all the time. She acted sad, he acted concerned. Or he acted moody and she acted cheerful. Or she acted annoyed and he acted like a fool to get her out of it. It wasn't like real acting, the kind they did in films. It was a different kind of acting, because the feelings were real, but it was like the two of them were trying the feelings on for size, like clothes to see if they fitted, and to see if they suited them.

He quite liked it when she was annoyed with him. It did suit her. She had dark eyelashes, and when she was being annoyed she looked down, so that all you could see was the eyelashes and the wide mouth turning down at the corners. It made her look mysterious.

Once, he'd made her cry. What his pals had been saying about her had been getting to him, so he'd decided to chuck her. They'd gone for a walk in the graveyard. It had been a lovely sunny evening. Everything had been fine except that at the back of his mind he knew he was going to have to tell her it was finished. They went into a bit of the church that was sort of half inside and half outside. In the cool shadows they'd kissed and canoodled as usual. Then he'd told her. She'd turned away, but he'd seen the long black mascara tears trailing down her cheeks.

He'd felt so bad about her crying and had missed her so much that a few days later he'd knocked on the door of the girls' bogs at dinner time and asked for her. When she'd come out, he'd taken her along to the maths corridor and asked her if she'd have him back. She'd thrown her arms around him and looked happier than he'd ever seen her before.

Maybe it wasn't all acting, even if they didn't know how they should do it or say it.

He noticed that she'd stopped chewing her gum and was still looking really annoyed. He asked her if she'd finished with it, could he borrow it?

It didn't work.

In the end he had to tell her. About the roller-skates, the cinnamon sticks, the Kia-ora man, the Morlocks in the wardrobe and the zombies of paradise. About the nightmares and being scared of the dark when the lights went down at the matinee. What he couldn't tell her about, what he couldn't find words to explain, was the idea that all the folk around them were just like the zombies of paradise, and when they left the cinema it was like the siren sounding. The Morlocks would be waiting for them. . . but he couldn't tell her all that. She knew it anyway. She knew that if she missed her bus and had to walk home and got in late, the Morlocks would be waiting for her, stirring the cauldron.

She listened to it all and when he'd finished whispering

it in her ear she moved away from him and said, 'Is that all?'

But she kissed him quickly on the cheek, looked at him as if she was looking from far away and smiled. It was just a little kiss, but one of the things he liked about Christine, although everybody said she was a dog, was that she was a great kisser, she had all these different kinds of kisses. All of her kisses made him feel good inside, made him feel like himself, like he was acting in a film but the part he was playing was himself. It was magic, and sometimes when he was with her he wanted to shout something out but he didn't know what.

He put his arm around her and let his fingers play with the gold chain of her locket. She went back to the film, her mouth opening and closing as she chewed her gum.

David Bowie was watching fifty televisions at once, all showing different programmes. He kept changing all the channels with his remote. Christine's hand covered his mouth before he could shout it out: 'Nothin much on telly the night!'

Anyway, it wasn't very funny. Not worth getting thrown out for. But Christine was laughing because of what she was doing, putting her hand over his mouth to shut him up. She was still laughing a bit when he moved his hand up to her neck, pulled her closer and kissed her on the mouth. Then the laugh died away in her throat as they started kissing seriously. He could taste her lipstick and her chewing gum, feel the tips of her teeth and her moist, soft tongue. He stroked her neck, then ran his hand down over her collarbone. . . before he could go any further, she caught his hand in hers and squeezed it.

After a while they broke apart and watched the film.

David Bowie was having his nipples removed with a

scalpel. Christine hissed, 'Don't you dare!'

Anyway he couldn't think of anything very funny to shout out, except maybe, 'Ohyah!'

What would it really be like to fall to Earth? Sometimes he wondered about that. Sometimes he could even feel that he really had just fallen to Earth, like when he looked along the row and saw all the faces staring up at the screen. It was like seeing people for the first time. Not one at a time, the way you usually looked at them, but sitting there in a row, like a line of aliens, like the zombies of paradise.

*

They held each other close in the newsagent's doorway, waiting for the bus. They kissed, but his mind was only half on what he was doing. He wanted to tell her that she wasn't like the others, not a zombie of paradise, and that she suited her nose or it suited her, and that he liked her eyes, her mouth, her hair, the way she laughed. . . He wanted to tell her something he'd never told anybody else.

Why couldn't he just say it to her, just look her in the eyes and say it? Of course, it wasn't like saying something ordinary, although going by the films, people said it to each other all the time. He should forget about looking into her eyes when he said it. He should just, after a really long kiss, a serious kiss like this one, whisper it in her ear, and it would sound as loud and as real as the soundtrack of a film. Or just say it, say it like he meant it, say it like he wasn't acting at all.

'Here it comes.'

She snatched another quick kiss and broke away from him and hurried to the door of the bus. She turned to him, smiled and waved as the bus door opened. Then she went on, paid her fare and found a seat next to the window so that she could smile and wave again. It was only when the bus started to pull away from the stop that he panicked inside and he didn't care who heard as he shouted it out.

Kreativ Riting

'TODAY, we are going to do some writing,' says PK. 'Some creative writing. You do know what I mean by creative, Joe, don't you?'

This is what he says to me. So I says to him, 'Eh. . . Is that like when ye use they fancy letters an that?'

'No, Joe, it is not. Creative writing has nothing whatsoever to do with "they fancy letters an that",' says PK.

So I made the face like Neanderthal Man and went, 'UHHH!'

We call him PK cause his name is Pitcairn and he is a nut. So anyway, he goes round and gives everybody a new jotter each.

'For God's sake now, try and use a bit of imagination!'

Then he stops at my desk and he looks at me like I am a puzzle he is trying to work out and he says, 'If you've got one, I mean. You have got an imagination Joe, haven't you?'

This is him slaggin me, ken?

So I says to him, 'Naw, sir, but I've got a video.'

That got a laugh, ken?

So then PK says, 'The only trouble with you Joe is, your head is too chock-a-block with those videos and those video nasties. Those video nasties are worse than anything for your brain, Joe'

Then Lenny Turnbull, who sits behind me and who is a poser, says, 'What brain? Joe's no got a brain in there, sir, just a bitty fresh air between his lugs!'

That got a laugh, ken?

So I turns round in my seat and I give Lenny Turnbull a boot in the shins, then he karate-chops me in the neck, so I slap him across his pus for him.

PK goes spare, ken?

Except nobody takes any notice, so he keeps on shouting, 'That's *enough* of that! Come on now 4F, let's have a bit of order round here!'

So then I says, 'Sir, they video nasties is no as bad as glue is for your brains but, is it?'

That got a laugh, ken?

Then Lenny Turnbull (poser) says, 'Joe's got brain damage, sir, through sniffin too much glue!'

'Glue sniffing. . . solvent abuse. . . is no laughing matter. Now let's have a bit of *order round here!* Right, I'm going to get you all to do a piece of writing today. You've got a whole two periods to do it in, and what I'd like all of you to do is empty your mind. In your case, Joe, that shouldn't be too difficult.'

This is PK slaggin me again, ken?

So I says for a laugh ken, 'How no, sir? I thought you said my mind was chock-a-block with video nasties?'

Then PK says, 'That's right, Joe, and what I want you to do is just empty all that stuff out of your mind, so that your mind is completely blank, so that you've got a blank page in your mind, just like the one in you jotter. . . understand?'

'But sir, this jotter's no blank. . . it's got lines in it!'

'Joe, your head probably has lines in it too, through watching all those video nasties.'

Everybody laughed at that, so I made the face like Neanderthal Man again and started hitting my skull with my fist and went, 'UHHH! UHHH!'

'Joe, I knew you'd hit the headlines one day,' says PK.

Nobody laughed at that, so PK says, 'You are a slow lot today, aren't you?'

So I did the face again and went, 'UHHH!'

'Right. As I was saying before I was so rudely interrupted, what I want you to do is empty out your mind. It's a bit like meditating.'

'What's meditatin? Is that like deep-sea divin an that?' says Podge Grogan, who sits beside me.

'Not quite.'

'Of course it's no!' says Lenny Poser Turnbull.

'Well,' says Podge, 'it coulda been! That's what it sounds like, eh Joe? Deep-sea divin in the Mediterranean an that.'

'Aye, that's right enough. Deep-sea meditatin! Ah've heard o that!'

'Away ye go! Deep-sea meditatin! Yez are off yer heids, you two!' says Lenny.

'Meditating,' says PK, 'as far as I know, has nothing to do with deep-sea diving at all, although when you think about it, the two activities could be compared. You could say that deep-sea diving and meditating are. . . similar.'

So me and Podge turns round in our seats and looks at Lenny Turnbull.

'See?' says Podge. 'Deep-sea meditatin. Tellt ye.'

'They're no the same at aw,' says Lenny. 'Ah mean, ye dinnae need a harpoon tae meditate, eh no sir?'

'Ye dae in the Mediterranean,' says Podge.

'Aye,' I says, 'it's fulla sharks an that, course ye need a harpoon.'

'Aye,' says Lenny, 'but you're talking aboot deep-sea divin, no meditatin!'

'Well Lenny,' says PK, 'maybe you could tell the class what meditating is.'

'Aw, it's what they Buddhist monks dae.'

'Yes, but how do they do it?'

'Aw, they sit wi their legs crossed an chant an aw that.'

'Naw they dinnae,' says Podge Grogan, 'cause Ah've seen them. They dance aboot an shake wee bells thegither an that an sing Harry Krishner, that's how they dae it!'

'That's different,' says Lenny, 'that's no meditatin, eh no sir?'

'Well no, I don't think so. In any case, there are different ways of meditating, but basically you have to empty your mind. You'll find it's harder to do than you think. Your mind will keep thinking of things, all the little things that clutter our minds up every day.'

'How's that like deep-sea divin, sir?' says Lenny.

'Well, it's hard to explain Lenny, I just meant that when you meditate you sort of dive into your mind, you dive into the depths of your mind and that's what I want you to try to do today. If you're lucky, you might find something you didn't know was there.'

'Dae we get tae use harpoons?' says Podge.

'No,' says PK. 'Pens.'

Everybody goes, 'AWWW!'

'Now listen,' says PK. 'It's quite simple really. All I really want you to do is write in your jotter whatever floats into your mind. I don't want you to think about it too much, just let it flow. OK?'

'OK, PK!'

'Anything at all. It doesn't have to be a story. It doesn't have to be a poem. It doesn't have to be anything. Just whatever comes into your heads when you've emptied out your minds. Just let your mind *open up*, let the words *flow* from your subconscious mind, through your pen into your jotter. It's called Automatic Writing, and you're lucky to get a teacher like me who lets you do something like Automatic Writing especially first two periods on a Wednesday.'

This is still PK talking, ken. Then he says, 'I don't even want you to worry about punctuation or grammar or anything like that, just let your imagination roam free – not that you worry about punctuation anyway, you lot.'

So I says for a laugh, ken, 'Sir, what's punk-tuition? Is that like learnin tae be a punk?'

Everybody groaned. PK rolls his eyes and says, 'Joe, will you just shut up please?'

So I says for a laugh, ken, 'Hear that? First he's telling us tae *open up* and now he's telling us tae *shut up!*'

That got a laugh, ken?

Lenny Turnbull (poser) says, 'But sir, what if nothing comes intae yer heid when ye're sittin there wi yer pen at the ready?'

'Anyway,' I says, 'how can I write anyway, cause I've no got a pen?'

'Use your harpoon!' says Lenny.

'You can borrow my pen,' says PK. 'But it's more than a pen you'll need to write, Joe, because to write you also need inspiration.'

'What's that, a new flavour o chewing gum, or what?' says Podge Grogan.

So everybody starts laughin and PK goes spare again, ken. Then he brings this cassette out of his briefcase and he says, 'Right, I want you to listen to this piece of music I've got here, so that it might give you some inspiration to get you going. Just listen to the music, empty your mind, and write down whatever comes out of the music into your heads. OK?'

'OK, PK'

'What is it sir? Is it The Clash?'

'No it is none of that Clash-trash. That Clash-trash is even worse for your brain than video nasties *or* glue, Joe.'

Everybody laughed, so I did the face.

'UHHH!'

'If the wind changes, your face might stay like that, Joe. Right, now stop wasting time. The music you are about to hear is not The Clash, but a great piece of classical music by Johann Sebastian Bach.'

'Who's she?' says Podge Grogan.

'*He*,' says PK, 'was a musical genius who wrote real music, the likes of which you lot have probably never heard before and probably won't know how to appreciate even when you do. Now I want you to be very quiet and listen very carefully to this wonderful classical piece of music and just let go, let go, and write absolutely anything the music makes you think and feel about. It's called "Air on a G string".'

'Hair on a g-string?' I says.

Everybody fell about, ken?

'Come on now 4F, let's have a bit of order round here!'

Then Lenny Turnbull says, 'But sir, can we write *absolutely* anything we want, even swearin an that?'

'Absolutely anything you want to,' says PK. 'Just listen to the music and *let go*. I promise no member of staff will see it – except me. If you don't even want me to read it, I won't. The choice is yours. You can either read out what you've written to the class, or you can give it to me and I promise you it will be destroyed. OK?'

'OK. PK'

Then Lenny Turnbull says, 'But sir, what about sex an that – can we put sex in it as well?'

'Hold on a minute,' says PK.

So I says for a laugh, ken, 'Hear that? First he tells us to *let go*, and now he's telling us to *hold on!*'

That got a laugh, ken?

Then PK started clenching his fists so the knuckles went white, and he glared at me and his face went beetroot like he was ready to go completely raj.

'Look here you lot, we haven't got all day. You've already wasted nearly a whole period already with your carry-on and I am sick to the back teeth of having to RAISE MY VOICE IN HERE TO MAKE MYSELF HEARD! Will you please sit *still*, keep your hands on the desk and YOU, Joe Murdoch, are asking for *trouble!* One more wisecrack out of you and you will be out that door and along that corridor to pay a visit to the *rector!* Do I make myself clear?'

I sort of make a long face.

'As I was saying, you may write anything you like, but I don't think this piece of music will make you think about sex, because it is not an obscene bit of music at all. In fact it is one of the most soothing pieces of music I know, so *shut up* and listen to it!'

So then PK gets the cassette machine out of the cupboard where it is kept locked up in case it walks and he plugs it in and he plays us the music. Everybody sits there and yawns.

Then Podge Grogan says, 'Sir, I've heard this before!'

'Aye, so've I!' everybody starts saying.

Then Lenny Turnbull says, 'Aye! It's that tune on the advert for they Hamlet cigars!'

So then everybody starts smoking their pens like cigars and PK switches off the music.

'Put your pens *down!* Any more of this and I'm going to keep you in over the break! I am aware that this music has been used in an advertisement, but this is not the point of it at all. The point is, it was written centuries ago and has survived even until today, so *belt up and listen to it!*'

So we all sat there and listened to the music till it was finished, but nobody got any inspiration out of it at all. So then PK says, 'If anybody is stuck, you could always write something about yourself. Describe yourself as you think other people might see you. 'Myself As Others See Me.' Now I've got a stack of prelims to mark, so I want you to keep quiet for the rest of the time and get on with it.

So that's what I did, and here it is. This is my Kreativ, autematick, deep-sea-meditatin ritin:

MY OWN SELF AS OTHERS MITE SEE ME

MY NAME IS JOE MURDOCH AND I AM SHEER
MENTAL SO WATCH OUT I HAVE GOT A GREEN
MOHAWK IT HAS GOT SKARLIT SPIKES ON MY
FOUR HEAD I HAVE GOT A SKUL AND
KROSSBONES ON MY BLACK LETHER JAKET I
HAVE GOT AT LEAST 200 KROME STUDS NOT
COUNTIN THE STUDS ON MY LETHER BELT AND
MY DOG KOLLAR ON MY NECK I HAVE GOT A
TATOO IT SAYS KUT ALONG THE DOTTED LINE
ON MY BACK I HAVE GOT NO FUTURE ON MY
BOOTS I HAVE GOT NO HOPE IN MY POCKET I
HAVE GOT NO MONEY AND MY DAD STOLE THE
LED OF THE DALEITH EPISCAPALIEN CHURCH
ROOF AND I GAVE HIM A HAND AND WE DIDNET
GET CAUGHT HA HA I AM A WARRIER AND I AM
SHEER FUCKEN MENTAL SO WATCH OUT O.K.

THE END

And now I will take out my kreativ riting to PK and tell him I
don't want to read it out to the class and I don't want him to
read it either. I will tell him I want it to be *destroyed*.

That should get a laugh, ken?

Media Studies

WHEN HE WOKE up, David Law heard his mum and dad moving around in the kitchen downstairs – his mum's nervous steps on the linoleum, the squeak of his dad's wheelchair – then he remembered what he'd done, and that this was the morning the *Murkirk Gazette* would come. Soon he'd have to get up, get dressed, go down and face them.

He shut his eyes and tried to get back to his dream, an erotic dream – that was the word, *erotic*, although a year ago he'd've called it *dirty* – but now he'd lost the thread of it. Had it been about Anne, his girlfriend at school? Somehow he didn't think so. He could just remember odd bits of the dream: a white blouse and a black tee-shirt, his hand unbuttoning the blouse and moving inside it, over the black tee-shirt, then feeling the tight, firm breast with the nipple as hard as a nut, pulling the tee-shirt up, cutting open the tee-shirt with the scissors – that's right he'd had a pair of *scissors* in the dream. . . then the short black skirt riding up over a thigh as she sat down next to him, his hand with the glue-brush in it – glue-brush? – reaching over and moving in there, over that black nylon-sheathed thigh, pushing the glue-brush up into the deep, hot secret place between. . . And Jazzman just standing there watching all this going on, as if it happened every day in Media Studies.

Suddenly he remembered the face in his dream. Of course! It hadn't been Anne, his girlfriend – she was too 'nice' to be in dreams like that, and anyway she didn't get Media Studies, because she was too brainy – but another Ann, Ann Erskine.

She was fourth year as well, but she wasn't in his class for anything except Media Studies. It was his best subject – the only subject he'd ever come top in. Last week Jazzman – his name was Mr Logan, but everybody called him Jazzman because he was always playing jazz records in his room at dinner-time – had got them all to shove the desks together in the middle of the classroom so that they could spread out the newspapers and cut out headlines and photographs from different papers and paste them in their project folders. And Ann Erskine had ended up sitting next to him. He didn't think he'd been watching her at the time – he'd never fancied her. He'd always thought she was a slag – but now he had to admit that he must've been taking it all in, because it had all been there in the dream.

Ann Erskine wore her skirts tight and had dyed auburn hair in a side-parting over one eye. She wore this thick black eyeliner and heavy purple eyeshadow. Her lips as well, sometimes she wore this black lipstick that made her look like something out of *The Night of the Living Dead*. She always looked sort of bored with school, as if she was thinking about something else the whole time, something else only she knew about. He had heard she was *fast*.

Look at those *legs*, thought David, but somehow the subtitle didn't bring a picture on to the screen What a *body*, he thought, but again the words made no movie flicker and unfold on his inner screen, his dream-screen. Maybe the projectionist had packed up and gone home, thinking there wasn't any need for another showing.

He opened his eyes and looked around the dim bedroom: that wallpaper with its repeating pattern of tanks, helicopters and ships, soldiers, pilots and deep-sea divers. . . It had been up for years now the original blue background, a strange mixture of sky and sea, was torn in places and riddled with pinholes and Sellotape-marks. He'd put up so many pictures of his heroes, cut from newspapers, magazines and album sleeves, then made a mess of the wallpaper when he'd taken all the pictures down again – he'd decided he didn't want to have heroes any more, that having heroes was really pretty naff.

That was one of the things he'd learnt from Jazzman, from doing Media Studies. Jazzman was always saying that hero-worship was bad for you, whether you were the worshipper or the hero. When they'd done the unit on 'Pornography in the Popular Press', about page-three girls in the *Sun* – 'Titillating Tits' he'd called his own project – Jazzman had argued with the class for nearly a whole period. Everybody had said there was nothing wrong with it, but Jazzman had said there was, because it was exploitation, not just of page-three girls, because they earned loads of money after all, but exploitation of the men who looked at them. It was encouraging grown men to worship images of women instead of caring about real women, like hero-worship except in this case the heroes were bare-breasted blondes and brunettes. That was what David like about Jazzman – he came out with phrases like 'bare-breasted blondes and brunettes' in the class.

His mum had created hell about the mess he'd made of the wallpaper, then last week she'd started making plans to get new wallpaper, but he'd told her he didn't want any new wallpaper. He'd rather keep the room the way it was, with its massacred boy's wallpaper – it looked sort of OK like that. Then he'd told her he wanted to paint the room, and had even offered to go and buy the paint and do it himself, but there had been a raging bloody argument about the colour, because he'd wanted to paint it black. Imagine it, he'd said to Raymond King, the pal he hung about with after school, imagine it black all over, no pictures or nothing, not even one, just completely fucking *black*. . . Raymond, who still had album sleeves and posters all over his room, even the ceiling, had just shrugged and said, 'Sounds really eh. . . what's the word? Boring.' Even Raymond hadn't seen what would be pure ace about a completely black room.

He'd have to leave off about wanting to paint the walls black for a while, because this morning there was going to be another screaming row, with his mum and dad doing the shouting.

He shut his eyes again and thought about the other Ann. He still had the scissors in his hand – that was kind of weird but in a way he liked the weirdness – it made it more like a movie. The blouse, unbutton the blouse first, then feel that firm breast under the black tee-shirt, cut it open, careful, that's it. . . He didn't think she'd been wearing a bra in the dream but now he put one in anyway, a black lacy bra. . . then one snip with the scissors in the middle and it flew open. Now the glue-brush , painting the nipple with the glue-brush. . . Get down to the skirt now, cut the skirt up the front. . . He found it hard to keep the other Ann's body on the screen for very long, and even when he did it kept changing , blurring with other images he'd seen in movies, magazines and newspapers – all those 'bare-breasted blondes and brunettes'. The scissors and the glue-brush kept getting in the way as well, and sometimes Anne, his girlfriend, would barge into the fantasy and drop her schoolbag, heavy with maths and science textbooks, on the desk between him and the other Ann, then the movie would break down, the screen would go dark, there were numbers flashing across it, and in his mind David booed just the way he'd booed as a kid when the film had broken down at the Saturday matinee.

He'd seen the other Ann again this week, in the science wing. McKenzie, the chemistry teacher, had been giving him a lecture in the corridor outside his classroom door.

'If you're no interested in the story of combustion, laddie, that's yer own lookout. There's always one, isn't there? The wise-guy, the funny man, the class cabaret. Ye think ye're hilarious, eh Law? I'll tell you something: life's no joke. Ye're a wastrel, Law, destined for the dole queue. Don't think I don't know ye've been in trouble wi the police already. It's common knowledge in the staff room. But ye'll no get away wi it in my classroom, son, ho no. An ye can sneer at a Chemistry O-level if ye like, laddie, but take it from me: without some qualifications under yer belt, you'll no go far. . . '

In the middle of it, the other Ann had come round with a

circular, but McKenzie had made her stand and wait until he was finished with him. So she'd stood there listening to it all, then at one point David had looked at her and she'd looked away at the floor. . . but, yes, she'd smiled! Fuck the story of combustion, David imagined himself saying. The fantasy David then shoved McKenzie aside and swaggered off along the corridor, giving Ann Erskine a provocative glance as he passed her. . .

A clatter of dishes from the kitchen below brought him out of it. He lay completely still in the bed, listening to all the sounds from the kitchen. Sometimes he felt like he'd just arrived, just come down to the planet Earth and was seeing and hearing everything for the first time. This was what it was like now, listening to the babble of the morning news on the radio, the clatter of the cups and plates and cutlery being laid out on the kitchen table, the squeak of his dad's wheelchair, his mum's tense, high voice and the growl of his dad's answer. It was his answer to life as much as to her or what she was asking, full of scalding bitterness.

He listened to the two voices going on like that. They sounded like water and fire. His mum's voice shook, trembled, quivered, trying to put out the crackling fire in his dad's He wondered if their voices had always been so opposite. Maybe at one time, long ago, before the world began, water and fire had been the same substance, the same element. He tried to imagine liquid flames, but he couldn't – *If you're no interested in the story of combustion, laddie, that's yer own lookout!* – then he thought about his own voice and tried to remember how it sounded. Then he sang a few words of a song he liked – wasn't his voice like a mixture of water and fire, of his mum's voice and his dad's? He couldn't make out what they were saying to each other down there, but he knew this was the morning the paper came, that they were waiting to read about him in it, about what he'd done that Saturday night after he'd walked Anne home. They were probably talking about it now – either that or trying not to talk about it. But the not talking about it could be worse than the talking about it.

His head and his arms and his legs and his hands and his feet – in fact every part of him – felt heavy, like lead, as if it was molten lead running through his veins instead of blood. Maybe, during his sleep, he'd been paralysed. He moved his hand an inch or two under the bedclothes to make sure he wasn't paralysed, then he wondered what it would be like if he was. His dad's legs were paralysed after an accident at the foundry, and now he was living on the compensation and something called Mobility Allowance. Paralysed. The word sounded rubbery, like that rubbery sliced meat his mum sometimes bought. Half a pound of Paralysed, please. Fancy a wee Paralysed sandwich? He imagined shouting downstairs to his parents: 'Help, *help!* I'm paralysed!' That would teach them. Or if he'd been struck down in the night with some mysterious fatal illness – then they'd be sorry. . .

He pictured the gathering at his graveside – his mum having a good cry there, pushing up her glasses so as to wipe away the tears with her lipstick-smeared hanky; his dad bent double in his wheelchair, scowling with his own guilt as he threw a handful of earth on the coffin; the cops who'd arrested him both with their hats off, their walkie-talkies silent; the people in the court who'd looked him up and down and passed judgement on him; McKenzie, the chemistry-vicar, reciting the periodic table and shaking his head, praying to the God of combustion for his lower-than-O-level soul; Anne

Media Studies 169

in her neat school uniform, except that now it's black, even the blouse is black, and the skirt is tight and short, like the other Ann's and she's wearing eyeliner, black lipstick, pulling a black handkerchief out of her pencil-case. . .

He heard the clack of the letterbox, the soft thud of the paper on the hall floor, then the babble of the radio swelling as the kitchen door opened and his mum hurried out to get it.

They'd all read it. Anne's dad would read it. He was a director for a firm that manufactured, so he'd told David when he'd met him, surgical equipment – walking frames, artificial legs, things like that. David hadn't been able to help smirking about this – it was just the thought of all those plastic legs on the conveyor belt – and ever since then he'd felt her dad's disapproval when he phoned up Anne. Now he'd see that his daughter was going out with a juvenile delinquent, a criminal, and he'd forbid her to meet him. He wondered if Anne would meet him anyway, in secret, but somehow he couldn't imagine her doing that. But what about the other Ann? Maybe seeing his name in the paper would make her look at him with a new respect? It wouldn't worry her anyway, she wouldn't condemn him for it, and suddenly this seemed to David more important than anything, this not worrying and not condemning, and he wanted to talk to the other Ann more than anybody else he knew, and he swore to himself that he'd never call her a slag again, even in his thoughts. And Raymond – what would Raymond think? Raymond was doing well, he was getting good marks at school, and lately he'd been acting cool. Maybe this thing in the paper would make Raymond want to steer clear of him. And all the teachers would hand it round – *'it's common knowledge in the staff room'* – and Jazzman, what would Jazzman think of his star pupil? Maybe he'd get them to do something about it in the class, something about petty crimes and the way they were reported in the local paper, then the way more serious crimes were dealt with. . .

David wondered how his case would be reported. Maybe if there had been a spate of serious crimes, his would only get a little paragraph, hardly noticeable. But if not, there might be a headline, not a big headline of course but a headline all the same. He was curious to read about himself, about how they would describe him, but still he didn't move. How much longer could he lie here like this, not moving a muscle, paralysed? And how could a few words printed on a piece of paper cause so much trouble, even change his life? It was the words that caused the trouble, not what he'd done.

He could imagine the little drama that would happen when he did go down. His mum, hands wet from the dishwater, wringing them dry in the dishtowel, going on about how she'd always done her best to give him a good home, how she'd worked all her life, worked her fingers to the bone, weeping and wailing that she'd never had his chance in life, his chance of a good education – and now look at what he does with it, the swine! Dragging my good name through the dirt and I don't know how I'm going to face the neighbours after this, after all we've done for you, you turn out to be a common criminal! Then his dad would get stuck in spitting fire, jabbing at the crackling pages of the paper with his pipe, throwing the paper on the kitchen floor, roaring that he'd been roasted alive in the foundry all his life and for what? Two paralysed legs and a son who was a criminal, a criminal!

Water and fire, water and fire.

'David! Get out of your bed this minute and come down here! Your father wants to talk to you!'

He heard his dad's voice booming above the noise of the radio, a loud eruption of threats and curses. Then the kitchen door banged shut.

This was going to be the worst bit, worse than getting caught, worse than going to the court.

It'll blow over, he told himself, and he tried to think about that time to come in the future when it would have blown over, when everyone would have forgotten what he'd done, as if just by thinking about it he could magic it into now. He remembered playing the same game as a kid in the dentist's waiting room: don't listen to the noise the drills make, don't think about the injection, the pain. . . think about next Saturday, at the matinee, watching the film. . . One drill makes a high, whiney noise, the other makes a low, growling noise, but on Saturday, this Saturday coming, I am going into the pictures, I am sitting down with my bag of popcorn and my juice, the lights are going down and the curtains are opening and the film is just going to start. . . concentrate on *that!* But the noise of the drills hadn't let him imagine the film he might watch, and now his mum's voice had the same effect.

'David, get out of your bed at once!'

When the kitchen door banged shut again, he could hear her worry and her panic, even in the clatter of the plates, even in the sound of the water rattling into the kettle. It didn't matter what she was saying – he could hear the meaning. Then his dad's rumbling voice, cursing and bellowing. The two voices went on like that, clashing and interrupting each other, lamenting and condemning, as if no matter what the words were they were always saying the same things. *It's terrible, terrible! We'll just have to look on the bright side!* Then his dad's answer. *There is no bloody bright side!*

He tried to remember doing what he'd done, but now it didn't seem real, like something that had happened to somebody else a long time ago.

It had been about going away. He'd been talking to her about leaving Murkirk, going to Edinburgh, Glasgow, London, Paris, travelling the world. . . but Anne hadn't been in the mood for it. She'd told him he'd get a job on a milk-float if he was lucky, the way he was going, and that after school he'd get stuck in Murkirk for the rest of his life. When he'd talked about Media Studies, trying to make it sound like something really modern and complicated, and how he might go into photography or journalism, she'd laughed and said, 'Yeah, weddings and funerals for the *Murkirk Gazette!*'

That had done it. On the way down the hill from her house – the goodnight kiss hadn't been up to much – he'd started touching the parked cars when he walked past them, then trying the doors. One had opened. He'd got in out of the cold and had sat there for a long time, just thinking about what she'd said. And she was probably right. Weddings and funerals for the *Murkirk Gazette* was the most he could hope for. It would be Anne who'd get away to university, she'd be the one who'd travel the world. He'd fiddled with things on the dashboard and had switched on the headlights, then he'd taken the handbrake off and felt the car move forward, very slowly at first, then less slowly. He'd started to steer it guiding it down the hill as it gathered speed, just freewheeling without the engine, that was the good thing about it, it had felt good just to be *moving*. Eventually the car slowed down and he steered it to the side of the street and put the handbrake on. Then the cop car had drawn up alongside.

David climbed out of bed, walked over to the window

and opened the curtains, then screwed up his eyes when the light hit them. Birds were singing in the back garden, and even they seemed to quarrel and accuse.

I'm Glad That Wasn't Me

THE TAXI shuddered as Gus paid the driver and waited for the receipt. Gus shuddered with it as he looked through the tinted glass at the down-and-out. He stood on the corner scratching his itches, grinning at nothing with tobacco-stained teeth, shifting his weight from one bow leg to another, trying to trap a passer-by between the separate stares of his wall-eyes. Every day he was there, dressed in the same ripped and stained rags he'd been wearing since he'd first shown up on the street – his legs and back buckled as if by a great weight, an endless labour. His face and hands and bald scalp were burnished red, as if he'd been boiled alive like a lobster, or baptised in fire. At the same time he looked clownish – swaying from side to side as he walked, eyes askew. One day last week, when he'd turned the corner into the street, Gus had been troubled by the tramps' elongated shadow falling across his path like a bad omen.

The tramp had been coming into his restaurant almost every day for the past two weeks, a disarming grin smeared across his face, smacking his tobacco-flecked coins on the counter and requesting a pot of tea for one. Gus had put up with him, and there was no real reason not to. The man was polite, more civil than many of the regulars. He took his tray with its pot, its tea-strainer, its little jug of milk and its cup and saucer to a table in the corner, where he sat for an hour or so smoking if he had anything to smoke and contemplating his image in the wall-mirror. One day he'd sat there puffing away at a fat cigar, and though he'd no doubt cadged it from someone on the street, in a burlesque way the cigar had suited him. On other days, Gus'd suspected the guy of falling asleep.

Who was he? Where did he come from? More to the point: when would he go away? Things were definitely getting worse in the street.

When the driver handed him the receipt Gus opened the door farthest away from where the down-and-out stood and crossed to the other pavement. Even so he thought he heard the man calling out behind him – a polite 'excuse me'. The politeness sounded practised – a kind of irony.

He decided not to hear him and hurried along the street. He was late, and already one or two of the dealers were opening up. In the last year or two the street had become infested with antique shops, displaying in their windows few genuine antiques – it was mostly old sideboards and dressers, sanded and varnished, and the odd grandfather clock that didn't work. Some of the humblest household objects from his childhood were now, apparently, sought-after items – old biscuit tins, clockwork toys.

Maybe instead of opening a restaurant, he should have

Selected Stories

gone into junk, but he doubted if he could compete with some of the dealers who came in regularly to complain about the price of everything and lament how bad business was. They were wide. He was sick of the restaurant, of dealing every day with food and with the public, but he was also sick of the street and the people who worked in it – including himself, maybe.

When he'd opened the place seven years ago, the street had been different. There had been a couple of second-hand clothes shops, a place that repaired violins, a record shop which specialised in obscure imports and sheet music. There had been a communal feeling. His had been the only restaurant, and the food had been thought of as unusual, even slightly exotic, at the time. Now it had become commonplace, and three other lunch places had opened up. The people he'd liked best had left. Those who'd stayed had all had children and operations and tax bills and – business had become business.

But business was not good. He'd scarcely broken even on his first two years, and since then he'd become disenchanted with the work and had consoled himself by spending too much money – meals out with Nina, the woman he saw regularly but didn't live with, presents for her ten-year-old son, holidays abroad for the three of them – Greece, Turkey, Majorca. Over the last two years the tax man and VAT people had started taking him seriously – examining his accounts closely, presenting him with outlandish bills and threatening to put him out of business. If he ever came through these tribulations, it would be as a slightly changed person, and he wasn't sure he liked the idea of the slight change. He'd been here too long. He wanted out, but for the moment there was no way out. He had to make the business pay to meet the outstanding bills.

The street, among those who had survived in it, had come to be called The Street.

He hurried down the stairs and greeted Paul, his backup, who was waiting for him and reading a book. *Waiting for Godot*. Paul was a student of English Literature, making some money in the summer. He shut the book and pointed at the tray of morning rolls, telling him in detail how they'd been pissed on by a dog.

'So what else is new? Where's Lucy?'

'She'll be along.'

He glanced at Paul. Since he and Lucy lived together, they usually came to work together. Maybe something was up. Paul's thin face, with its sharp features, had set in an expression both hurt and spiteful.

Gus unlocked the door and they went in. He switched on the lights, the coffee machine, the hot water urn, the fan, the immersion heater. Paul started hacking apart a cabbage for the coleslaw.

Lucy came in, said sorry for being late and, without even acknowledging Paul, began peeling the beetroots she had remembered to boil yesterday afternoon. Something was definitely up. Lucy was a good worker, the best. She took care over the way she did everything, but at the same time she was efficient, fast. If there was no real work to do, she cleaned, dusted, put flowers in vases, polished mirrors, pictures, windows – she brought light into the place. If she and Paul split up, he might lose her.

He made the first flask of coffee and gave Lucy hers just the way she liked it, with the merest drop of hot milk, and was rewarded by her quick, frank smile Maybe Paul was in a mood, maybe they'd had an argument, but she wasn't going to let it affect the way she was with others. If he'd been ten years younger and unattached, he could have gone for a girl like Lucy – or, maybe she could have gone for him.

An American couple, tourists, all sweaters and slacks and moneybelts, came in wanting coffee and omelettes. Gus told them he wasn't open and didn't do omelettes. When they apologised cordially, he gave them the morning papers and told them he'd bring it to the table when it was ready. Paul gave him a dirty look over the shredded cabbage. There wasn't time to be making omelettes for tourists – there were too many other things to do. This was true, but what Paul didn't know was that he couldn't afford to turn away customers.

Lucy placed her first salad under the counter, behind the glass – beetroots, celery, orange, watercress, arranged in such a way that it looked beautifully simple, almost Japanese – and offered to beat the eggs for him. Paul rammed the carrots into the shredder and hunched his shoulders.

Gus was the restaurateur, he could do what he wanted, he was the owner. Big deal. He was also the cook, the *maître-d'* and the accountant. Nowadays he sometimes had to be the dishwasher and floor-sweeper too. In a small place, you had to be too many people, you had to be all things to all men. Edinburgh was like that, a small place.

He should have settled somewhere else, but despite many long periods spent travelling in the seventies – India, Sri Lanka, Thailand, Malaysia – and in the eighties – the States, Mexico, Peru – he had always been sucked back to Scotland, and more specifically, Edinburgh – as if some force were pulling him back. Nowadays everyone in Scotland was talking about

I'm Glad That Wasn't Me

Europe as if it had just been invented. It was like listening to kids thinking of opening their garden gate. He'd explored Europe so long ago that he could barely remember it.

He whisked the eggs and chopped some fresh basil he'd picked up by chance at the market yesterday. An omelette, properly cooked in the French way – maybe his experience of Europe had come in useful after all – was an art. Good food required both spontaneity and dedication. The simplest things could be the best. His own taste in food was like that – pasta with home-made pesto, green salad, good bread, a simple dry red wine.

When he thought about taking someone on, he always asked them to peel a potato. Some had done it before, others hadn't. Some had shredded the skin as they peeled it, others carved a careful spiral. It wasn't that he rated one way over another – he could just imagine working with somebody when he watched them peel a potato. Lucy had weighed the potato in her hand, looked at him and asked him what it was for, and said that was a waste of a potato. He'd taken it out of her hand and asked her when she could start.

He made the omelettes and took them to the tourists, then their coffees. He hung around near their table for a minute, pretending to make small arrangements to a table nearby but in reality hoping for a compliment on the omelettes. When none came he went back to the kitchen area and started on the lunch dishes. You need some feedback, some appreciation. When none came it was like being snubbed.

He had nightmares about sauces that burned, about those inspectors from the Department of Health who had invaded the kitchen without warning one day and examined his wooden spoons, his pots, his toilets. One of them had drawn his attention to the crumbs of food and grime trapped in a groove in the rubber seal of the fridge, and had ordered him to ventilate the toilets more adequately for their return visit the following week. There was a recurring one about the woman who had found a lump of jagged glass in her mayonnaise. The jar had broken, and he had salvaged some of the mayonnaise. She had complained quietly, discreetly, when she could have taken him to court. He'd offered to pay for her lunch, which had only added insult to injury. No, she had made her point in the most polite way possible. She would not take it any further. She would not make a fuss. She would never eat here again, that was for sure, but she would not condemn him because of the lump of glass in her mouth. She was the kind of customer he could do with.

The compliment came when they ordered more coffee: the omelettes were *really* delicious, and they had never tasted parsley like that before – was it Scottish parsley?

When he'd laid out the trout in the oven dish and trailed the sauce over them, he put the dish aside and stopped for a coffee. He sat down at the staff table and leafed through a paper without reading it. The pizza and quiche that hadn't sold yesterday were OK for today. The trout was prepared, so he needed two more hot dishes. He knew what they would be already: Aubergine Parmigiano, because he had the aubergines and had to cater for vegetarians, and Chicken with Mango, both of which he'd done the groundwork for yesterday afternoon. The aubergines were salted, washed and presently congealing in a box in the fridge. The chicken had been roasted and dissected into portions. All he had to do was the sauces.

He had to keep getting up to serve people from the street who needed coffee before they opened up their own shops. Then he made the sauces, got all the hot dishes ready for lunchtime, but today there was no lunchtime rush. That happened sometimes. When everything was ready and waiting, twelve o'clock came and went and no one came, then one o'clock. Maybe it was the unusually hot weather. The weather good or bad, was never good for business. The few regulars who trickled in today – they got on his nerves, but he needed them – didn't want his hot dishes but asked for finicky combinations or half-portions of salad. He told Paul off for cutting the tomatoes too thick for the tomato salad and for not using the basil.

By two o'clock no one was speaking to each other and the trout were already destined to become a cold trout mousse for tomorrow. He sent Lucy out for the cream cheese and told her to take her time and enjoy the sunshine.

He sat at the staff table drinking coffee, reading the papers and staring out the barred window. Since the restaurant was a basement, the only view was of the street literally at street level. He watched people's feet going by. Eventually he saw a girl's legs go by he wanted to go to bed with. Then the legs came down the stairs and he realised whose they were. She was too conscientious to linger in the sun and was already unwrapping the cream cheese and starting on the mousse. She was one of those people who would rather be doing something than nothing. Salt of the earth, but he wished she was happy.

It was three in the afternoon and the place was empty when Gus recognised the shoes of the down-and-out. They were heavy, shapeless, battered and soft, as if his feet were wrapped in layers and layers of soiled bandages. The man's steps had a slow inevitability about them, never really leaving the ground. His feet came down the stairs the way a child's would – both resting on each stair before going onto the next.

Had it taken him all day to raise the price of his pot of tea?

Gus lit another cigarette and pretended to engross himself in the crossword so that Paul would have to serve him. He didn't look up as the man shuffled past him but he could hear his laboured breathing, like the sound of coals shifting in a fire, the clatter of the tray as he hoisted it from the tray-rack, the crash of his assorted coins on the counter. Then the disarming politeness as he spoke, as if a dishevelled devil disguised a slick, well-mannered angel, 'Pot of tea for one, please.'

He was aware of the swathed bulk of the man swaying in and out of his field of vision as he tried to concentrate on the crossword. Paul, who still hadn't made it up with Lucy and was having a bad day, served him with pointed reluctance, barely concealing his resentment. He banged the teapot down on the tray, smashed the money into the till-drawer and turned away.

'Excuse me.'

Gus looked up, thinking the down-and-out was talking to him, but he wasn't. He was trying to get Paul's attention.

'Excuse me.'

Gus was about to intervene when Paul turned round and eyed the down-and-out with distrust.

'Are no strainers available?'

Gus almost laughed aloud. You had to admire the man's audacity.

'No.'

The man was about to take his tray and go, but suddenly Gus found himself on his feet. It was a policy in the restaurant to give every customer a tea-strainer with their pot of tea. It was meant to be one of the small, personal touches which might distinguish the place from others. These standards had to be maintained.

'Give the gentleman a strainer.'

Paul's eyes rounded with affront, then he sighed emphatically and turned away. He took his time about finding a tea-strainer, only to drop it with disgust on the tramp's tray.

'Thank you.'

He lumbered with his tray around the dividing wall and headed for his favourite seat in front of the mirror. He was their only customer.

What did he think about when he sat there in front of the mirror? Was he horrified by the sight of himself, of what he'd become? Or did he admire himself as a man who'd broken free of everything, even his own life?

Paul sat down opposite him with a belated lunch – the only portion of the Aubergine Parmigiano which would be eaten – and a glass of white wine. He opened his book and read as he ate, shovelling the food into his mouth without looking at it. That was what happened to most of the food you made – people ate it without noticing it.

'People are bloody ignorant apes.'

Paul looked up from his book with a narrowed eye as he crammed another forkful of the Parmigiano into his mouth.

'It's a quote from that.'

He nodded at the book in Paul's hand.

Paul raised his eyebrows briefly. He seemed to think he

Selected Stories

was the only person who read, and was never quite convinced when he mentioned a book.

'Have you read *Mercier et Camier*, the novel Beckett based it on?'

Paul shook his head and tilted his glass of wine this way and that.

'You should.'

But the student wouldn't be drawn. When he'd finished eating, he put the open book face down on the table and asked him for a light. As Paul took the lighter and lit up, he gave a backward nod of his head towards the corner where the down-and-out sat and said, 'That guy has to go, Gus.'

'Why?'

'He smells. He's scaring off the other customers.'

'What other customers?'

'Exactly.'

'He isn't the reason they're not coming in. It's a heatwave out there. We need to put some unusual cold drinks on the menu. Edinburgh tap-water, with ice and lemon.'

Paul wasn't in the mood for humour.

'That guy is bad news, Gus, and you know it.'

'So are a lot of our regulars.'

'You know what I mean, Gus. He's the kiss of death. If you don't want to tell him, I will.'

'If anyone tells him, I will.'

'You're the boss.'

Paul flicked his ash into the ashtray, though it didn't need to be flicked, and smoked his cigarette intensely. When it was half-smoked, he stubbed it out fussily, shut his book and took his plate into the kitchen area, where he stood with arms folded and glared at the door, as if defying anyone to come

I'm Glad That Wasn't Me

in. It was hard when there was no custom. It was hard for everyone.

Gus thought, '*Godot* doesn't seem to be teaching him much in the way of compassion for down-at-heel wayfarers.' Yet in a way the student was right.

He thought of a woman – he didn't know her name but she was a good customer – regular, appreciative, well-heeled – who often came in with her teenage kid. Their enthusiasm for the lemon cheesecake was heartening. She paid him the compliment of ordering one to serve at a dinner party. More than once she'd hinted that she'd like to run a restaurant herself. She probably imagined it as an extended dinner party. It didn't occur to her that the lemon cheesecake had become a daily chore for him, a meaningless ritual – he could no loner bear to taste it. But he'd concealed his nausea at the thought of making an extra one and had agreed to do it. The last time she had come in, now that he thought about it, was on one of the down-and-out's first visits, and she'd encountered him at the counter. He'd bumped into her tray. The teapot had over-turned, and some tea had splashed on her arm. The tramp had apologised, then grinned and said,

'I'm glad that wasn't me!'

She'd eyed him with something like awe and replied that it was nothing.

She had behaved well, as one should, but she hadn't been back since.

Something had to be done about the down-and-out.

He found the recipe for Aubergine Pie which he could apply to the Parmigiano – all he really needed to add was some fresh basil, which he had. While he was rolling out the pastry, Paul chopped the basil and put it to him.

'He's been sitting there for an hour, Gus. The guy's asleep. Somebody should go over, clear his table.'

He didn't want Paul to do it – he would do it with such bad grace – but he didn't want to do it himself. He asked Lucy. She was cleaning the glass of the salad counter, but she didn't mind. Paul looked at him with disgust.

He finished rolling out the pastry, laid it in the oven dish and started trimming it with scissors.

The scream was clean and startling – it sounded almost wholesome. They ran into the restaurant area, he clutching his rolling pin, Paul the knife he was using. They met Lucy rushing the other way, her hands covering her ears as if to block out the sound of her own scream.

He walked over to the table in the corner. The man had become a slouched statue of himself. He had not poured his tea. Gus put a hand on his shoulder and turned him a little. The grin had soured into a grimace, the green eyes had locked in their askew stares.

He turned to Paul, whose eyes were wider than he had ever seen them.

'An ambulance? You want me to call an ambulance? What's wrong with the guy, Gus?'

'Nothing's wrong with him. He's dead.'

Lucy screamed again. He told Paul to take care of her – it sounded like he was telling him to take care of her all the time, not just at the moment – while he made the call and locked the door.

He didn't want to leave the dead man. He sat down on a chair next to him and held his hand. It felt stiff and calloused, like the broad claw of a crab. He did not say anything. He was vaguely aware of people being turned away at the door, of

Paul buzzing around, keeping people out and gesticulating at Lucy, who was now at the staff-table, her head in her hands. He closed his eyes and waited for the ambulance to arrive.

He poured some brandy into an empty tumbler and took it back to the table in the corner. He sat down and looked at himself in the wall-mirror – worried, tense, unhealthy. He thought of the corpses he had seen – in India, in Sri Lanka, in Peru. And the deaths he had lived through here in Scotland – his father floundering in his bed, gasping like a landed fish, a look of strained incomprehension on his face. His mother's slow, inexorable death, the erosion of her body and then her mind, until she believed that her bedside locker in the hospice was bugged. By comparison, the death of the down-and-out seemed serene, as if he had chosen it. And he knew this had been his first real death – the first death he felt truly involved in.

The others in the street would be waiting for him in Dr Jekyll's, the pub on the corner, waiting for the story of how the down-and-out had died. There was so little to tell, really, but already, in his mind, he was rehearsing how he'd relate the event – and in the pub, the other dealers would all chip in with their anecdotes about the down-and-out – maybe he'd find out who had given him the cigar – all relieved as hell that he was gone, then they'd close in on him to ferret out and relish every detail of the death, as if it concerned them. 'I'm glad that wasn't me!' – already he could hear himself quoting the down-and-out to the others, and they would smile, nod their heads, narrow their eyes and agree.

He stood up, cleared away his glass and his ashtray, switched everything off, put on his jacket, made to set the alarm, then he realised he hadn't swept the floor.

Strange Passenger

GOING HOME always felt worse than leaving. The train hadn't changed in all the years I'd been taking it: the same stops at stations where no one seemed to get on or off; the same unexplained delays, blocked toilets and litter-strewn carriages with worn seats. It was always either empty and freezing or, like today, overcrowded and stifling. It was a sultry afternoon. I hadn't slept after my eldest sister Angela had called to tell me the news about Dad. She'd been called to the hospital after midnight and had sat with him. She'd left the room for a few minutes and when she'd gone back, 'he was *very dead*'. Somehow the phrase was much more specific than just 'dead'. She'd seen something I hadn't, something I couldn't quite imagine: our father being very dead.

My reaction had been – but had there been any real reaction? Hadn't I just made the sorrowful and shocked noises appropriate to the occasion?

Then I'd gone back into the bedroom to tell Polly. Her reaction was more dramatic, and it embarrassed me. Tears sprang into her eyes – maybe my father's death reminded her of the death of her own father? Or maybe her emotions were riding high in any case. Before the call, we'd been building up to an argument all evening. She'd first mentioned that her period was late a few days ago and it had come up again tonight, after the spaghetti bolognese and the bottle of cheap red wine. This time she'd wanted to talk about exactly what we were going to do if she was, and my unwillingness to discuss it had made her angry and tearful. She'd demanded to know how I felt about it, but I'd been coolly evasive, treating the whole thing like a hypothetical ethical dilemma from Moral Phil.1.

After the call, of course, I'd had the perfect excuse to drop the whole question of the pregnancy: my father's death. So, although she'd held her arms out to me I hadn't gone to her. Instead I'd told her I wanted to be on my own for a while and had gone to sit in the kitchen. I'd sat there for a long time, trying in vain to realise what had happened, trying to find the reaction in myself I knew should be there, but I'd found nothing except a vague numbness, an inability to feel. The more I'd tried to focus my mind on it, the more remote and abstract it had seemed. Of course, I was a final-year student of Philosophy, so maybe everything had become a bit remote and abstract. I'd tried to think of my father in his life, of the good and fond memories of him I undoubtedly had, but even this proved to be impossible. The recent image of him as he lay dying in hospital, paralysed down one side of his body and having lost the power of speech, obliterated the others. Added to this was a sense of anticlimax the death brought with it. He'd been dying for a long time, all the family knew it, and it was difficult to feel anything like shock.

So I'd sat up through the night, smoking my thin, hand-rolled cigarettes, trying to feel something real about my father and experiencing only an uncomfortable awareness of myself – of my own physical movements as I sat there smoking, but also the movements of my thoughts, such as they were. I wasn't really in my thoughts, but apart from them, like someone reading about himself in his own diary. Could this be how grief started, I wondered – as a kind of dissociation, a kind of absence of feeling? Maybe Nietzsche, the unwilling subject of my unfinished and, I suspected, unfinishable dissertation, had written an aphorism about it somewhere, but if so I couldn't remember in which book, or what it said. Wouldn't he equate grief with guilt, and thence the life-denying instinct of the herd? Anyway, although I was half-buried in my footnotes to *Beyond Good and Evil*, I was beginning to have doubts about academia. Hadn't my father once said to me that you shouldn't have to look up a book to know what you think? Didn't that apply even more to what you felt?

And wasn't Nietzsche partly to blame for the way I was acting about Polly? I'd been living with her for two years, but still didn't feel quite committed to her. The idea that she might be pregnant made me feel less so. Nietzsche encouraged me to give the V-sign to commitment when it suited me. I mean, would the Overman, who was capable of creating his own moral values, worry about such things? Of course he wouldn't. There were no absolutes. Anything was permissible. Nothing was taboo.

I'd gone back to bed briefly that morning, but hadn't been able to sleep. Then Angela had called up again to tell me about the arrangements. The body would be transferred to Agnew's, the undertaker's in Murkirk, that morning. The funeral would be in two days' time.

There was this persistent, pulsating ache behind my temples. My hands were clammy and swollen and I'd bitten my fingernails to the quick. My shirt adhered to my back like a membrane, a second skin I longed to shed. I shuddered despite the heat. I was bothered by the nearness of the other passengers, especially the two who sat on either side of me. That asthmatic old lady on my left was the last thing I needed. She kept wheezing and muttering under her breath, and her sickly perfume hung in the air like a premonition of something rotten. The dumpy, crew-cutted teenage boy on my right was just as bad. He kept crunching his crisps noisily and jiggling his thigh up and down on the seat to the demented beat of the heavy-metal music on his pocket radio.

I felt like tapping him on the shoulder and saying, 'D'you mind? I'm in mourning.'

But no, that would be melodramatic, another way of falsifying what I felt, if I felt anything. For the moment, I felt only the intense discomfort of the journey. I rearranged myself in the seat, trying to make more room for my legs and elbows between the two on either side of me. On the seat opposite there was a young couple with a crying baby. The mother was harassed, the father sullen. The baby kept crying and being sick, and they kept having to search in their several bags, which were crammed together on the floor between us, for bottles and tissues and baby-wipes. I couldn't imagine me and Polly with a baby. I didn't want to.

I watched the baby opposite kicking its legs and drumming its chubby fists in the air. Its screwed-up face seemed to swell and redden, as if about to burst, every time it drew breath to cry. It looked to me like anger itself as it cried as hard as it could cry. The mother was rocking it furiously, but I could see she was too much on edge, at the end of her tether with it. Then the father held his hands out to take the baby and the mother sighed with exasperation and passed it over to him. He held the baby close to his face, so that his nose came into contact with its head – he was *breathing* on it! Then *he* began to rock, slowly, backwards and forwards, and as he did he murmured something to the baby, or maybe he was humming a tune to it. He looked almost as if he was dancing, from the waist up, slowly, as if he was remembering being at the dancing and it was a slow slushy number, like 'Please release me, let me go. . .' It was working. The baby's cries lessened and soon it fell asleep.

Could I have done that? I wondered, and stared with a kind of appalled admiration at the father. Christ, he was a young guy, about the same age as me, probably younger, but he looked older, unshaven and exhausted, his unkempt black hair drooping over one eye. He wore a nylon, short-sleeved, open-necked shirt printed with the kind of pattern you sometimes saw on tumblers, made up of intersecting circles and triangles and lines.

He went on rocking, humming and staring into space, as if he was still at the dancing, then he noticed that I was watching him, flicked the hair out of his eye and smiled at me, and his smile seemed to say it all. Look at me, the smile seemed to say, look and be warned. This could be you, pal. I wanted to say something, but I didn't know what to say. Well done? That seems to have done the trick?

The wheezing old lady beat me to it, but she spoke to the

mother, 'Ah doubt she's gonnae be a daddy's girl! What's her name?'

'Tracy.'

The old woman wheezed and said it was a lovely name.

Jesus Christ, if Polly was pregnant, she might want to have the baby. Not that we'd discussed it properly last night, but now it seemed to me that she'd been less against the idea than she should be. Maybe that was because she knew she wasn't, but maybe not, maybe she knew by intuition that she was and felt OK about it, even if it would mess up her last year at the art college. There was no accounting for what hormones could do.

What would we call it – Kandinsky or Zarathustra?

The light, which had a steely glare, was hurting my eyes. I tried shutting them, but then the pounding in my head seemed to louden, jarred to a crescendo by the thud of the carriage door every time it slid open and shut as the slow train rumbled and lurched along the track, which needed to be relaid, to Murkirk.

When my restlessness became insufferable, I stood up and walked to the next carriage, which was just as crowded as the last and just as airless. One or two of the passengers eyed me as I moved up the train, but without curiosity – if anything they looked furtive and threatened.

Was I just imagining it, the hostility and the defeat in their eyes, or was it there to be seen, almost a public statement, deliberate and unanimous? Or was it just that I was seeing things strangely today – because my father had died, or because I hadn't slept, or because I had a head full of *The Anti-Christ*?

The herd. They were what Nietzsche called the herd, and

I moved among them as an outsider, a strange passenger. When I came to the front of the train I found a free window in the corridor where no one was standing. I tried to open it, but it was jammed shut. I leaned against it and, shielding my eyes from the sun with a hand, peered out through the glass – almost opaque with grime from the train's endless journey through the Central Belt. The first thing I saw was, around a squat black church with a mean little spire, the huddled stones of a village graveyard. Even then, I had to prod my own mind to make the connection this should have had with death.

It was the same landscape I'd seen so many times from the train, industrial, with short stretches of what could be called countryside in between, but these were so featureless and haphazard that they seemed like brief interludes in the interminable story of the factories, the warehouses, the car parks and the housing schemes. . . the backs of those drab brown houses, with their coal bunkers and their drying greens and their kitchen windows, looked like stunted, blighted faces.

The same landscape, but something about it was changing, and it was like the change was taking place right there before my eyes – a boarded-up building that had been a working factory, I was sure, the last time I'd seen it; a corner of wasteground where a school had been demolished but nothing had been built; a shop up for sale; a vandalised bus shelter; a gang of teenagers sitting on a wall. Unemployment had stamped on the faces of these small towns and villages, leaving them with broken teeth and empty eyes, and it would stamp on them again.

My education had taken me away, but one day I might have to return – to work in a school here, teaching kids how to pass exams and get out, or fail exams and stay and be forgotten except as statistics in the unemployment figures. I might have to work here where others wouldn't find work, because I might have to be a teacher – what else could I do? If Polly was pregnant, and if she went ahead and had the baby – Christ! I'd have to do something for money. On the other hand, she might be late. She'd been later than this before.

I turned from the window and started to make my way up the train, because it was slowing down as it neared the station, and already I was surrounded by it, the herd of shuffling, muttering Murkirk folk. They sounded resigned to having arrived at their destination.

The funeral parlour was modern. I had not expected this, especially in Murkirk. The plate glass doors, the expansive foyer furnished with maroon leather chairs and mahogany wood-panelling – all smacked of a business venture whose success had proved to be beyond the scope of its founder's most outrageous dreams.

I crossed the foyer to the reception desk. I looked through the glass at a woman who sat there typing something. She was in her late thirties, but there was something older about her. Her dress, for one thing, belonged to the late fifties or early sixties, the time of bouffant hairdos, heavy eye make-up and twin-sets and pearls. And she wore these winged glasses, almost like the kind my mother wore, and they made her big brown eyes look like dead leaves stuck to a window pane.

'Can I help you?

For some reason I wanted to shock her.

'I've come to see my old man.'

She ignored the casualness of this and asked me for the

name, opened a desk diary and ran a manicured talon down a column.

'D'you have an appointment?'

'No.'

She admonished me briefly over the specs.

'It didn't occur to me that he'd be busy.'

That hit the target all right. She wasn't amused. She wasn't shocked either, but she gave me a quick, hard look, a look I'd seen before, full of a kind of hostile curiosity. It was the look of those who'd never left Murkirk and never would, never step outside their lives and look in. It was the look, I decided, of the herd.

'I'll just see if Mr Agnew can make arrangements, if you'd like to take a seat.'

I decided to make myself plain, so I bleated at her before walking away to the waiting area. She looked at me steadily as I uttered the bleat, but I knew it was hopeless. Already she had me pigeonholed as a drug addict or a weirdo.

I resented having to wait. I resented the place, with its ugly, fake-antique furniture. Wasn't this coffee table, with its pile of magazines, the limit?

Who'd want to read a magazine while waiting to visit their dead? But apparently people did, because here they were. I picked one up and opened it to see a picture of a mother holding a towel to the cheek of her baby's face. The baby was smiling, his or her bright blue eyes gleaming with glee, the rosy cheeks shining with health and vigour. The mother was smiling too, a caring, reassuring smile at the baby. It was an advertisement for fabric softener, but to me it was another reminder. Christ, I wasn't ready for it. My own father had just died, I wasn't ready to step into those shoes.

Mr Agnew was not what I'd expected an undertaker to be. He hurried from a door at the rear of the reception area and stuck on a smile for me as he approached, extending a clean – the word I thought of was 'pampered' – hand. A strange thought shot through my mind as I shook the hand – that maybe he washed his hands before handling a corpse as well as after, as if afraid that the living might contaminate the dead. A whiff of aftershave – or was it something else? – accompanied a businesslike manner as the face of Mr Agnew came too close for comfort.

It was not an undertaker's face. No solemn, sunken eyes or deathly pallor. Nothing sepulchral. No mournful moustache framing a bejowled, doom-heavy mouth. He looked, if anything, obscenely healthy, with the ruddy complexion of those who eat well and get plenty of fresh air. He explained that because I hadn't made an appointment, it would take a few minutes to make the necessary arrangements so that I could see my father. His demeanour was irrepressibly that of the businessman. It wasn't just the pin-striped suit and the brisk manner. It was also the way he narrowed his eyes when he looked at me, as if sizing up a cadaver of the future. True, there were other gestures and mannerisms more suited to his profession: a restrained tone of voice as he spoke, a certain inclination of the head acquired by the habit of commiseration, but these did little to disguise the manner of man he was. As he walked away, I thought I sensed something amiss with him, some discomfort, as if he hadn't found time for something or had forgotten to put something on his agenda, like clipping his toenails. Maybe attending to the minor needs of so many other bodies made him neglect the demands of his own? It was the way he walked that made me think of this – it looked like it pained his feet to come into contact with the floor. Maybe his shoes were just a bit too tight.

I waited again.

I tried to remember something about my father, something that would suit the dignity of the occasion, but what came into my mind wasn't dignified – it happened on a weekend visit home.

When I come into the house, they are in the kitchen. My father is sitting at the formica-topped kitchen table, reading the *Murkirk Gazette*, while my mother finishes off making the tea. After the usual greetings, my father says to me, 'Where the hell's fire have you been?'

I smile. It's what he always says when I come home.

'That's where I've been.'

My dad laughs and cries out, 'Hear that, Mary? Says he's been tae hell! He's met the devil hissel!'

My mother is too busy laying out the food on the plates to pay any attention.

She puts my plate down on the table in front of me. There is protein there and carbohydrate, and as a concession to fresh vegetables a fried tomato dominates the colour-scheme of the platter, alongside which, on the table, she puts two slices of plain white bread, liberally margarined, and a cup of strong, heavily sugared tea.

'Tae hell and back! D'ye hear that, Mary?'

My mother, confused by this loose talk of hell and wary of my father's moods – even when they are good, she knows how quickly they can change – ignores him and says to me, 'Ye'll enjoy that, son.'

'He hasnae ate a meal since he was last hame. Look at him, skinny izza rake! Play a tune on his ribs! Is that aw ye're gien him?'

My mother tuts agitatedly.

I am beginning to feel some indefinable discomfort I've often felt when my father jests with my mother like this. I look at the mixed grill in front of me and say, 'I'll never eat all this, Mum.'

'You will so.'

I half expect her to add that I'm a growing laddie, but she doesn't. Still, there's a hint of command in her scandalised tone of voice. Maybe she has always made me do what she wants me to, not by being strict, but by the opposite stratagem – by indulging me in her love. Maybe in the very act of giving, of providing, she makes me feel obliged to her. Anyway, I know that anything left on the plate will be in the nature of a filial insult, a criticism of her personally.

'Is that aw he's gettin for his tea?' my dad exclaims, running a hard palm over his bald, pitted scalp and shaking his head in mock disbelief.

My mother adjusts her glasses, which magnify her eyes to make them look permanently affronted, takes her hanky from her sleeve, sniffs into it and glares at him, daring him to go on.

'I thought ye'd have killed thon fatted calf, Mary.'

She raises her eyebrows, and executes a kind of little mime show, closing her eyes and spreading a hand over her chest, as if about to faint. When she laughs, it is forced and shrill, like the cry of a panicking bird. My father's humour always makes her think of things she'd rather not think about. His jokes are tainted with politics or religion and they never cease to put her on edge.

'Did ye no defrost thon fatted calf in the freezer? Ah mean, the boy's been tae hell and back and he comes hame, the Prodigal returns, expectin a fatted calf, at least wan, tae be slaughtered for him. . .'

'Aw, stop it. . . please!'

She tries to change the subject.

'Are ye enjoying your tea, son?'

Here I echo my father, 'It's the first decent meal I've had since I was last here, Mum.'

'It is not!'

She is frowning and smiling at the same time. The idea is as pleasing as it is scandalous.

'I'm sure Polly feeds you well,' she adds, sceptically.

'It's no the same as his Mammy's, eh no son?'

I nod and smile and try not to show that I'm having trouble with the black pudding. The egg, the greyish sausages, the tattie scones, the fried tomato and greasy, fatty bacon are going down OK, but I'm definitely having trouble with the black pudding, which is soggy in the middle and partially uncooked. To make matters worse, I remember my father telling me off as a boy for not eating my black pudding at Sunday breakfast.

'Shovel it doon yer gullet!' had been his exact words then.

As if reading my thoughts, he gives me a penetrating look and says the same thing now, 'Shovel it doon yer gullet!'

My mother looks worriedly at all the food I've still to eat.

'Finish your tea, son. There's more black puddin if ye want it.'

'There's a fatted calf in the freezer there,' says my father.

My mother closes her eyes, holds her hands up in a parody of despair and exhorts, 'Aw please, don't!'

I raise a clot of the dried blood to my lips. I know my

mother is watching me and waiting. I'm beginning to feel queasy, and when I take a mouthful of the grisly black pudding, I taste the metal of the fork – it's a worn fork that has lost its shine and gone grey. The metallic taste of the fork lingers in my mouth and I feel nauseous.

It's now that it happens.

My dad, playing the fool, reaches over to filch a sausage from my plate.

'Gi' us a wee bitty that fatted calf, Prodigal!'

My reaction is instinctive, almost a reflex – it's not that I desperately want to keep the sausage. It's his mischievousness I'm reacting to. Maybe I'm just not in the mood for it and he senses this and does it all the more to tease me. Anyway, I raise my fist in a warning gesture. But, and this is the strange thing, somehow the clenched fist takes on a life of its own, all restraint dissolves and, without meaning to, I punch him so hard on the arm that he drops the fork and recoils in pain. He screws up his face and bellows in outrage.

My mother's mouth falls open in horror, and I suppose that my own mouth does something similar, because I am truly astonished at what I have done. I have hit my father, hit him hard, I have hurt him. Then I see the anger flaring in his piercing blue eyes and I know I have to run. And I do run, and with good reason, because my father is chasing me through the house, shouting and cursing. And here is another curious thing. Although I'm scared of what he might do to me if he catches me, I'm also laughing hysterically. I glance over my shoulder as he chases me up the stairs, and the sight of his enraged, inflamed face makes me giggle all the more. I am still giggling as I shut and lock the bathroom door on him, and the sound of his fists beating on the door, and the sight of the door shuddering with the violence of his fury – all of it only makes me laugh all the more uncontrollably, doubled up on the toilet seat, laughing like a madman – and in fact I am mad at this moment, I have stepped into the realm of madness, because I have broken a taboo.

A few minutes later, when my father has stamped his way back downstairs, my stomach rebels and pumps its multi-coloured contents into the disinfected sink. Time itself seems to lurch inside me as I retch my mother's mixed grill out of my system and into that of the plumbing, which gurgles noisily as if in complaint. And through it all I am still shuddering with insane laughter.

I was still shuddering with insane laughter when Agnew returned. He looked disturbed, but intrigued to find me as I was, writhing in the chair helplessly.

'Are you all right?'

His concerned frown and solicitous hands – one on my shoulder, the other open and offering itself to be grasped, the fingers like such fat, pink sausages – made me worse. The spasm of laughter became all the more acute, and I could feel the sweat breaking out on my forehead and my face burning as I tried to contain it. Obviously he thought I was hysterical, or just mad, or both, but when I tried to suppress the laughter by looking away from him, I caught sight of the po-faced secretary, and that set me off again. He nodded to her and said something, and in a moment she was there with a glass of water. I took it and tried to drink it. I spluttered. I choked, I coughed. But, slowly, I was recovering, and Mr Agnew, experienced as he was in the many and diverse manifestations of grief, assured me that my reaction was very common, very common indeed, and that I was still in a state of shock, but that this would pass, it was a stage in my coming to terms with my loss.

Eventually I regained my composure, brushed the solicitous hand from shoulder and said, 'Where's the body?'

Agnew led me along a short corridor from which several doors led off. He opened one of these and ushered me into a room that wasn't a room. It wasn't an anteroom either, because the coffin was there. I could see it out of the corner of my eye, along one wall, on a purpose-built shelf of some kind. I didn't look, but waited until he'd shut me in there with the corpse. He took a while to go. He hung around at the door, holding it open. I felt like telling him to fuck off and leave me alone with my father's corpse. Instead, I looked at him. That was enough to send him scuttling along the corridor, like a spider running away from some dangerous victim caught in its web.

There were subdued lights, tastefully concealed behind louvred panels, and from somewhere came the steady hiss of an air-conditioner. I half expected to hear some suitable morose Muzak to come wafting from concealed speakers, but no – this was Murkirk, not California. There was one upright chair, against the wall opposite the coffin. I moved it to the side of the coffin, but before I sat down, I looked.

The emaciation of the old man's head could not be disguised by its presentation, which involved a collar of fluted pink satin. The patina of powder and tint made it seem, if anything, less lifelike than the face of a corpse, slightly masklike. The sharp ridges of the cheekbone and jaw were clearly visible, and his mouth, no doubt vivified by Agnew's hand, still looked like a rip in a piece of coarse canvas that had been sewn up hastily. The eyes, too, looked stitched shut.

The old man looked nothing like my father, though no doubt he had been someone's father. No doubt he had worked hard like my father, if not in the pits or the steelworks then in a factory or a brickworks. Or maybe not – who could tell?

I had a mind to complain about being shown the wrong cadaver, but, after all, I hadn't really come to see my father. I had come to see death and here was a good example of death. The fact that I didn't know the deceased hardly seemed to matter. At the same time, it was as if my father was mocking me. Hadn't he told me, the very night I'd thumped him, on the way back from the Dryburn Working Men's Club, that when he died I should come to see his dead body, because everyone had to see a dead body some time, because it was part of growing up? And now he'd dodged out of it, got someone else to stand in for him, reneged on our arrangement.

I sat there for a long time, paying scant attention to the corpse, but remembering that night in the Working Men's Club in Dryburn.

He's still mad at me for hitting him, although I've apologised, and he's feeling the need to get back at me. A pal of his, Aleck, has sat down with us, and when Aleck asks me what I'm studying, my father gets stuck in.

'Nietzsche by Christ. Slave for thirty year doon the flamin sufferin pit tae send him to the Uni and this is how he thanks me. Nietzsche!'

'What's wrong with Nietzsche, Dad?'

'He wants tae know what's wrong wi it! You tell him, Aleck

– knock some sense intae him, will ye?'

Aleck shrugs and smiles, exposing the gaps in his teeth. He is an emaciated, unshaven, ferret-like man and his baggy brown raincoat makes him seem all the more skeletal as he moves around inside it restlessly, his beady, close-set eyes darting from his almost empty glass to the bar and back again.

'Eh. . . Ah wouldnae know about that. Only book Ah ever read was Wells what's-his-name.'

'H.G. Wells – great writer. *The War Of The Worlds. Invisible Man.* You tell him, Aleck.'

'Naw, eh. . .Wells Fargo, that's the boy.'

'Aye, Wells Fargo! He'd be better off readin that than what they're gien him at the Uni! Nietzsche by Christ! A flamin sufferin Nazi.'

'No he wasn't, Dad! His philosophy was distorted by the Nazis! They *used* him!'

But I can hear the plea in my own voice, a shrill note that sounds like my mother.

My father flicks his ash with a disparaging gesture, brushing a smaller, weaker man aside.

'Oh? Is that so? The master race, eh? The Nazis used that – eh, Aleck?'

'Naw, Ah've definitely no read that wan. Ah dinnae go in for science fiction. Gimme a guid western any day.'

'Science fiction! Ye're right there, Aleck! The master race, by Christ – science fiction right enough!'

'But Dad, you've got to keep in mind the context . . .'

'Context! D'ye hear him, Aleck! D'ye hear what he's tryin tae tell me now, his faither, a trade union activist for twenty year in the pits! Context! Ah'll context ye, ya sod ye!'

Aleck smiles uncomfortably and says, 'Mine's identical.

Selected Stories

Cannae unnerstand a word he says since he went tae college. Naw, Wells Fargo, that's what Ah enjoy.'

'Hear that? Here's a man who's only read Wells Fargo, an you're tellin him tae think aboot the context! What d'ye mean, *context*?'

I take a long drink of my pint. I want to conceal my hesitation, or better still drop the subject, but my father won't let me off the hook.

'Eh?'

'I mean. . . the rest of his philosophy, Dad. In *Beyond Good and Evil*, his critique of Christianity. . .'

'Oh? there's anither context as well as that wan. It's cried History! It's cried Belsen! That's right, Aleck?'

'Aw aye! History! Terrible stuff!' says Aleck, shaking his head from side to side vehemently and grimacing, as if history is a food he can't stand to eat and is scunnered by the very mention of. His eyes dart from father to son and back again, as if he's trying to work out what this argument really is about.

'I do know that, Dad, but Nietzsche thought. . .'

'Oh, ye do, do you? Would ye listen tae it, Aleck? Thinks he kens it aw, no let his auld faither tell him onythin!'

'Aye, mine's identical.'

'Hasnae even read Marx – wid ye credit that? Calls hissel educatit! Hasnae even read *The Ragged Trousered Fellae* and he talks tae his auld faither aboot Nietzsche. You've read *The Ragged Trousered Fellae*, eh Aleck?'

Aleck looks doubtful and moves around restlessly in his seat.

'Well, Ah might've read it a long time ago. . .'

'See Aleck's read Robert Tressell an he's juist a panel-beater!'

'I've read it as well, Dad!'

'Oh, ye have, have ye? Mawn then – tell us what it's aboot.'

I open my mouth to begin, then shut it again and shake my head in exasperation, but my father persists.

'Mawn! Tell Aleck here what it's aboot, cause if ye cannae – what guid's yer flamin sufferin education, eh?'

'It's about this group of housepainters. . .'

'Naw it's no! It's aboot the oppression o the workin man by the rulin bloody classes – that right Aleck?'

Aleck, bewildered, agrees hastily.

'Calls hissel educatit! Doesnae even ken what *The Ragged Trousered Fellae*'s aboot! Needs an auld ex-miner like me tae explain it tae him!'

Aleck smiles uneasily and chips in, 'Eh. . . Ah couldnae say for sure Ah've read that wan masel. A good story, is it?'

'A *great book*. Shows the working man how tae fight back.'

I chip in, 'The only thing wrong with it's the ending.'

My father's eyes widen in outrage.

'Oh? Is that so? and what, for the benefit of us ornary workin men whae havnae read Nietzsche, is wrang wi the endin? *Eh?*'

I can hear the dangerous rise in his voice and I know I shouldn't pursue it, but there's no going back.

'He kills himself. It doesn't offer hope.'

'Ah like a happy endin maself,' suggests Aleck, tentatively.

'He kills hissel cause that's what happened! Robert Tressell committed suicide!'

'He died of tuberculosis, Dad.'

He waves this aside with a hand.

'Anywye, that's no the point, eh no, Aleck?'

Aleck shrugs and smiles, then, seeing that both me and

my father are looking to him to settle the dispute, thinks better of his smile and starts nodding, then shaking his head furiously.

My father looks at me with exaggerated outrage.

'You'd bloody kill yersel if you'd had his life, ya swine ye!'

'Whose life, Dad? Tressell's or Frank Owen's?'

'Same thing, eh, Aleck?'

Aleck looks from my father to me and back again. He's clearly getting fed up with the argument.

'It's *not* the same thing, Dad! There's a difference between fiction and autobiography! Or there should be, but with *The Ragged Trousered Philanthropists*, maybe there isn't, maybe that's what wrong with it, maybe that's why it doesn't offer hope!'

But I know that I'm faltering, that I'm sounding muddled and strident, like a wee boy on the verge of a tantrum.

My father waves my words aside, laughing scornfully, then settles back in his chair and beams at Aleck, basking in his victory. It's as if all he has to do is get me arguing, get me riled and anxious to prove my point, then that proves that he's won.

'Would ye listen tae him, Aleck! That's how they're learnin him tae talk up at the Uni! Comes back here an tells us he's read Nietzsche, a flamin sufferin German Fascist. . .'

'Aw leave him alane, he's just a boy. Mine's the same. They'll grow oot o it.'

Aleck leans over the table to me and consoles, 'Never mind him, son. You stick in at yer studies, eh? Here's tae ye, son!'

Aleck raises his glass and drains what's left in it.

'I'll get the drinks,' I say, as decisively as I can. I want to escape to the bar, but I'm not sure about whether the money in my pocket will cover the round.

My dad senses this and seizes on it.

'Oh ye will, will ye? Make mine a double. Aleck here'll have the same.'

'A wee nip'll dae me fine, son.'

'Naw it willnae. We'll have two doubles, and two half pints!'

I tug a handful of coins from my pocket and start to count them out on the table. It's obviously not enough. My father beams with satisfaction as he flourishes a ten-pound note.

'There ye are, ya fascist parasite! That's yer parental contribution! Keep the change! See Aleck? He takes his poor auld faither's hard-earned money tae buy hissel books on reactionary German philosophy, then Ah have tae buy him his drinks! It's criminal, is it no?'

'Aye, mine's identical.'

I hear my father mention the Hitler Youth as I leave the table and suddenly everything seems comic, but with some of the tragic inevitability I remember from Aesthetics 1, in Aristotle's *Poetics*. Here I am, home, where I should belong, but don't feel that I do. Not any more. I look around the bar at the faces, all the faces of the men and the women here. Even if I want to be one of them – will they still have me?

A local band has set up their equipment on a small stage in a corner, and as I walk to the bar they start playing – there's no escaping it – 'The Green Green Grass of Home'.

But it's later, walking up the road from the club, that the subject comes up. I ask him what he thinks happens after death. Nothing, he says, but there's apprehension in his eyes. Then he tells me that by the time he was my age he'd seen plenty dead bodies, that it was part of growing up, but that I didn't have to look so down in the mouth about it – I'd see his soon enough.

So he knew he was going to die soon.

The knock at the door brought me back to the present. I hurried out. Agnew was still looking concerned about me. And there was something else in his look, as he showed me out to the front door, a kind of professional interest, as if I was an interesting example of something he'd heard of but not actually seen before, a rare species of mourner.

'All right?'

'It wasn't him.'

He smiled a sad smile, a smile laden with understanding and condolence, a smile he had developed for the purpose, a smile that helped to explain the inexplicable.

'I know how you feel, many people feel the same when they lose someone they dearly love.'

Before closing the door behind me I looked over at the secretary and bleated at her again. She looked utterly terrified.

There was almost an hour to kill until there would be a bus to Dryburn – the godforsaken little village where my parents lived. It wasn't even home. They had moved there when my father's pit had been closed and he'd had to retrain as an engineer.

I meandered the streets of Murkirk with a restlessness I could barely contain. I passed Lemetti's Cafe, still the same glass door with the sign advertising coke, and the brass handle, where I'd spent so much time sitting around with school-friends after school and on Saturday afternoons. I found myself outside the churchyard and I went in. It was a place I hadn't set foot in since schooldays, when I'd sometimes come here with Annie, my girlfriend at that time, for want of anywhere else to go. It seemed poorer now, shrunken and drab. Of course, we'd come here at night, when the darkness could be our accomplice. It had seemed a different place then, with darkness and a moon and the town clock gonging on the hour. . . But I could couldn't quite remember it in detail, couldn't remember how we'd talked to each other, couldn't quite see Annie's face in my mind. I was stuck in the present, in this crude, sweltering summer's afternoon. The graveyard seemed offensively public, giving so little privacy from the town around it that I found it hard to believe that we'd thought of it as *our* place. Now it looked like what it was for – a place where you dump the dead, with haste, then hurry away.

The older graves looked like badly made beds with lumpen blankets and awry headboards, as if the dead had bad dreams and were troubled by restless nights. Why did I see it like that, this ordinary little bit of ground? Why was I seeing everything like that today, as if everything had taken on a life of its own? My father had died, that must be it, and everything else was too alive. I felt something stirring inside me – a feeling to do with death maybe, or maybe it was to do with life. Either way, there was more disgust in it than loss. Maybe it was Sartre's *nausée*? Maybe I was going to throw up?

I wandered into the arched vestibule area of the church. The statues of the king and queen were still lying there, hands clasped on their chests, in their separate beds of stone. Though I'd often come in here with Annie, and we'd canoodled behind these outstretched, eroded figures, I'd paid no attention to them at the time. Now the figures had a surreal quality, as if the stone had become a thick fluid, a kind of dead grey jelly. Even the solid stone walls of the church, as I looked at them, seemed to clench and move apart like blackened knuckles, and the flagstones under my feet were like flesh. It seemed to me I could see the pores of the stone opening and closing. I walked over to read an inscription above the statues and my foot disturbed a used condom among a heap of litter and leaves. That brought the pregnancy back and the image of a ghostly foetus I had seen in a colour supplement.

Go away, little ghost, don't haunt me.

Before the funeral everyone gathered at my sister Angela's house. My mother, buttoned up in her coat, a dark headscarf round her hair, sat on the edge of her chair and smoked her cigarette nervously. It was her usual way. There was nothing in her eyes or her voice to give away how she was feeling. My older brother Jim, dressed in a blue pin-striped suit that dated from before his marriage, from a dark time in his past when he had run a bingo hall in Doncaster, looked more careworn than the last time I'd seen him. Of course, he'd had to drive up from Norfolk, so maybe he was still tired from the journey. His blonde wife Rita, who'd always struck me as a happy person with a raunchy sense of humour, looked strangely subdued and uncomfortable in the grey dress she was wearing. Maybe it wasn't just the dress – we were all a bit uncomfortable. My other sister Carol, heavily pregnant, was feeling breathless and exhausted. Max, her boyfriend, usually such an easy-going guy – his hippy wedding to his ex-wife had been featured in the *Daily Mail* with a photograph and the caption: WOULD YOU LET YOUR DAUGHER MARRY THIS MAN? – even he seemed on edge. And then there was me, with the black tie borrowed from one of my mum's neighbours and suit jacket and corduroy jeans that didn't quite match for colour.

I felt uneasy as well. Maybe we all felt a bit shabby in the room, which Angela had gone to great pains to decorate and furnish in a way that suggested both luxury and restraint. Angela didn't seem herself either – less businesslike, less brisk. There were dark marks under her eyes – maybe she was just exhausted.

Of course, somebody was missing.

Only Arnold, Angela's husband, seemed perfectly at home in his role as host, serving out the drinks. When he'd done that, he stood in the bay-window and practised his golf swing as usual. He did it without thinking, it didn't matter where he was or who was in the room with him. It was like breathing.

He started talking about the death. He was talking to me, maybe just because I was nearest, but soon the others were listening as well. Apparently he'd been with him at the moment he'd died – when Angela had gone out of the room.

'I wouldn't have missed that experience for anything in the world. I was talking to him, telling him what was in the paper, you know. . . ah, it's kind of problematic to communicate with someone who can't verbalise a response, especially a man like your father, a man who needed to talk. But, ah, he just looked at me and suddenly I knew he was going. It was, ah. . . like he was *letting* go, then he looked at me and he said 'Jesus Christ', and that was it. He went. He just went.'

'He went,' I repeated, under my breath. 'He went. He just went.'

My sister Carol was sitting beside me on the sofa, and she gave me a puzzled look.

I was finding it hard to keep down the laughter. What was this laughter inside me? This desperate, uncontrollable thing inside me that could only come out as laughter? Was it the divine laughter of Zarathustra, the cruel and remorseless laughter of the free spirit? Maybe not – anyway, I couldn't let it out, not here, not now. It would seem like I was being deliberately perverse.

My mother was taking in Arnold's words as if a great mystery was about to be revealed.

'Oh, would ye credit that!' she said.

My brother-in-law went on, glancing at me as he said, 'Strange last words for someone like your father, an old communist of his ah. . . calibre, don't you think?'

I didn't really want to think about it at that moment, but like my father, my brother-in-law had the knack of coming out with things no one wanted to think about, the unwelcome truth – or, if that wasn't available, a provocative lie.

I didn't answer. I was looking at Carol, at the swelling under her dress. She was eight months pregnant. Birth was the mystery to me, the true horror, not death.

Angela countered her husband briskly.

'Oh for heaven's sake, Arnold, you're not seriously suggesting that dad saw the light at the last minute! How ridiculous.'

'I'm not suggesting anything of the kind, all I'm saying is that you wouldn't expect a man of his political ah. . . disposition to ah. . . invoke the name of Christ with his last breath, that's all I'm saying.'

My mother, anxious to find some mystery here, blew her nose and looking at the floor with wide, portentous eyes, ventured, 'Ye never know, Angela. He was a lapsed Catholic, remember'

Angela closed her eyes with forbearance, then said in a measured voice, 'How could I forget? I was there when he threw the priest out of the house!'

My older brother Jim shifted around in his seat uncomfortably and said, 'You know Dad – he was probably swearing.'

Angela added, 'He was probably so sick of looking at you, Arnold, that he gave up the ghost!'

Arnold adjusted his grip on the four-iron and chipped an imaginary golf ball at her in reply.

My mother closed her eyes and said, as if pained, 'Oh, what a thing to say, Angela!'

But wasn't her reaction to Angela just like her reaction to my father? She felt more comfortable with Arnold's way of talking, because although she couldn't really understand it, he made everything sound like it had come out of a book.

At that moment I saw Carol's stomach move and she gasped. Everyone stopped talking. Max asked her, 'Was that the baby moving?'

Carol nodded and said it had been moving around a lot.

There followed a conversation about the position of the baby – apparently it wasn't in the right position. Everyone was eager to think of the birth rather than the death. Except me. I sat there staring at Carol's bulge with stupefied dread. No. Not for me. Not yet.

Carol noticed me looking at her and asked if I wanted to feel the baby kick. Then she took my hand and placed it on her stomach. After a moment, the baby kicked and I recoiled in horror, as if the baby had given me an electric shock. There was general laughter about this, then Jim said, 'Couldn't've hurt that much!'

Rita laughed too loudly. Angela gave her a dirty look. Then she gave me a severe, questioning look – she knew something was up. When I left the room she came out after me and confronted me in the kitchen, so I told her that Polly might be pregnant. I found myself smiling a little as I told her – after all, being the youngest I was the only one who hadn't had kids and I suppose part of me wanted to beat my breast in a manly display of potency, but Angela's reaction scared the hell out of me. It was like I'd told her that somebody had died. She shut her eyes, sagged into a chair and put her hands to her brow.

'Oh my God. She'll have an abortion.'

'I don't know if Polly would.'

Angela looked up at me in utter disbelief.

'But she must!'

Then my mother came through and I retreated into the back garden.

My nephews were playing football. Although there were only three of them, they were taking it seriously and for some reason I really wanted to join in, but when I did I felt awkward, I couldn't give myself to the activity of controlling the ball at my feet. Maybe my nephews sensed this, because they became strangely quiet as they passed the ball to and fro.

The phone rang just as the hearse arrived at the front door and everyone started getting ready to go. Angela answered it, then told me calmly, but it was as if she was restraining a scream, that it was Polly.

I hadn't expected her to call – she'd be busy all day hanging her show. I told her I had to go, that the hearse was there outside.

'I just thought you'd like to know. My period's come.'

'Has it? Oh. That's good.'

Angela, who happened to be walking past me at that moment, squeezed my arm and closed here eyelids with relief.

Then everyone was walking past me through the hall and out the front door.

'Tell everyone I'm sorry I couldn't be there.'

'Sure, Polly. Good luck with your show. Everybody understands.'

'Will you be coming back tonight?'

'I said I'd stay a couple of days at my mum's.'

'Oh.'

She sounded disappointed.

'I won't stay long. A couple of days. Listen, Polly, I'm sorry about the other night. . . Things'll be better when I get back.'

'Will they?'

'Yeah. Everything changes, eh?'

She agreed with that although she sounded puzzled by it. I was puzzled by it myself, but it sounded like the right sort of thing to say under the circumstances.

Everyone looked at me strangely as I ran out of the door punching the air, unable to hide my jubilation. I was off the hook, I wasn't going to be a father, not yet. I was still free. First I had to help bury my father – if it was my father there in that long wooden box in the hearse.

If it was him. That was all I could think about during the ceremony. If Agnew could show me the wrong body in his funeral parlour, maybe he could make the same mistake when it came to burying him. We were all standing there looking long-faced, watching the coffin on the conveyor belt with squeaky wheels as it slowly disappeared into the dark place beyond the curtain, where presumably the cremation happened, but maybe we were attending the funeral of the old man I'd seen in Agnew's. I thought about him again now, and as the image of that lifeless head came into my mind, the certainty that it had in fact been my father struck me forcibly, almost as if my father himself had struck me a blow. Of course it had been him, there had been no mix-up with corpses! Confronted with his corpse, I had failed to recognise him – maybe I hadn't wanted to – and how my father jeered at me in my head. As the speaker from the Humanist Society went on with his little speech, my father's rasping, derisive laughter coursed through me like a pungent antidote. Jesus Christ, he was haunting me, the old bastard was taking me over! I had to let it out, but as soon as it started to come to my lips I tried to stifle it, so that I began to shake all over and splutter. The others were looking at me and I made a coughing fit out of it. When I'd recovered I glanced along the row at the others and saw that Carol too was shuddering, her head in her hands. But she was actually crying. I envied her. She'd cried after she'd seen him in intensive care, wearing the oxygen mask. Why hadn't I felt like that? I was impatient for the ceremony to be over. My mind kept asking me the wrong questions. How much was the visiting humanist paid to deliver the secular oration? Did they burn the coffins with the bodies, or did Agnew instruct his men to whip the bodies out and save the coffins from the flames – wouldn't that make sense? What a waste of good wood a coffin was, when you thought about it. . . and all those wasted flowers! The smell of them pervaded the place, and the claustrophobia of my own thoughts and oppressive heat made me itch to be out.

The house was strange. My mother had been busy cleaning it, eradicating every trace of my father. I sat, slumped in front of the television, vaguely irritated by my mother's busyness. Wasn't there something strange about it? The way she had collected together all his clothes, washed and ironed them, then folded and tied them into neat bundles. . . it was weird. His other possessions, his razor, his shaving mug and mirror, his spectacles, his tobacco tins, his cigarette-rolling machine, his haversack for work, with its sandwich tin and its flask, his shoes, his walking sticks – all these relics of my father had been assiduously gathered together, some thrown away and others packeted and labelled and put in the bag with the clothes – the black plastic bag I was to take to the rest-home in Murkirk before I took the train back to Edinburgh.

My mother made me a cup of tea before I went. I looked around the room. It seemed different, tidier and more arid without my father, without the mess of newspapers and ashtrays and cups and plates he created. Still I could feel the back of my head settling into the dent in the armchair where his head had rested, despite the clean antimacassar she'd placed there.

'What did he look like, son?'

'How d'you mean, Mum?'

'Angela said his head went a funny colour all down one side just after he died.'

'It wasn't a funny colour when I saw him.'

'Did he look peaceful?'

'He just looked dead, Mum.'

She looked hurt and disappointed by that. I didn't want to get annoyed with her, but she was annoying me. The way she'd cleaned the house so briskly, obliterating all trace of my father. This business of having to take the bag of his things to a rest-home – as if the old folks waiting to die in there would appreciate a gift of a dead man's things. And what about me, what about my feelings? Didn't it occur to her that I might not enjoy taking this black bag of death to a rest home? And her curiosity about how he'd looked, as if she half regretted not having gone to look at the body herself. Now she wanted to know the details of its physical condition. It was her eagerness to find out about this that bothered me most and I wished I hadn't told her that I'd gone to Agnew's. Maybe, like me, it hadn't come home to her yet that he was really dead. Maybe like me, she had yet to feel the loss.

I kissed my mother and asked her if she'd be all right on her own. She told me she would, that she had her work to go back to in the morning and that she could always phone up Angela if she needed to talk to somebody. I picked up my bag and slung it over my shoulder, then said goodbye and heaved the other bag on to my other shoulder. It was heavy.

My mother stood at the window until I reached the gate, then she waved. I held up my one free hand in reply. Then I watched her adjust her glasses, look along the street first one way then the other way, before turning away from the window and going to meet herself. It was the first time she'd been alone for a long time – maybe she'd never really been alone? I wondered what she'd do, what she'd think about in that empty house on her own.

When the bus moved off, the bag sagged forward and let out some air. It made a noise that was eerily human, like a sigh of resignation. Every time the bus turned a corner the bag leaned towards me a little. It kept shifting its position in the seat, as if it wasn't comfortable. When the bus stopped at a bus stop and people came on, I noticed them glancing at the bag. Maybe they wondered what was in it. I knew. I knew what was in it all right, and for the first time I had a sense of my father's sudden absence, and the huge emptiness he left behind him. It was inside me, that sudden absence, that huge emptiness, and I wondered if it would ever shrink or be filled.

As the bus moved off, the bag lurched forward in the seat and I had to catch it to stop it falling. For the rest of the journey I kept my hand on it, holding it steady on the seat beside me. It made a strange passenger.

A Good Night's Sleep

JUST WHEN he was maybe beginning to fall asleep at last, George Lockhart, an insomniac, thought he heard something bumping softly against his door. He opened his eyes to the darkness and listened. There it was again, against the door of his flat, soft but insistent.

He tried to rearrange himself more comfortably in the bed and sighed a sleepless curse. The noise had been getting to him lately. All the noises from the street below. Lockhart lived on the third floor of a tenement building in Edinburgh and although the street he lived in wasn't one of the busiest, there were always these noises puncturing the quiet – squeals of taxi-brakes, car doors being slammed, the Muzak from the late-night bar downstairs. When the bar closed, a few of its customers usually stood around on the pavement outside, gabbling loudly. Once they'd said their repetitive goodnights, there was usually a lull and sometimes he managed to get to sleep before the Chinese restaurant closed up. The staff always seemed to be having controversy as they set the alarm, locked up, ignited the engines and roared off to the casino. Often too there were bands of students being extrovert on the way home from their pubs and their parties, and more than once that inflated laughter had set him thinking about his own student days, the flats he'd lived in then, the parties he'd gone to, the girls he'd gone out with. . . set him thinking, and so kept him awake. Worse were the tribes of drunks, branding the night with their threats, their slogans and their chants. And then there were the miscellaneous voices of the night – the garbled, gruesome shouts of the forsaken and the damned.

Something bumping softly against his door.

Sometimes there were noises from the building itself as well as the noises from the street. The old guy with the limp who lived upstairs. He was always coming home wildly drunk, and Lockhart would have to listen to his demented monologue as he heaved himself up the stairs, stopping every few steps to argue with some remembered or imagined enemy. Worse were his bouts of song. Amplified and distorted by the stair-well, they sounded like the wails of a wounded, cornered animal. And of course there were the people through the wall, the new people who'd moved in recently and who were always having rows. They'd had one of their disputes tonight, complete with slamming doors and breaking glass. A strained silence, then the muted duet of argument that meant they were over the worst of it. After a while, he'd heard them going out. He was anxious to be unconscious before they came home and started kicking their shoes off, playing their blues records and making it up in bed – their good times could be just as noisy as their bad.

Selected Stories

Now this, surely not the wind, in any case not worth paying any attention to.

It was urgent that he fall asleep immediately because, as well as an insomniac, Lockhart was a teacher of Communication and General Studies, with the first year first thing in the morning. He'd got them having a series of discussions recently on the Problems of Modern Society. They'd done Pollution. Unemployment. Race Relations. Last week it had been Drugs and tomorrow it was what?

He turned over and tried to concentrate on not thinking about anything, so that maybe he wouldn't and therefore go out like a light – as if sleep could be crept up on from behind and be taken unawares. Of course he knew, from the yawning years of wrestling with his demons, as the dawn light seeped through his curtains, that sleep couldn't be crept up on, couldn't be taken unawares. It had to take you – a bit like orgasm and, as far as Lockhart was concerned, nowadays every bit as longed for. It was months since he'd slept with anybody and now he didn't know which he needed most – the sleep, or the anybody.

He punched the pillow, clenched his teeth, rearranged his legs and his arms. It was one of those expensive beds, scientifically designed for the sleepless, but single when all is said and as such harder than some. He tried not think of Elaine, his ex-wife, sleeping in their old, comfortable double bed – alone? – and tried not to start worrying about what to do with Ben, their son, when he took him for the weekend. . .

He heard it again then, against the door of his flat, softly bumping. It wasn't anyone knocking and anyway – why knock? There was a doorbell. And it was too soft to be the old guy with the limp staggering against the door on his way up to his own. This was a different kind of pressure on the door, ceasing and coming again, not making much noise maybe but enough to keep insomniacs awake. Surely it couldn't be the new people, locked in a passionate embrace against his door, unable to wait until they'd unlocked their own?

He propped himself up on one elbow, switched on the bedside lamp and gave the clock-without-a-tick a dirty look. The time it told was wasn't the right time, because Lockhart had developed the habit of setting it ten minutes fast, so that if need be he could take ten minutes longer to surface in the morning – as if time could be stolen from Time. Even so it said 01.45 – the wrong time for a visitor. Maybe it could be that stray cat he'd invited in not so long ago for the remains of a Chinese carry-out – back for its banana fritter? If so, he'd wring its neck.

But no, there it was again, something leaning then not leaning on the door, something bigger than a cat, something heavier and by the sounds of it, less likely to go away.

Tying his dressing gown on, Lockhart stamped along the chilly hallway in his bare feet, switched on the light and unlocked the door.

'Yes?'

The young girl sitting on his doormat looked up sharply as she spat out this affronted 'Yes?', for all the world as if he'd just barged into her bedroom. Maybe he had. He apologised.

'I'm sorry, but I heard. . . I wondered what the. . . '

Lockhart held the door half-closed and moved from foot to foot in the icy draught, scarcely able to believe that she was there on his doormat, talking to him with such emphatic scorn.

'What are you doing. . . out here?'

'I was *trying* to sleep!'

'Out *here*?'

'What does it look like?'

He had to admit that it did. She had spread out an assortment of brightly coloured but tattered clothes on the landing and had bundled others up into what looked like a makeshift pillow.

He watched as she took a pair of lumpy woollen socks from a plastic carrier bag and tugged them on over her jeans, every so often glaring up at him suspiciously. He went on staring helplessly as she tied on her worn sneakers, taken aback by her presence – by those glowering dark eyes, by the delicate cheekbones and lips. She was young – in her twenties, maybe younger.

'Don't you have anywhere to *live*?'

'I wouldn't be here if I did, would I?'

'No. . . I suppose not.'

'You suppose right. I'm homeless, that's all. I've been sleeping in stairs for a long time now.'

'But. . . you're young!'

'So? A lot of young people are homeless nowadays. . . haven't you heard?'

The teacher of communication and General Studies hopped around in the icy draught and had to admit that he hadn't.

'Well you have now. Goodnight. George.'

He was startled by her use of his name, then laughed nervously. Of course, it was on the door. She echoed his nervous laugh perfectly, then dropped it suddenly and averted her face.

'But surely there must be somewhere you can go. . . a hostel, maybe?'

'Which hostel is that?'

'A hostel, I don't know, for the homeless.'

'They don't let me in any more, so I sleep in stairs. Tragic, isn't it? If you know what *tragedy* is.'

Lockhart found himself thinking of a grey-haired king wandering around in the homeless wilderness of a first-year literature option, the fool at his side, but the doorstep at two in the morning was no place for a tutorial.

'Are you a student?'

'What's it to you? You a teacher?'

Lockhart nodded. The girl stopped blowing into her hands to laugh derisively.

'I might've know it. You look like the sadistic type.'

Lockhart ignored this.

'Where were you living before?'

'Before what?'

'Before you weren't.'

'Listen, teacher, listen carefully. I had to leave the place I was in. Now I don't have anywhere else to go, so I'm homeless. Got it? Sleep well.'

'But that's terrible!'

'No it's not. I'll die, that's all. I'll die and I don't care anyway and don't start telling me you do because you fucking well don't. Nobody does.'

She glared up at him as she spat out the words. Lockhart stood there holding the door and saying nothing. What was there to say to a young girl who was going to die on your doormat at two in the morning?

'You wouldn't have a *cigarette*? Oh, I don't suppose you *smoke* though, do you?'

Lockhart replied stiffly that he did smoke, told her to wait a minute, then let the door swing closed on her. He could lock it now, go back to bed, forget her, get a good night's sleep yet if he dropped off right away. After all – why should he have to bother with her? Why did he feel obliged to try and do something to alleviate her plight? Maybe it was the way she sneered as she spoke to him, as if he personally was somehow to blame for her situation.

Back in the warmth of his bedroom, Lockhart lit a cigarette for himself and donned his socks. He could offer her the boy's room for the night. What harm would it do? Or if she preferred, she could just get some rest on the couch until the morning. Or he could call the police. Wouldn't a cell be better than the cold stone landing of a tenement stair, with a doormat for your mattress?

He yawned his way back out to the door. As he stooped to give her the cigarette and the lighter, he noticed the frayed hole in her old pullover and thought he caught a whiff of something bad – like rancid butter, but worse. As she handed back the lighter she bared her teeth in the parody of a smile and said, 'Thank you *so much*. You're *so kind*.'

He wasn't used to being the target for such venom and didn't know how to react. He hovered over her in silence, holding the door with one hand and smoking with the other. She looked up at him once, laughed sarcastically and looked away. At length, he came out with it.

'OK. You can stay the night here. My son isn't here at the moment. You can take his bed.'

He was just about to add that it was only for one night, that he had to get up early for work and that he'd want to see her gone in the morning, when she interrupted.

'No way.'

'But I'm offering you a place to *sleep*!'

The word echoed in the hollow stairwell. She glared at him insolently, over her shoulder, her lips parted slightly as if ready to laugh at him at any moment. Then she flicked her ash on the doormat, looked away and shook her head.

'Come on! It's a bed for the night!'

'I've heard that one before!'

'Oh for Christsake, I'm not going to. . . *do* anything.'

She glanced at him with blatant accusation, as if to say that because he'd mentioned it, he must have thought about it.

Lockhart groaned with emphasis and waited. He thought she might be hesitating, but it was taking too long and so he told her that he had to sleep, had to get up early and he hoped she'd find a place to stay soon.

As he turned the key in the lock he heard her, on the other side of the door, bid him a quiet goodnight, all hostility gone from her voice, without that sharp edge of scorn.

Lockhart thumped the light switch with the side of his fist and padded back along the hallway to bed. Turning over and over in the warmth of it, trying not to think about her out there on his doormat, he heard it again, the soft bumping sound as she leaned back against the door. She must be trying to get comfortable, or not comfortable exactly but into a position for sleep. Lockhart endeavoured to do the same. Then he heard her coughing, weakly at first, then it was a harsh, hacking cough that echoed in the stairwell. She was definitely going to die out there and she didn't care – *And don't start telling me you do because you fucking well don't. Nobody does!* – and Lockhart wondered if he'd maybe been too impatient with her. Yet he felt angry too, angry with her arrogance. How dare she not care about herself! Why should he care about her, if she didn't? Why should anyone?

Again he heard her cough.

When he could suffer it no longer, he climbed out of bed again and switched on the lamp. Then he heard the voices outside, in the stair. It was the couple next door, the new people. He couldn't make out what they were saying, but the man's voice was raised. His wife's voice was high-pitched, accusing. He thought he heard the young girl – her sneering rejoinder. After a few minutes the voices subsided. Then he heard the key rattling in the lock of the flat next door. He hurried out and unlocked his door in time to catch his neighbours closing theirs. The woman was already inside, but the man stopped on his threshold when he saw Lockhart. There was no sign of the young girl. Lockhart found himself apologising again.

'Sorry. I heard the. . . I wondered what the. . . '

'Oh, it was just some junkie sleeping in the stair.'

'Really?'

'Yeah. I told her where to go.'

'Did you? Where?'

'Where do you think?'

Lockhart glimpsed his neighbour's tight little smile before the man turned and stepped into his hallway.

'See you.'

'Yes, goodnight.'

They locked their respective doors.

Lockhart switched off the lamp, then stepped over to the window, parted the curtains and peered down into the dark canyon of the street. He couldn't see her anywhere, but her voice was still there in his head, bidding him a quiet goodnight as he locked the door on her, as if she'd felt able to own up to her helplessness only with the door between them.

He turned from the window but didn't get into bed. What was the hurry? The luminous digits on the clock told him in any case that he'd never get a good night's sleep now. He stood in the darkness of the room, listening to the woman through the wall kicking off her shoes one by one, to the voices resuming their duet, to the music with its thudding bass, the man's laughter and the woman's shrill cry of mock surprise. . . Didn't they have work to go to in the morning, these new people? He had the first year, and another of the many Problems of Modern Society. It had to be homelessness.

He climbed into bed, closed his eyes and immediately began to drift into a deep, deep sleep, then he heard it again, against the door of his flat, soft but insistent.

The Long Way Home

GEORGE LOCKHART, the teacher who was still learning, lingered in his cramped classroom long after the nightclass had shambled out of it, tacking things up on the walls.

The class had been the first unit in a module he'd put together on the History of the Working classes – and it hadn't worked. Even his 'Day in the Life of a Coal-heaver', which he'd enjoyed making up, had sounded trite and unconvincing in his mouth. Towards the end of the session a fainthearted feminist had pointed out that so far he hadn't touched on the plight of working-class women during the period in question. He'd said that this was history's omission, not his, but although this seemed to satisfy his questioner at the time, Lockhart now felt that he'd passed the buck. If he knew anything about history, he knew that people usually blamed it for their own failures.

So although it was a warm evening and he itched to be

out, he rooted out a book with a token chapter on the plight of the wives and conscientiously slogged his way through it, taking notes. While he was doing so an image of his mother from an old black and white snapshot floated into his mind. Wearing her nylon housecoat and with her hair tied up in a headscarf, she was leaning out of the window of their council house and wagging a warning finger at whoever was taking the picture.

Flicking through the book to look at some of the illustrations, Lockhart paused at one of a typical working-class interior, with the clothes-pulley above the range and the bed in the recess. Meant to illustrate privation, the solid and cosy look of the room made him think of his own modernised little flat with repugnance and long for the long-demolished home of his childhood. It was then that he'd looked up at the bare walls of his classroom and so he'd started – photographs, facsimiles, anything he could find to brighten the place up a bit. The simple pleasure of decoration had engrossed him and for the first time this term he'd been able to forget about time. He'd had to sprint for the train into town.

Emerging from the station in Edinburgh, he looked for a taxi but any he saw were taken. The streets were crowded because there had been a game on, and packs of drunken supporters roamed around chanting and singing. Most pubs were on the point of closing and people were spilling into the streets, less anxious to get home than usual because it was a warm night. Lockhart dodged between the revellers, wielding a weighty briefcase. He decided to take the long way home and stop in somewhere for a late pint, but the one or two pubs still serving were packed to the gills.

Almost home, he turned the corner into his street and

Selected Stories

barely avoided stepping on an enormously fat woman who lay on her back across the pavement, howling loudly. Her friend, a tight-lipped blonde with no-nonsense eyes, leaned over her and yanked at an arm.

'Ah'm warnin ye Margaret, get up!'

Margaret rolled around on the pavement, trapped in her outrageous distress, and howled some more. As Lockhart steered his way round her, the friend caught him by the arm. He jumped, as if electrocuted, and raised the briefcase as a barrier between them. She hung on tightly to his sleeve. His impulse was to shake himself free – he was on his way home and it had been a tiring day – but the earnestness of her eyes held him where he was.

'Ye've got to help me, gimme a hand to get *her* on her feet.'

She yanked her thumb at the fallen woman. Lockhart hummed and hawed, then reluctantly leaned his briefcase against the wall and said he'd try.

'Right then Margaret. This gentleman's gonnae help ye up – so *move* yersel, or else!'

Together they heaved in vain. Margaret went on rolling in her pain, heedless of anything else, howling inconsolably.

'What's the matter with her?'

'She's upset.'

As if that explained everything. Lockhart didn't pursue it. The main thing was to get her on her feet and get home, but as soon as they'd succeeded in raising her from the ground, she sagged and sat back down. Added to the weight of her, there was the ponderous burden of her reluctance. Abandoned to her howling, she had become oblivious to her surroundings and didn't notice a group of supporters on the other side of the street, jeering and catcalling. Her short black skirt had ridden up around her hips, exposing moons of white flesh between her stocking-tops and her knickers. The friend held a skinny finger out in front of Margaret's tear-stained and convulsing face, then yanked at her lank black hair.

'Margaret, Ah'm warnin you, if ye dinnae get a grip. . .'

'Come on, Margaret, time to go home!'

The fallen Margaret paused not to listen but to gasp for air and go on howling. The friend grabbed her face in one hand, pressing her fingers deeply into the loose flesh of the cheeks and shaking it violently. She slapped the howling woman hard and yelled,

'Move!'

'Don't hit her! Let me talk to her!'

'Ye're welcome! Go ahead and try!'

As he leaned over the howling woman to do so, a bead of her bright blood dropped on to his shirt-cuff. Blood was trailing from her nose and running into her open mouth as she howled. The friend crouched beside him and dabbed at Margaret's face with a handkerchief.

'Look at what you've done!'

'She asked for it!'

Between her swollen eyelids, Margaret's brimming eyes seemed to gaze uncomprehendingly at Lockhart's face for a moment as she gasped for breath. She gazed at the blood-stained handkerchief, but if she saw it at all, it merely confirmed that she'd been deeply abused and so she howled all the more.

Lockhart squeezed her hand and tried to reason her out of her grief, every so often looking over his shoulder to see if anyone was looking.

'Listen to me, Margaret, I don't know what's wrong with you, I mean I don't know what's upset you so much, but whatever it was isn't worth it and you just can't lie here in the street like this. In the morning everything'll seem different, you'll see! So I think you should get up now and let your friend take you home! I'll help you!'

The friend yelled in Margaret's ear, 'Hear that, Margaret? This gentleman's gonnae help ye hame, so move or we're gonnae dump ye here!'

But Margaret had dumped herself here and had howled herself beyond the reach of reason or threat. Heaving her into a sitting position and propping her against the wall, Lockhart and the friend now hooked her under the armpits and wrenched her to her feet. Though the wall helped to support her, she lurched and wobbled unpredictably. Her feet flopped around like landed fish, then one of her shoes flipped off. Lockhart reached down to retrieve it – an absurdly dainty creation in red patent leather – then he felt Margaret come down on him. Compressed against the wall, one hand holding aloft the shoe and the other hand trapped beneath a wide thigh, Lockhart let out a high, panicky laugh. The friend yanked, slapped, threatened and kicked. Margaret rolled over on her side and went on howling. Lockhart sprang to his feet and reached for his briefcase.

'Look, I'm sorry, but I have to get home.'

But the friend caught him by the lapel and pulled him face to face with her.

'Ye cannae leave me like this! Help me get her back to the flat! Help me an Ah'll gie ye what ye want!'

Lockhart wondered what she thought he wanted. He shook his head and picked up his briefcase.

'It's no far. . . please!'

'OK. One more try!'

Again they heaved. Suddenly, like Sisyphus on the crest of the hill, they were moving and gaining momentum. Their steps at first slow became comically rapid as they veered across the street.

Halfway across, Lockhart felt his legs give way under him and saw the ground rolling over his head. As they fell, the briefcase burst open and a pile of unmarked essays spilled out over the street. A taxi rounded the corner and screeched to a stop, blaring its horn at them. Seeing the 'FOR HIRE' sign, Lockhart jumped to his feet and waved his arms about. The driver looked him up and down and shook his head. Lockhart staggered to the driver's window and pleaded.

'Look, I don't know these people, but one of them's in a bad way and we've got to get her home.'

He pointed to Margaret, who was howling into his open briefcase, her bloodied cheek stuck to the first page of someone's essay, her hand flailing at a pile of the others.

'Her? No way.'

The friend stuck her head in the driver's window and swore at him. Lockhart pulled her away and stuck his own head in, tugging pound notes from his wallet.

'I'll make it worth your while.'

The driver eyed him with contempt and leaned on his horn. Margaret reared her head and responded with hers. The friend shouted abuse at her. Lockhart wrung his hands and begged.

'That's all very well, but what happens at the other end? Who gets her out the taxi and in her door?'

'I do,' said Lockhart. He felt the friend pressing against

him and squeezing his arm. Finally the driver sighed with professional weariness and told them, to make it snappy.

The decor made him think of a lounge bar, with its embossed maroon-and-gold wallpaper, the black leatherette sofa, the white wrought-iron coffee table with the glass top, the electric fire with fibreglass coal and simulated flames and the artificial sheepskin rug. What had he expected – a clothes-pulley above the range? No, but maybe something more like his parents' living-room as he remembered it, with the solid wooden sideboard and the three-piece suite and the china cabinet in the corner. Looking round the room, he found the authentic detail he wanted. In an alcove to the side of the feature fireplace, three ducks were flying in a diagonal line.

Maureen – she'd told him her name in the taxi, leaning into him on a corner – was undressing Margaret and putting her to bed in a narrow boxroom next door. It had taken half an hour to get here. Once inside the taxi, Margaret had stopped howling and fallen asleep, like an enormous baby lulled to sleep by the motion of the pram. It had taken ages to manoeuvre her out of the taxi and up the three flights of stairs to Maureen's flat. On the way up, she'd woken up and started howling again. A teenage girl who had been babysitting Maureen's son had opened the door to them. Now she seemed to have gone. Margaret was howling still and every so often he could hear Maureen cursing her as she struggled to put her to bed.

He spread out the soiled essays and notes over the coffee table to see if they were salvageable. The door opened and a fair-haired boy of seven or eight stood there clutching a Hero Turtle.

'Hello there.'

The boy didn't answer, but stared at Lockhart with big, serious eyes – the likeness was clear. The boy eyed the briefcase and the papers spread out over the table.

'Are you C.I.D.?'

Lockhart laughed nervously.

'No, I'm a teacher.'

'A real yin?'

'I think so.'

'Ye are not.'

'I am so.'

'Prove it.'

Before Lockhart could try, the boy had gone, chopping him up with an imaginary sword as he went and shouting, 'I hate teachers!'

He heard Maureen yelling at the boy to tell him to get back to his bed, then some whispering – a deal of some kind was being made between mother and son in the hall – then she came into the room carrying a half-bottle of whisky and two empty glasses. She had taken her coat off and he saw that she was wearing a black dress gathered at one shoulder toga-style and held at the waist by an ornamental belt of silvery hoops.

'You're ma friend for life, George, honest.'

She sat down beside him and opened the whisky. She poured two huge measures and passed him one. They clinked glassed and drank.

'Let's have some music, eh?'

She half-walked, half-danced across the floor to the music centre. She ran her finger down a rack of cassettes and chose one. A slow, smoochy number oozed from the speakers.

Maureen swayed to the rhythm of it as she walked towards him. She smoothed her skirt out at the back before she sat down.

'What's aw this then, yer homework or what?'

'Some essays I had to mark.'

'They're marked now, eh? You a teacher?'

'Your boy doesn't seem to think so. He wouldn't believe me.'

'Ye don't look the teacher type. He hates the school, hates the teachers.'

'I know, he told me.'

'He's a cheeky wee swine so he is, takes after his dad.'

Lockhart looked towards the door uneasily. Maureen laughed and nudged him.

'Dinnae worry aboot *him*, he left me six year ago.'

'I'm sorry.'

'Don't be. Better off withoot him.'

'I see.'

'I've worked for everythin Ah've got. Everythin ye see in this room. That carpet, that fireplace, this settee.'

She spread her fingers of one hand and patted the sofa, then she placed the hand on his shoulder, tilted her head, wagged her shoe and began to hum along to the music.

'Are ye gonnae put away yer homework, or what?'

As he did, a loose page fell from the pile of papers and Maureen bent down to pick it up. Her dress was short, and Lockhart glimpsed the long space between her thighs. She looked over her shoulder at him and smiled.

It was on, it was definitely on.

Maureen picked up the page, smoothed it out on the coffee table, frowned and read.

'The plight of working-class women. Margaret kens aboot that!'

'What's wrong with her?'

'What isnae?'

She rolled her eyes and handed him the piece of paper. He stuffed it into the briefcase with the others. He'd have to sort them out later, tell the class he'd been in an accident, these things happened.

'Yes, but what got her so upset?'

She groaned and refilled her glass, moving closer to him so that he could feel the pressure of her thigh against his. Lockhart squirmed a little to give his erection more room.

'Well, it's a long story but basically what happened is that Margaret got her books at the brewery. . . that's where she was workin, in the bottlin plant. Some job that – talk aboot soul-destroyin? Ah used tae work there masel, so Ah know what it's like, believe me. Now Ah'm in the office. Ah took a course on shorthand and typin, so it's no sae bad. Anyway, two days efter she gets her books, she gets a letter frae Northern Ireland an Dennis – that's her fiance – says he's decided tae break it off wi her because o how he's no ready tae settle doon yet and aw that. He's in the army like. And the thing is tae, she thinks she might be pregnant, because he was back on leave a few weeks ago and she hasnae had a period yet. Then, tae put the tin lid on it, she gets tellt tae leave her digs for bein behind wi the rent, so Ah says tae her never mind, men are bad bastards the lottae them anyway, so Ah says she can kip in the boxroom for a bit, till she gets hersel a new place an a job an that. So that's what's wrong wi her. She's depressed. She's been depressed since she moved in here. So the night Ah says tae her, come on Margaret, you'n me are gonnae go an have a night on the toon, but we didnae get as far as the disco. She wis knockin them back in the pub, drunk as a skunk, then some guys start trying tae chat us up, complete arseholes, an yin asks her what circus she's in – the fat lady. That was enough for Margaret. She just started bubblin. Talk aboot a red face? Ah was mortified. Then in the street, she just couldnae stop howlin. Ah donno what Ah'd've done if you hadnae come along!'

As he leaned forward to put his glass down he felt her fingers stroke his neck loosely.

'What about you, eh? You married?'

'Divorced.'

'Kids?'

'One. A boy.'

'So we're in the same boat then, eh?'

Lockhart nodded. Maureen took his hand and stood up.

'Let's dance, eh?'

Lockhart took his jacket off and let it fall on the couch. Then they were holding each other close and moving very slowly round the room, her head resting on his shoulder, his hands moving down her back. When the number finished they were down on the sheepskin. It had been a long time since he'd done it like this, on the rug in front of the fire. When he suggested that they go to bed, Maureen smiled at him with a kind of relieved resignation, then she took him through to her room.

The room was small and made to seem smaller by Maureen's gigantic bed – a relic of her marriage? – which had fitted bedside tables and a padded headboard. Lockhart undressed quickly and climbed in while she went to the toilet and switched things off next door.

When she came in she was wearing a black camisole, with suspenders and stockings – the works. She sat down on the bed, slid open a drawer and took out a contraceptive and a candle. She lit the candle, swearing as she spilled a spot of hot wax on her wrist, and stuck it in a candlestick. She turned in the bed to face him. She tore open the packet, took the condom out, then deftly unrolled it over his cock. He entered her slowly and soon they were moving in rhythm together. It quickly became an urgent, desperate fuck as their mutual hunger became clear, but something began to intrude. It was Margaret – she had started up again, sobbing and howling in the boxroom. Maureen gripped his shoulders harder and told him to forget her, she'd settle down soon, then they went on – all the more urgently, it seemed, because of the distraction in the background. It reminded him of the times with Elaine, when Ben had been a baby – chasing the orgasm had been like running for cover from the baby's cries. At her climax, Maureen cried out with what sounded like exasperation. He let himself come a moment later, surprised at the ease of it. He pulled out and lay on his back beside her. Maureen coughed harshly as she tried to catch her breath.

'I should cut down on the fags.'

'Me too.'

'Want one?'

'I'll share one.'

As they smoked, they listened to Margaret's grief, sometimes muffled by the pillow, sometimes spilling out of her freely in long, ululant howls.

'Ah wish she'd fucking shut up.'

'She can't help it.'

And obviously she couldn't help it. Long after Maureen

had turned over on her side, pulled the covers up over her ears and fallen asleep, Lockhart went on listening to it, until it sounded the strangest thing on earth, this woman sobbing her heart out in the boxroom next door, insuppressible syllables of something which couldn't speak, had never found words for its condition. Even as he drifted into sleep he could still hear it, that something that couldn't speak, swelling and subsiding, voicing its elongated vowel of despair from century to century.

Where I'm From

'WHERE is this?'

Before answering his son, George Lockhart pulled up alongside a disused shop. Above its boarded-up window, painted
letters spelled out 'NEWSAGE' – the remainder of the legend
was hidden by an eczema of shredded posters and a rash of
graffiti.

'This is where I'm from, Ben. That's called Arkin's Park.'

'Doesn't look like a park.'

Lockhart had to admit that his son had a point. The
neglected space behind the solitary shop could hardly be
called a park. The grassy expanse Lockhart remembered had
shrunk to a mean corner of overgrown wasteground. Off in
the distance, beyond the railway, there was nothing. There
was just an emptiness where once the silhouette of the pit
wheel had risen above a dark bing.

'I admit it's not how I remember it.'

Lockhart imagined himself as a boy. The unkempt, straw-coloured hair hanging over one eye. The skinny, suntanned arms and shoulders. The dirty, faded jeans and tee-shirt. In one hand, a grey tennis ball – every now and again he would bounce it on the ground, or throw it up in the air and catch it with ease. It had felt so right to throw that ball up in the air and catch it with ease. He had refined it, so that he could catch the ball behind his back. In the other hand, a stick, both weapon and pencil. He could threaten people with it and draw things in the dirt.

In the middle of the wasteground stood a brick shed with a rusted corrugated iron roof and a padlocked door.

'What are we stopping here for?'

Lockhart pulled out his cigarette packet and held it up.

'You know you can't when I'm in the car, it's bad for my irritation.'

'I'm getting out. Coming?'

'I don't want to get out.'

Lockhart turned to look at his son. The boy slumped in the seat, his heavy spectacles askew on his nose, a baseball cap drooping over one ear, the earphones of his personal stereo dangling around his neck. On the seat beside him there was a stack of sci-fi comics. Because of the skin problem his face looked permanently flushed, with an opaque quality that seemed to mask expression. Overweight, strapped in the seat-belt, wired to his machine, with his stack of comics, he made Lockhart think of a sullen invalid wheeled out into the sun against his will.

He'd been looking after Ben for the past week. During the school holidays, he and Elaine, his ex-wife, looked after him week-about. He'd be taking Ben back to her place – it had once been his place too – in an hour or so. In a few days, Elaine was taking him on holiday with her to Greece, so this was Lockhart's last day with his son for a while.

He'd taken him lots of places, maybe too many, over the past week. He regretted bringing him here, especially on their last afternoon. His idea had been to show him something – where his father came from, where his grandparents had lived – in the hope that this would give him a stronger sense of something: his background, himself.

They had stopped first at the primary school, but it had been long since closed and converted into a block of flats. He had taken Ben around the playground – now a car park – pointing out what he could, remembering small events of his own childhood, and had been dismayed by his son's patent indifference. Then he'd driven to a new housing estate which had been a cornfield when he was a boy. He turned the car around and drove away, telling him about how they had hidden themselves in the corn to share their plunder of stolen apples, how they'd used a corner of the field as a racetrack for their bikes and as a football ground. He'd even remembered how sometimes, as it was getting dark, an older boy – dressed for the dancing in suit, shirt and tie – would join in the game for a few minutes before strutting off into the night. He'd tried to explain to him that this was a kind of ritual, that the boy wasn't just showing off his new suit, but was having a last kick of the ball, a last shot at childhood before meeting the new, more threatening game of the dance hall. Ben had listened dutifully but none of it had prompted his curiosity. By the time he had found the house where he'd been born, Ben had started whining to go home.

Where I'm From   249

'Tell you what. I'll get out, go for a walk, have a smoke. You can stay here, OK?'

'Not on my own.'

Lockhart smacked the back of the passenger seat with the palm of his hand and cursed.

'So what do you suggest?'

'Open a window.'

Lockhart shook his head in exasperation, shrugged and cranked the window down. When he lit the cigarette, Ben coughed sarcastically and scratched at his peeling skin.

'What did we come here for? You said we were going for a drive.'

'We've been for a drive.'

'You didn't say we were coming here.'

'I thought you might be interested to see where I grew up, where your grandparents lived, but obviously I was wrong.'

If Ben felt any interest his eyes betrayed no flicker of it. He fiddled with his digital watch, making it emit a tiny repertoire of buzzes and bleeps.

'Did you hear me? This is where I grew up.'

'I heard.'

Ben ejected his cassette, turned it over, pressed the 'play' button and manoeuvred the earphones on to his head.

Lockhart found himself shouting, 'Switch that damn thing off!'

He yanked the earphones from the boy's head. Ben let out a high whine of outrage, then his face buckled into an ugly caricature of anguish as he cried loudly and deliberately, his pale eyes overflowing.

'Shut up!'

But Ben went on howling with abandon.

'You're not a baby, for christsake! Switch that damn thing off!'

Ben stopped crying as suddenly as he had started, rubbed his eyes with the sleeve of his shirt, then stabbed at the 'stop' button with his thumb.

'Don't you think at your age, you should stop having tantrums? Don't you think it's time you grew up?'

'Time you grew up yourself!'

Lockhart threw his head back to declare a scathing laugh.

'See that shop there?'

Ben glanced at it briefly, then looked glumly at his father. His watery blue eyes, made unnaturally large by the thick lenses of his spectacles, looked vaguely affronted.

'Every morning before school and every afternoon after school, on my bike, I delivered the newspapers for the shop. On Saturday I delivered the late pink final and Sunday the Sunday papers. It was a seven-day week, Ben, and I handed over that money to my mother. . .'

'Late pink what?'

'Final. The late edition of the paper was printed on pink paper.'

'Why pink?'

Sometimes his son's curiosity irritated him as much as his indifference.

'I don't know, it just was.'

'Can we go now?'

'See that building there? Guess what that was used for when I was a boy, Ben.'

Ben barely glanced at the grim brick shed with the rusty roof before sighing emphatically and answering.

'Search me.'

'Scout hut.'

He had thought this might interest him since Ben was keen on the Scouts.

'What a dump.'

Lockhart stubbed out his cigarette and cranked up the window.

'Are we going now?'

'I want to show you one more thing.'

'What?'

'The pit where my dad – your grandad – worked.'

'I don't want to see it.'

Lockhart gripped the steering wheel tightly.'

'OK. Get out.'

Though he didn't look round he could sense his son looking up at him with alarm.

'Go on, get out. Some fresh air'll do you good. I'll be half an hour at most. You can wait for me.'

'*Here*?'

'If you go past that hut and over the other side, there's a path that runs alongside the railway. Go along it till you reach a bridge. Over the bridge, there's a swingpark. I'll meet you back here in half an hour.'

'I'm too old for swingparks.'

'Since when?'

'Since last year.'

'Because you started at high school, is that it? Just because you're a whizz at computer games, you think you're too smart to enjoy a swing?'

'The sun's bad for my skin.'

'So don't take off your shirt, turn your cap round the right

　　　　　　　　　Selected Stories

way so the peak keeps your face in shade. You can't let a bit of sun defeat you.'

He had given this or similar advice on countless occasions. He no longer had to think about the words, and he was sure Ben no longer listened. It had become a kind of routine between them.

'I'm not getting out. I'll come to the pit with you.'

'No you won't. You're not interested, so what's the point?'

Lockhart leaned over and unfastened his son's safety-belt. The boy glared at him.

'You heard me, Ben. Out.'

'But Dad. . .'

'No buts. Out you get.'

Ben looked at him in disbelief, the wide, shallow pools of his eyes threatening to spill their tears again. Even as he lumbered out of the car he kept his eyes on his father, as if expecting him to smile, tell him he was joking and that he should get back in.

Lockhart pulled the door shut and waved Ben away with a hand. As he watched his son step awkwardly into the area of wasteground behind the shop he felt an acute and useless pity for him.

He started up the engine, giving it too much gas, and drove away. As soon as he'd turned the corner he began to feel bad. He'd caused the argument, by expecting his son to be interested in something which was too abstract and remote for him to imagine – his father's background.

He had lost the will to go and look at the pit himself. Anyway, he knew it would be a flattened site. He would drive around for five minutes, then go back for Ben.

Where I'm From   253

On the way to Elaine's Lockhart tried to make amends. He asked about the planned holiday to Greece, the Scouts, his fossil collection, his friends at school, the music he liked listening to, the sci-fi comics he was so keen on. Ben answered the questions reluctantly. Only when the sci-fi comics were mentioned did he seem to betray any real interest. Lockhart listened to the names of the comics he liked best, and was treated to a summary of some of the stories – more intricate than he'd have suspected – and one story in particular.

'It's about this alien race called the Numen who have to leave their planet because it's invaded by the Triludans. . . '

He was relieved to draw up outside Elaine's ground-floor flat in Edinburgh. He got Ben's bag out of the car and carried it up the path to the door. Ben followed him. He rang the bell, but there was no answer.

'I'll get it'

Lockhart was surprised that his son had his own key to the door. He watched him open the door and hold it open for him before stepping inside.

It was the first time he'd stepped inside for a while. More often than not, he dropped Ben at Elaine's door and she at his. The hall had been redecorated and he stood in the middle of it uneasily, reluctant to go any further.

'Are you coming through, or what?'

Ben opened the kitchen door and waited for him.

'I'll stay till Elaine gets back.'

In the kitchen, Ben switched on the kettle and asked him if he wanted coffee. Lockhart nodded, sat down and watched him. His son had suddenly become animated. Maybe he was just pleased to be home. This was his home, no matter how often he came to stay at his place.

Selected Stories

'So where is she? She was supposed to be here by now.'

Ben shrugged.

'She'll be back. You can go if you want. I'll be OK.'

'I'm not in a hurry, I'll wait.'

Ben made him coffee then busied himself around the kitchen – opening the fridge, pouring himself a glass of juice, making a peanut-butter sandwich. He seemed eager to talk.

'Dad? You know that place we went today?'

'Uh huh.'

'Is that really where you grew up?'

'Yes. What about it?'

Ben was tilting his head and looking at him strangely. 'You don't go there anymore though, do you?'

'Well, no. Today was the first time for years.'

'Why not?'

'Hmm?'

'If you like it so much, why don't you go there more?'

'I never said I liked it. I just said it was where I grew up.'

Ben sat down at the kitchen table opposite him and appeared to consider this seriously while he chewed his sandwich. He stopped chewing to ask, 'What did you leave it for?'

'I left when I went to college.'

Ben nodded slightly, as if this made sense, and said, 'That was what Mum said.'

'What?'

'That's why she left the place where she grew up. She took me there the weekend before last.

'Lockhart spluttered on his coffee, then laughed.

'She took you to Fort William? You're kidding!'

Ben nodded once and took another bite.

'That must've been great for you. Fort William! The centre of the Universe!'

Ben stopped chewing, held his glass of juice halfway to his mouth and looked at Lockhart steadily.

Lockhart started back-pedalling.

'I don't really mean that. I know it's where Mum's from. . .'

Ben interrupted him quickly, wagging the crust of his sandwich in the air.

'It's a dump.'

'Maybe it doesn't seem that way to her. Anyway, why did she take you there? It's not as if she has relatives or friends there now . . .'

'Neither do you.'

'What?'

'You don't know anybody in the place you grew up either, do you?'

'Well, no, I suppose you're right, but Fort William's a lot further away.'

'Only in miles.'

Lockhart, taken aback by the perspicacity of this, could only mutter his agreement.

'Anyway Dad, I thought where you grew up was a worse dump than Fort William.'

'You're right.'

They heard the key in the front door and Ben jumped off his chair and ran to meet his mother. Lockhart stood up, stepped into the hall and stopped there when he saw Elaine. She was bending down to hug Ben and she had a parcel under one arm. She looked at him and said breathlessly,

'Sorry I'm late. There was a traffic jam. . .'

He shrugged and waved a hand loosely to say it didn't

matter. He moved from foot to foot as she turned back to Ben, who was pawing at the parcel. When she laughed, Lockhart felt the slight queasiness of remembered happiness, remembered desire.

'I think it's what you wanted. Here.'

Ben took the parcel and ran with it into his room. Elaine straightened up and looked directly at him.

'So. How has it been?'

'OK, I think. I think he's glad to be home.'

'For a day or two, then it'll be, "When's Dad coming to take me?" '

Lockhart shook his head and smiled at the suggested compliment. He looked at his ex-wife. She brushed a loose strand of hair away from her eyes and smiled at him. She looked attractive to him, but tense. She had always been tense.

'How are you, Elaine?'

'All right. Busy. You know what it's like.'

He nodded.

'I suppose I'd better go. I hope the holiday goes well.'

'We'll send a postcard.'

Something made him pull her to him and embrace her. She was slightly surprised, but only slightly. He had done it often enough since their separation. He held her tightly, too tightly for the occasion. He wanted to tell her how hard he had been finding it without her, but as he raised his eyes he saw Ben framed in the bedroom doorway, brandishing his present. It was some kind of laser gun. He had forgotten about it as he looked at them embracing.

They broke apart, but didn't let go of each other completely, to face him. Lockhart saw the look of mingled hope and hurt in his son's eyes. It was the boy who spoke.

'This planet is where I'm from. What a dump!'

He exterminated them in a cacophony of zooms and zaps, in a blaze of fluorescent, strobic light.

Say Something

WAIT FOR ME Pete, will you, wait. Stop running away, will you, wait! Look Pete, it's a doll. Somebody's gone and lost their dolly, Pete. Pete. Look, it's one of those dolls that can talk, Pete, I used to have one exactly like this. You pull the cord, see, like this. . . Hear what she says, Pete? She says she's thirsty, Mummy. I'm thirsty too, Pete. Hear what she says, Pete? She says she wants a dwinkie. I wanna dwinkie too, Pete. A big dwinkie, Daddy! I wanna gweat big dwinkie! I want. . . I want to sit down, Pete. I've got to. . . sit down. Just for a minute. I'm sorry, I'm really, really sorry but. . . I've just got to sit down for a minute. I just want. . . one cigarette, Pete, then I'll come upstairs, OK? OK, Pete?

Shit. Oh fuck. Look at that. I've gone and dropped my make-up things all over the stairs!

Say something, will you, don't just stand there. Pete! You don't care, do you? You don't. I've dropped my make-up things all over the stairs. Somebody's gone and lost their dolly. A little girl's gone and lost her dolly, but you don't care. Do you, Pete? No, you don't care. You just stand there. You just stand there looking like. . . like you. There's nothing else like it. You. You in a huff. You in a black, black mood. Oh say something, will you for Pete's sake!

For Pete's sake! That's a good one!

She's laughing too, Pete! Did you hear her? She thought it was funny, didn't you dolly? It made you laugh, eh dolly? Yes. Funny Mummy. But it didn't make Daddy laugh, did it dolly? No. Because nothing makes old huffy Daddy laugh tonight, does it? No. Cause old Daddy-waddy's gone into a gweat big huffy-wuffy, hasn't he? Yes. Shall I tell you why, baby? He's gone into a gweat big huffy-wuffy cause funny Mummy went and got boozy-woozy at Daddy's de-part-mental party! Naughty Mummy! And now old huffy-Daddy isn't going to speak to her for days! Is he, baby? No! Isn't that a terrible thing, baby? It is. It is a terrible thing, isn't it? Not to speak to somebody for days. Isn't it, Pete? *Pete?*

Please, Pete, say something, anything. Tell me I'm drunk as a skunk. All right, I'm drunk as a skunk. I know I'm drunk as a skunk. So what? Am I not s'posed to get drunk any more, hmm? Am I not supposed to enjoy the party? That's what parties are for, isn't it Pete? For enjoying getting drunk as a skunk. You said so yourself, Pete you know you did. You said just enjoy it, just be yourself. You said just enjoy the party Isabel, just be yourself *Isabel*. You called me Isabel, you know you did. That's why I got drunk. I was nervous, Pete. I'm sorry, I'm really. . . really sorry. Oh shit. Oh, fuck. I couldn't help it. I got nervous cause you called me Isabel. You did. Instead of Izzy like you usually do. So I knew you didn't really mean enjoy the party, you didn't really mean be yourself. You meant behave yourself *or else*.

Or else what?

You meant be decorative, that's what you meant. Be the New Blood's dec'rative fiancée! Be my formal little fiancée, wear the frilly, floral thing I bought you for that purpose! Yes! Act like a wifeling, be the New Blood's pretty wife-to-be! If she's lucky! If she behaves herself! As long as she doesn't get drunk as a skunk at the departmental party, eh Pete? As long as she doesn't go and do something really inconsiderate, like get herself pregnant again, for instance! Oh, that would really be the end, wouldn't it Pete?

That's what you meant, you know you did. You meant speak when you're spoken to, otherwise keep your mouth shut. You meant don't be yourself. For christsake, don't be Izzy! Not tonight! Not at the departmental party! Don't be natural, don't be relaxed! Not with the professor, at all costs! For godsake, don't say what you think! Don't disagree with the professor! Not about literature! Heaven forbid! Not about the role. . . the portrayal of women – that's the word, isn't it, portrayal? – of women in Victorian fiction. Oh no. That's the professor's speciality. Women in Victorian fiction. Women in bloomers, in stays! He's an expert on bloomers and stays! That's his baby! Don't shoot your mouth off about the suffragettes, he's much too learned to disagree with! Learned! Old letch. His eyes were all over me, you fool! And the others, the others were worse. Your so-called colleagues, Pete. And that young one with the little beard he was trying to grow, the little pubic beard – what was he called again? You know the one I mean, Pete, the one wearing the jeans. The one with the cock in his jeans and the little pubic beard, the one you thought I fancied, Pete – who was he, and how come you've never mentioned him before? No you don't have to tell me, Pete, I remember. His name was Mike. He told me, he introduced himself over the vol-au-vents. He must be about the same age as you, Pete. Or is he younger? And another of the new bloods, eh? Is that where you got the idea of growing a beard, Pete? So that you and Mike could scratch your pubic beards together in the staff club over a couple of mature malts?

I don't like you with a beard, Pete. I know I said it suited you, but that doesn't mean I like it, right? Oh, it suits you. It suits you too much, just like the pipe. And I mean, you have to look older than the students to have some authority over them, eh Pete? Maybe you should get a walking stick, that would do the trick, wouldn't it, Pete? A knobbly old walking stick, and you could use it like the pipe, Pete, use it to point to things. Things like the students. I mean, you've only had the job for a month, it's a one-year contract, but already you look like you're in with the bricks. That jacket, Pete, that tweed jacket. I never thought I would live with a man who wore a tweed jacket. You are really boring, Pete, you know that? I feel sorry for myself, I really do.

Come on, Pete, you can tell me about Mike – is he a friend or an enemy? A rival? You should watch him, Pete, he's got horrible little close-set eyes like a ferret. What he was doing to me with his ferrety little eyes. And the wives, did you notice the wives, Pete? Christ, Pete, you don't really want me to look like one of them, do you? The professor's wife – did you see what she was wearing, Pete? She was wearing the fucking curtains, Pete! And the shoes – Jesus, Pete, who the fuck did she think she was— Shirley Temple on acid? And the others, did you look at them, at what they were wearing, Pete? Have you ever seen so many cardigans in one room? Like a fucking cardigan convention, if you ask me. I looked at them, Pete, and they looked at me. Oh yes, they incinerated me with their eyes. That's a good word, eh Pete? Incinerated? I know where I learnt that word, Pete.

Say something, Pete. Please say something.

I'm not s'posed to say a word. I'm not s'posed to get drunk. I'm not s'posed to try, to try to enjoy. . . Admit it, that's what you meant, isn't it Pete? You meant don't dare enjoy the departmental party, or else. Or else I'd pay for it. All right, I'm paying for it now. And I'll go on paying for it for days. Won't I Pete? Pete?

You meant be Isabel. Be a good little dolly. I tried, Pete, I really did, but I s'pose I'm just Izzy, I'm fed up trying to be Isabel, so there. Put that in your PhD and smoke it. Somebody's gone and lost their dolly. Look at her, Pete. Isn't she pretty? And she can talk. Listen.

She says she's hungry, Mummy! I'm hungry too, Pete. Seriously, Pete, I was expecting something real to eat, not a cube of cheese and a chipolata impaled on a fucking toothpick. And the vol-au-vents, I still don't know what was in those vol-au-vents, but it tasted like cold tapioca, like wallpaper paste. Ugh! I'm ravenous, Pete, I've never been as hungry in my life. Come over here and I'll show you how hungry I am. No? What is it, are you scared I'll bite?

Say something. Go on, tell me I'm a drunken slut. Tell me how terrible I've been. How mortified you were when I dropped my wine. All over the white linen tablecloth, all over my new flowery dress, all over the stinking rotten carpet. I spoiled it all, didn't I Pete? The tablecloth, the dress, the carpet. . . Your chances of a ruined new. . . I mean a *renewed* contract.

Ruined your career, didn't I Pete? Just because I spilled a little wine, a little red wine. A little red wine isn't so bad, is it, Pete? It isn't as bad as blood, not as bad as spilling blood, new blood. You're the New Blood lecturer, aren't you? You should know. Tell me then, I need to know. Really I do. . . I really do need to know, Pete. It's worse, isn't it, to spill new blood?

Get your old ethics textbook out and tell me.

OK, don't. Don't say anything at all. Just stand there. Just stand there looking like you.

Your glasses are steaming up again, Pete.

I wonder why they do that. You know what, Pete, why is it that no one ever invented windshield-wipers for glasses? I mean, when your glasses got wet tonight, I mean when I threw that glass of wine over you, that other glass of wine somebody gave me to replace the one I'd spilled all over your career, well, remember how it went all over your glasses? Well Pete, now think about this. If you'd had a little button in your pocket you could've pressed to activate the wipers, maybe it wouldn't have been so bad for you, eh Pete? You men like pushing buttons, I've noticed that. You've pushed my button, Pete, and now it's time to drop the bomb. The only kind of bomb we women ever drop, Pete.

I'm really sorry for throwing the wine at you, Pete, but it was the way you were talking to me, through clenched teeth like that, the way you were gripping my arm and leading me out of the room. . . You were hurting me, Pete. At least no one saw me do that, eh? Isn't that something to be thankful for? At least you'd got me out of the room before I threw the wine at you. It would've been worse if you'd been wearing your contacts. How are your contacts, Pete?

Oh, yes, I forgot. I'm sorry I stood on one of your contacts,

Pete. But that's what happens in the academic business, isn't it? You end up with a fiancée who stands on your contacts.

Do your contacts get steamed up the way your glasses do? No, really, Pete, I'm curious, I'm interested to know. I remember being with you somewhere, Pete. Either the botanical gardens or a café with a lot of pot plants. Anyway, when we went in, your glasses steamed up. And I looked at you Pete, and you know what you looked like? You looked like a Dalek, Pete. A steamed-up academic Dalek. If you think I'm going to spend the rest of my lie with a steamed-up academic Dalek like you, you've got another think coming.

You've always got another think coming. That's what you're paid to do. You're paid to think, Pete, and you know it! But you don't think, you don't really think at all. You mouth your footnotes like flea-bitten animals grunting at each other in the zoo. That professor of yours looks exactly like a yak, don't you think?

Why are you gripping the banister like that? Hmm? Your knuckles've gone all white. You've gone white all over, Pete. What d'you think you're doing, palely loitering? Palely loitering. It's unhealthy. You've been taking too many of those tutorials. You look like a ghost. Worse, you're as white as a thesis. An unwritten one, one that just can't seem to get written. That one you kept telling me about the first time I got pregnant, that one you had to get finished then! That one you still have to finish! Then we'll move out of this dump. Then we'll get a bigger flat, have a baby! Not yet though, oh no! You just stand there looking like a silent seminar, like the ghost of an unwritten thesis, looking down at me like. . .

All right, go ahead and look! This is me Pete, this is who I am!

Say Something   265

At least I can still do that, Pete. I can still look at myself. Can you do that, eh? What do you think you see when you look in the mirror, Pete? Apart from a bit of designer pubic beard and a thorough understanding of your period?

I have a thorough understanding of my period as well. Don't you think I wanted it to come? Don't you think I've been praying for it to arrive?

You don't know what it was like for me to grow up. At the school I went to, I was expelled. That's what happened to me, Pete, I got fucking expelled. All right, I know you know about that, I know I've told you about that before, but I haven't told you why, not really. You know why I got expelled, Pete? I want to tell you this, I have to tell somebody this so I suppose it'll have to be you. I got expelled because. . . They had this school council, a kind of mini-parliament, except we were all girls of course because it was a girls' school – can you follow that, Pete? Just stop me if there's anything you don't understand – and so anyway, I was expelled because I brought up the subject of our periods at the school council. Seriously. You know what we had to do? If a girl was caught unawares by her period, which happened all the time, because girls of that age aren't always all that regular as I'm sure you'll remember if you think hard, Pete. But I'm forgetting – you don't think, do you, Pete? Oh well, just let me think for you and give your brain a rest. Anyway, the girl in question had to go through this great rigmarole to get a sanitary towel, right? She had to request permission to leave the classroom, she had to go to the games teacher, who had the key to the cupboard, the cupboard where the sanitary towels were kept. I'm sorry if this is disgusting you, Pete, but it's true. The truth is disgusting sometimes, the truth is never pleasant, otherwise

Selected Stories

it wouldn't be the truth. I expect you've read a book or two about the truth, Pete, eh? Your kind of truth. Anway, to get back to my kind of truth, this sanitary towel from the games mistress had to last you all fucking day. And the thing was, of course, everybody knew, when they saw you being led through the corridors by the games mistress to the cupboard, everybody knew. . . But that wasn't the worst of it, the worst of it was that when you'd finished with your sanitary towel, you had to put it in this disposal bag and give it to the janitor! Can you believe it, Pete? Can you understand what I'm telling you? That was why I was 'asked to leave school'. I raised the issue of the issue, and the disposal of, the sanitary towels with the school council.

Aren't you proud of me, Peter?

You fucking should be.

See? I called you Peter. I did. I called you Peter, Pete, so that's what you are to me now. Peter. All right, Peter, although I never thought I'd live with anybody called Peter, what about sex then, Peter? Isn't that what you want now? To atone for my sins at the departmental party in bed. And how.

Why don't you edit a volume on the subject, Peter? I could do your research for you, I could be your fucking research, and type out your boring footnotes, make the coffee, dress up as a schoolgirl-whore-nun who demands to be dominated. What d'you think?

Isn't there a monogram in it somewhere? All right, Peter, come on, dominate me. I demand to be dominated. Come on Pete, dominate me, all over. Really, it would make a fucking change!

No? Oh, so that's how it is, is it? No sex, please, we're English Literature. We'd rather interpret 'The Wife of Bath's

Tale' again, in the original! Of course, we wouldn't touch a real Wife of Bath with a fucking barge-pole, oh no!

Don't look at me like that!

Don't. Please. I'm sorry. I'm really. . . really. You know I can't stand it when you look at me like that. Like I'm some kind of despicable. . . thing. I'm not a thing, I'm Izzy. Don't you understand? Don't you like Izzy? You used to say. . . You didn't look at me like a thing. Maybe that's what you want me to be, Pete, is that it? A play-thing. And a work-thing. And a sex-thing. And a little wifeling-thing. I can't be all those fucking things! Not any more, Pete. That's what you want all your so-called colleagues to think, isn't it Pete? Oh here's the New Blood, with his thing! She's quite sexy, quite pretty, pretty good in the sack I imagine, I imagine she's quite the thing! Good for the New Blood, well done the New Blood!

This is what you really want, Pete? A doll. A doll called Isabel. Dress her up in a pretty floral thing. Take her to the departmental party. Then undress her again, take her to bed. That isn't all you want from me, is it Pete?

It's a pity she talks so much, isn't it Pete? Listen. She says she's sleepy, Mummy. I'm sleepy too, Pete. I'm so tired I could sleep for a hundred years, a hundred years, a hundred years. I could do that, Pete, but you wouldn't chop the trees down, would you? You wouldn't wake me with a kiss. No, because your kiss, with that little pubic beard of yours, would send me into a fucking coma!

OK, turn your fucking back on me, if you can't stand to look at me. Turn your back on everything, go on. Everything you can't deal with. It's yourself you can't deal with, not me.

A little girl's gone and lost her dolly, but you don't care, do you Pete?

I want you to care. Everyone has to care. I want to care for it. I don't want to lose it. Not this time, Pete. I want to keep it, to hold it, to care. I don't want to have to. . . You shouldn't make me have to. . . No one should be made to have to. . .

Losing It

HE KNEW it would do him no good to smash the monitor, but that didn't stop him. In one fluid movement he scooped up a heavy object – a glass astray, he found out later – and flung it at the screen, which burst with a strange popping noise as it imploded. There was the crash of broken glass falling inside the machine, then a light somewhere inside went out. That was it done: the computer monitor was fucked. He couldn't believe he had done it – he who depended on computers for his living. It would do him no good – unless it already had.

He was on his feet, breathing hard, shaking with anger. The computer went on making its neverending noise, even though the monitor was now completely fucked. He tried to remember the key command to shut it down – how the hell did you turn the thing off when you didn't have a screen? He reached for the computer manual on the shelf. What a hateful book it was, with its trite step-by-step explanations and its thick blue spine and its stupid, macho words like 'trouble-shooting'. He threw it at the wall and watched it splay open in mid-air and slap against the photo of his daughter Scarlet on the wall, before falling open at his feet like a shot bird. He kicked it across the room. A dangerous solution presented itself. Why not? The work was gone anyway, the work was lost. He bent down and wrenched the adaptor with all its plugs and wires from the socket. The buzz of the computer stopped, the anglepoise on his desk went out and the music he had on lurched to a stop. All that could be heard in the room was his own hoarse shout.

—Fuck you, bastard!

He stabbed a finger at the monitor, as if to say it had got what it deserved. Then he began to shudder with a strange laughter. It burst in his chest like an underwater explosion and his throat was crowded with it as it rushed to his mouth and spilled out in a froth of giggles. Possessed by this gleeless laughter, he marched back and forth in the room, shaking his head and flailing his arms as if having to swim upstream. He lurched back to his desk and sagged into the chair. He looked at the monitor, at what he had done. He had lost it. He had lost it completely. Completely lost it. He couldn't believe that all that careful, detailed work over the course of weeks, months. . . Almost a year's work had gone, had vanished into cyberspace in a split second.

He covered his face with his hands and groaned. It was unbearable to think about all the time he'd spent editing it and re-editing, designing and redesigning. It was almost finished – at least, he was getting towards the end of it, even if he'd have to go through it again. Now it wasn't there to go through again. It was gone. Had he taken copies on disks? Not for weeks, and the last time he'd tried to use those disks, they hadn't let him in. The computer had given him a message that the disks had become unreadable. He remembered feeling annoyed about this at the time, but had he taken other copies?

He rummaged in the open drawer and found a box of disks. Some of them had labels on them with 'Accounts' or 'New' or 'c.v.' or 'working documents'. Others had blank labels and others again had no labels, they were just disks that hadn't been used yet or disks that had been used and had stopped working, had become unreadable. Unreadable – it sounded like a criticism and this made him all the more furious as he flicked through the disks in the box but didn't find the damn disks he was looking for. When he had flicked through all of them he snapped the box shut and threw it back into the drawer. He was fucked. He was completely fucked. All that work, for nothing. All that work he would have to do again, like Sisyphus and his stone.

He thought of Sisyphus shouldering his stone, trying to get it to the top of the hill. But just as he's about to get there, the stone gains so much inertia and feels so heavy that it's impossible to push it any further. Then Sisyphus feels the stone rolling back down the hill a bit. Of course, he tries to stop it, but there comes a point when he can't – because of certain laws of physics and gravity and because he's fucked. And at this moment when Sisyphus decides or realises that there's no point in trying to push, there is a choice. The choice is: he can either jump out of the way and let the stone go, or he can stay where he is and keep pushing, in which case the stone will crush him in its downward path. It's not much of a choice, but it's a choice. And every time Sisyphus gets to this

Losing It

point, it occurs to him that there is this choice between life and death.

Of course, Sisyphus is a fly guy. He's outwitted death before, locking Hades in his own handcuffs with the oldest dodge in the book – 'Hey, show me how they work, sir. . .' – so Sisyphus jumps out of the way and lets the stone roll back down the hill, because even if he's doomed, he's outwitted death again. Sisyphus wants to stay alive, at any price. Even if it means rolling a fucking stone up a fucking hill for the rest of his fucking life. So he picks himself up and walks back down the hill – and this must have been the only good bit of Sisyphus's life since he'd got the stone-rolling job: the downhill stroll. At a leisurely pace, with rests.

He smiled a bitter smile, and felt a strange elation. He'd let the stone go. Maybe now it was time for the downhill stroll. He had to admit that it felt good to have let his anger out, let go of it completely. He couldn't remember losing it so completely for years – not with his kids, not with his wife, not with anybody. Not since he he'd been in a fight in the playground at school. Sitting on another boy's chest, drumming his fists on the other boy's head. And he hadn't been able to stop, because he was out of control. He'd lost it then. But he was an adult now. He had learnt the virtue of restraint, if it was a virtue.

To lose it with a computer like that. . . but maybe it wasn't the computer, maybe he'd lost it with himself. How could such a thing have happened? All that carefully compiled information had melted into nothing. It was gone. Had he at least taken a printout of the data involved? Yes, but the last time he had taken a printout had been before he'd decided to completely reshape and reorganise the material and he wasn't even sure if he still had it. He tugged open another drawer and rummaged among the clutter of letters and calculators and screwdrivers and photographs and batteries and lightbulbs and bankbooks – what a fucking mess that drawer was. Of course it wasn't in there. He didn't keep printouts in that drawer. That drawer was for everything else. He'd probably lost that printout, and anyway – that printout was so incomplete he'd be better to start again, start from scratch.

As he put a cigarette in his mouth and lit it, he noticed that his fingers were shaking. So he had smashed the monitor. So he'd have to buy a new monitor. But that was the least of it. He would have to start again. Virtually from scratch. If he could get into those disks, the ones that wouldn't let him in, he would be half way there. He would be where he had been six months ago, if they let him in. If not, it was gone, it was all gone. What would Louise think when she came home? What would Scarlet think, when she came in from school? What would they think when they saw the smashed monitor? What had happened to the ashtray? He reached into the guts of the monitor and found it, intact.

Though it was only half-past three, it was beginning to get dark when he loaded the cardboard box into the boot and drove around the city looking for a skip. They were like taxis – when you really needed one. . . He did see a couple, but they were being used by workmen, and he didn't like the idea of asking them if it was okay if he could dump something in their skip. Anyway, there were a lot of people around – people hurrying home from work, or hurrying to work, hurrying because it was getting dark and it was cold and outside was no place to be.

At this very moment Scarlet would be on her way home from school. He hoped she had her key to the door. If not, she'd have to wait until Louise got back. He took out his mobile and switched it on. It rang immediately, but he had to put it down on the passenger seat while he turned a corner and looked for a skip. He pressed the button and heard a woman's voice. It was his boss, asking him in a very measured way how he was and hoping the work was going well. He would have to tell her it was gone, that he'd need another three months minimum. It wasn't so outrageous. She would probably understand. When you told people that you had a problem with your computer, they tended to be sympathetic, as if you'd told them you had the flu.

He pulled out his mobile and thought about paging Scarlet – but of course, you couldn't do that from a mobile, so he pulled over at the first phone box he saw, turned his headlights off and climbed out of the car. In the phone box he took out his wallet and rifled through a wad of bills, receipts and money until he found the little piece of paper with his daughter's pager numbers on it and the list of number codes. He punched in Scarlet's number and heard the woman's voice thanking him for using this service, then instructing him to say his number, one digit at a time, after each tone. It was a cheap pager that used number-codes instead of text, and now he paused as he ran his eye over the list of codes. . . 604 – 'hugs and kisses'. . . 216 – 'stuck in traffic'. . . 1664 – 'fancy a beer?' . . . 220 – 'where are you?'. . . until he found it: 4164 – 'I'll be late home'. He spoke the numbers after the tones. The woman's voice read the numbers back to him and asked him to say 'yes' if they were correct or 'no' if they weren't after the tone. He said 'yes' and listened to the woman's voice telling him his message had been accepted, then he hung up, stuffed his papers back into his wallet, his coins into his pocket and went back to his car.

Would Scarlet have her pager switched on anyway? Would she switch it on, when she got out of school? Would she remember the number code? Would the message get through? Even if it did, what difference would it make? If she had her key, she'd let herself in anyway. If she didn't, she'd have to wait.

He pulled back onto the street and looked for a skip. Wouldn't it look odd, a man stopping his car and lifting a heavy box out of the boot and dumping it in a skip? He headed out towards the bypass. He'd been to the city dump once before, to get rid of some stuff the bucket men wouldn't take, some rubble and bricks from knocking the arch from the kitchen to the dining room, stuff they called builder's waste. He couldn't remember where it was exactly, but it was out towards the bypass somewhere.

As he accelerated he noticed that there was a new noise coming from the car, from somewhere underneath. The exhaust. A strange growling noise, as if something had corroded to the point of coming off. He'd have to have it replaced with a spanking brand new exhaust – but what did the garage do with the old one? And what happened to the files you dumped from the computer? You put them in the wastebasket and then you emptied the wastebasket, but then where did they go? Limbo files. In his first computer, there had been a thing called 'limbo files'. You could retrieve something you had erased or thrown away. Maybe the work was still there in the computer's memory, in the dump for discarded files. Maybe he could pay somebody to go through his mountain of trashed files, looking for the ones he wanted back, needed back. He couldn't believe all that work had ceased to exist. It had to be out there somewhere still. The growling was definitely there, persistent – underneath, towards the back of the car – he wasn't just imagining it.

He came to a mini-roundabout and didn't know which way to go, so he kept on going. He passed the car dump where he'd tried to get rid of his last car – a godforsaken place surrounded by a twenty-foot high fence. He'd driven into it one afternoon, when it was clear that it was time to get rid of his car, thinking that he'd get a taxi back into town once he'd sold it for scrap. He'd stopped the car in front of a wasteland of dumped cars, but he hadn't got out, because a lean alsatian leapt from the doorway of a hut and ran around the car barking fiercely. Sitting there in that grim place with the angry dog, in a car he wasn't sure would start again, he'd felt his heart panicking, like an animal trapped in his chest. When no one appeared and the dog kept on barking at him, he had started up the car and driven out of there. He'd got rid of the car somewhere else, a few days later.

A couple of miles out of town, he saw the sign: Waste Recycing Unit and the city council's logo. He pulled off the road and followed the track up to the gates. He was just in time – a man in a fluorescent boiler suit was just about to close them, but he pulled the gate back and waved him in. He followed the signs past the bottle banks and the recycling unit for car batteries, He found himself in a queue of cars, and he switched the engine off while he waited. Every time he started the car to move forward, the exhaust sounded worse. It was definitely the exhaust. He would have to get the car to a garage. The exhaust was fucked. He might even have to call the AA. He was going to have to get the car fixed, before he did anything about the lost work.

The dark machines glinted in the yellow overhead lights as they ground and crunched and squashed the stuff men threw into them. The machines seemed to be vehicles of some sort – at least they sat on what looked like tram-tracks. When his turn came, he opened the boot and lifted out the box with the fucked monitor in it. A man in a fluorescent boiler suit, a cap with ear flaps and gloves that made his hands look huge pointed to one of the machines. He carried it over to the machine and threw it in, then he stood back and watched the great metal jaws eating it and forcing it down.

He got back in the car and turned the key in the ignition. The exhaust sounded like anger itself as he changed gear and accelerated out of the place, with its infernal machines masticating in the darkness. Back in the town, when he was stopped at the lights on the way to the garage, he took his mobile out and switched it on. He pressed a button and heard a woman's voice telling him that he had no new messages, then he pressed the button to get his own number. He phoned his own number and got the ansaphone. He heard his own voice trying to be as neutral as possible as it told him: 'Hello, this is John. I'm sorry you got the machine. If you have a message for me, Louise or Scarlet, please wait until you hear the tone.' He waited until he heard the tone. He was about to leave the message when he lost the signal completely.

The Host

'SO. HOW. Was. The. Film.'

I was speaking in words but I didn't know what I was saying and my voice sounded thick and moronic and my mouth was dry and my heart was hammering and my skin felt like a cold chamois leather as I touched my face with my fingers – no doubt the way I would normally touch my face with my fingers if I was asking somebody about a film they'd been to see but nothing was normal because here in my room was a man with two heads.

For a horrible moment there was no response from anyone. Had the words come out of my mouth at all or had they come out sounding so strange that no one could make sense of them? Was it my drugs? Had I forgotten to take my drugs? No, I had taken them earlier. Had I got the dosage wrong? No, I distinctly remembered taking the correct dosage.

'Well, I thought it was not a bad film, but the book. . .'

I felt a surge of gratitude to Jim. He had heard my question and he was answering it. He was talking about the film, thank God, so for the moment the attention of the room was not focused on me. Had nobody noticed that I was trembling and sweating and finding it difficult to speak?

I tried to pick up my glass and get it to my mouth. I couldn't help turning a little to check that the man who had been introduced to me as Douglas really did have two heads. I had seen the other head quite clearly when he'd come into the room and shaken my hand – lolling on his shoulder, as if it couldn't quite support itself. I'd had to look away as I'd said my pleased-to-meet-you.

It was there all right, I hadn't imagined it. In the dim light of my room it was difficult to see the crumpled features of the face, which was as pale as a cauliflower, but I could make out two screwed-up eyes, closed tightly under wispy, whitish eyebrows. I could see no clearly defined nose, but the lips were unmistakable – they looked dry and cracked and unnaturally old. Unnaturally old – that is the meaningless phrase that came into my mind. The face had set into an expression which was both sour and aloof. The way the lips curled down at one side and up at the other made me think of a kind of bitter relish, as if the owner of the mouth might take pleasure in sarcasm. At the same time there was something dreadfully vulnerable in the face's frozen sneer and the way the head lolled against the back of the armchair Douglas was sitting in – to all appearances a dead appendage. And no one seemed to have noticed it. Douglas himself appeared to be completely relaxed, as if utterly unaware of his encumbrance. He struck me as a congenial sort of guy, probably in his early thirties. Apart from his other head, his

Selected Stories

appearance was quite ordinary. He had longish brown hair and a neat beard. He looked mildly interested in the world and had a constant, rather vacant smile. He wore a dark blue jacket, jeans and a casual, checked shirt.

But he had another head.

A red-haired woman I didn't know and whose name I hadn't taken in was disagreeing with Jim about the film and there were one or two comments interjected by the others – including Douglas. He didn't say much – as far as I could make out, he was agreeing with the general drift of the discussion about the film. He was quietly spoken, maybe even a bit shy, but it was the kind of shyness which hints at an inner confidence.

They were having this good-natured, not-too-serious sort of debate about the merits of the film they'd been to see – for all the world as if nothing was out of the ordinary. I felt a moment of relief. The hammering of my heart was slowing down to a steady, heavy pounding. Although I'd raised my glass of wine to my lips I still hadn't taken a drink. Now I gulped some of it down in the hope that it would steady my nerves.

Was I overreacting? I was with friends, after all. Jim was a friend, a good friend, I had known him since schooldays. He often went my shopping for me, and that meant a lot to me. One or two of the others had been coming to see me for over a year now. There were strangers, but Jim often brought people back after a late-night film. It was supposed to do me good, help me cope with my agoraphobia, which he thought he understood. At least he understood that it wasn't just the fear of open spaces. He knew that it went hand-in-hand with claustrophobia. He understood that my fear was the fear of people. So he brought them round. It was supposed to encourage me to overcome it – or so I'd thought. Tonight he'd gone over the score. There were too many of them tonight. I couldn't see them clearly one by one as people, they were blurred into the same animal. I kept seeing movements of the feet and the hands but I didn't know whose they were. But although I saw them as one, at the same time I felt desperately outnumbered. It was difficult to hold on to my self.

Had Jim brought all these people round out of a spirit of charity or therapy? Maybe it was also convenient for him. Maybe he didn't want to take them all to his place. Here he was, acting for all the world as if he was doing me a favour by crowding out my house with the entire membership, I shouldn't wonder, of the local film club – one of whom had an extra head.

I glared at Jim, hoping to convey my displeasure with him in no uncertain terms, but he went on elaborating on some crucial discrepancy between the book and the film. He'd never brought this Douglas back before, I was certain of that, but people in the company seemed to know him, or if they didn't, they seemed to have accepted the fact that he had two heads with no trouble at all. Or maybe they were being polite. Maybe everyone in the room was doing his best not to look at it or talk about it, but inside they were panicking just as much as me. Or could it be that they were being quietly supportive? After all, an extra head, one which seemed to serve no purpose, must be a dreadful disability and Douglas seemed to be coping with it incredibly well. Maybe later on, I thought – but only if Douglas brings the subject up and wants to talk about it – maybe then I'll ask him if he has ever thought about the possibility of having it surgically removed. Oh God – no! I couldn't possibly ask him that – what was I thinking of?

Douglas leaned forward to flick his ash into the ashtray on the coffee table. The head sprang forward to hang over his shoulder. With a start that set my pulse racing and almost made me yelp with fright, I noticed that one eye had opened a little and seemed to be peering at me as if from a great distance. When Douglas leaned back slowly – apparently he was listening to the postmortem of the film with interest – the other head still hung forward, leaning one cheek on the collar of his jacket. I shuddered as I made out for the first time the tiny, creased nostrils. The head had, I was sure of it, taken a breath.

'So what do you think?'

Jim had turned to put this question to me and everyone now looked to me, their host, for an opinion.

'Well. . . I mean obviously. . . not having seen it. . .'

'But would you go to see it, on the basis of what we've said, or have we put you off going?'

'Well, I wouldn't want to go to a cinema, but . . .'

What was I doing? Trying to make light of my own condition? Or drawing attention to it, to spare Douglas the attention of the room? But then, no one was looking at him, everyone was looking at me, and I didn't know how to go on.

Jim smiled and said, 'You asked us what we thought of the film.'

'No, you don't know what. . . I wasn't asking you what the film was about, what I meant was. . . what was it like to go and see a film, to sit in a place in the dark with. . . a crowd of other. . . I mean. . .'

I trailed off, trying to use the glass and the wine as an

excuse to interrupt myself. I truly could not go on, not only because I was talking nonsense but also because the image of a crowded, darkened cinema had come into my mind, with its rows of silhouetted heads. One or two people laughed, apparently under the impression that I was being deliberately obtuse out of a sense of mischief. Jim looked at me in a pointedly puzzled way. I spluttered on my wine. I made the most of it, pretending that it had gone down the wrong way and I was having a coughing fit. Someone sitting next to me obliged by thumping me on the back, but in the middle of it I began to wheeze with disbelief. The head had now opened both eyes and was looking around the room.

Douglas took the cigarette from his mouth and, without even looking at what he was doing, placed it carefully in the other head's mouth. The other head sucked on it with some difficulty, then Douglas removed the cigarette and went on smoking it himself. A thin jet of smoke came from the other head's mouth, which was as desiccated as a shelled walnut, then it gave a little cough. How can I explain how this little cough made me feel? It was like a baby's cough, alarming because it hints at an articulacy and a history no one would expect of it. The sound of it made me shudder inside, as if on the verge of tears. I had to suppress a heavy sob welling in my chest. But now it was doing something else. I watched the head's mouth in awe as its dark, liverish tongue licked its cracked lips before speaking.

'That was very interesting.'

The eyelids of both eyes had parted, but were still stuck together at the corners in a way that looked extremely uncomfortable. The eyes, deep blue in colour, looked enormous in the shrunken face. But it was the look in the eyes. . . How can

I describe it? There was infinite depth and distance in it, as if it was still looking at something in another world it had just come from. Yes, that was it, the head was waking up. The eyelids blinked rapidly to unstick themselves completely and now the dark eyes looked directly at me.

'I don't mean what you were saying, but the way you were pretending to cough. Most people don't cough unless they have to, do they?'

The voice was rather thin and chesty, with a squeaky quality that made it sound slightly comical. It was like the voice of a very old man, but it also sounded like the voice of a child, made harsh by some bronchial illness. The other head smiled with one corner of its mouth, then uttered another babyish cough.

I couldn't answer. I was aware of the babble of voices around us. Apparently Jim was being witty and people were laughing. No one was paying the slightest attention to me or the head which had just addressed me. They were having a good time, apparently, but I was breathing hard and trembling and my hands were sweating so much they felt gloved in oil as I tried to find something to say to this head, this other head growing out of a man's neck.

I looked to Jim to rescue me, but now he was engrossed in some kind of intellectual duel with the red-haired woman. Of course, it was transparent to me that they were flirting. If only that had been all that was going on in my room – but no, there had to be a man with another head that wanted to talk to me. Douglas himself showed no interest whatsoever in the head even though it had woken up so conspicuously. He seemed completely preoccupied with stubbing his cigarette out, refilling his glass and following the conversation.

The crumpled face was waiting with an infinitely patient sadness. I had to say something.

'I'm sorry. It's just that I. . . don't know how. . . I've never met a person with. . .'

'Two heads? Is that what you're driving at?'

'Well. . . I suppose so.'

The head, hanging at an angle so that it seemed to be peering around a corner, did its best to nod with resignation.

'It's more common than you think.'

'What is?'

'Two heads.'

'Really? I had no idea.'

'Lots of people have two heads. Ask him.'

The other head indicated Douglas with a movement of its eyes and gave out a sharp little giggle. I glimpsed a row of neat, square teeth. Douglas raised the wine glass to his other head's lips, taking care not to spill it. This he managed to do without so much as glancing at the other head. Even so a drop of wine dribbled from the corner of the mouth. Douglas put the glass back down and took a tissue from his jacket pocket, with which he dabbed the other head's chin – though there was little in the way of what would normally be called a chin. All this he performed while staring straight ahead, apparently quite engrossed in the discussion about the film.

For a moment I saw Douglas and his other head as a music-hall double-act – the ventriloquist and his dummy. As if by telepathy, the other head looked at me and said,

'A gottle a geer.'

It chuckled at its own joke and the sound of its gargling laughter made me want to cry again. I had to fight back the shuddering sobs which wracked me inside and threatened to burst out at any moment. I call the other head 'it' because that is how I thought of this extraordinary phenomenon, but now I was forced to confront the fact that 'it' was a thinking, feeling being – 'it' was, I had to admit, a person. Had the poor man been someone's other head all his life? It was an intolerable thought.

The small, puckered face smiled up at me.

'How old do you think I am?'

My attempt at congenial laughter, as if we were engaged in the everyday social game of guess-how-old-I-am, left a lot to be desired. The small face with its vast, deep eyes watched me steadily as I brayed unconvincingly, waiting for my answer.

It was very difficult to tell how old he was. The eyes were as steady and watchful as a child's, yet they had a terribly knowing quality, as if they had seen the worst atrocities of humanity – the kind of thing most of us only read about in the newspapers. I could no longer meet their consuming gaze, and I studied Douglas – his main head and face, I mean, but also his clothes and his hands – before venturing:

'Well. . . younger than me – thirty? Thirty-one?'

The other head snorted briefly and said,

'That's his age. What about mine?'

'I have no idea when you. . . came about.'

'Came about? Oh, you make the mistake of thinking I grew out of him. No, my friend, you have it all wrong. . .'

I was alarmed by the way one of Douglas's hands suddenly stabbed a finger emphatically at his own chest.

'You see, he grew out of me.'

The hand now flew up to uppermost side of the other head's face and scratched a loose flap of skin – it must be, I realised, an earlobe – then it swooped to the coffee-table and, in one fluid movement, lifted Douglas's glass of wine to the other head's mouth.

'My God, you did that!'

The other head drained the glass, set it down carefully on the coffee-table and smirked at me with pride, as if it had proven its point beyond question.

'My God. I see.'

The head nodded to me then, and with a look of profound sadness said softly,

'Now you see.'

And I did see. I saw Douglas in a completely new way, now that it was clear that his other head could control his body. His main head, his normal head – or the one I had taken to be 'main' and 'normal' – now looked gross, a bland and doltish growth which had brutally usurped the other head's place, pushing it aside and, for all I knew, drawing succour from it – like a fungus sapping the life of the tree from which it has swollen. His open, rather vacantly smiling expression now appeared to me as abhorrent as the sated leer of a callous parasite. The other head looked weak, drained of life, dying.

'Yes, he's taken over. I'm on the way out.'

'That's terrible!'

The other head smiled at me sadly.

'Oh, not so terrible. He's better looking than me. He's nicer, he'll get on all right. Less intelligent of course, and less honest – but that will be to his advantage. It was nice to meet you. You've been a very good host. But you look pale – you should get out more often.'

The other head yawned, winked at me, then the fragile eyelids drooped and closed. He snuffled a little before his breathing slowed to a barely perceptible whisper in the air.

Douglas leaned back and the head swung behind his neck and subsided among the shadows of the armchair. His dominant head turned to look at me, as if he expected me to speak. Everyone was looking at me, waiting for me to speak. Jim had asked me a question and now he was repeating it.

'Are you all right?'

I tried to pick up my glass, but my hand shook uncontrollably. Thankfully the glass was almost empty. Someone relieved me of it, there were other people's hands and faces everywhere, then Jim said something about there being too many for me.

'One too many, just one too many.'

I looked at Douglas meaningfully as I said it and his eyes widened with baffled alarm. He stood up, and there was a sudden consensus in the room – everyone was standing up, draining glasses, putting coats and scarves on. The blurr of all that activity made me feel nauseous, dizzy. Voices kept offering me their apologetic thanks.

Jim, crouching down beside my chair, asked me again if I was all right. This really was the last straw. He brings enough people to my house to fill a small cinema – one of them a double-header into the bargain – then he asks me if I'm all right!

I stood up, pushing him aside and shouted,

'I'm all right. Ask your friend there how his other head is. Ask him if he's all right!'

But Douglas was already shuffling hurriedly into the hallway, where a few of the others were already waiting to leave. Jim looked at me with puzzled concern.

'Take it easy now. We're going.'

'About time too.'

The Host

Jim turned and raised his eyebrows to the woman with red hair. It was evident to me that they had formed an unspoken pact. It would be back to his place, or hers, for sexual congress. But would it bring them closer to each other, or even to themselves? Somehow I did not think so. I suspected that their transaction between the sheets would leave both of them feeling lonelier than they had felt before, if either of them had ever felt truly lonely.

Jim said he'd call round in a day or two, thanked me for my hospitality and said they'd see themselves out. That was just as well, because I didn't feel particularly like standing around in my own doorway, exposed to the elements as I exchanged farewells with him and his army of film buffs. Let them go out into the street, under the empty sky. It was all right for them, they could do that with their eyes wide open and their heads held high, without the dread and the panic and the keeping near the wall and the scurrying for cover like a beetle when its stone is overturned.

When the front door eventually closed, I breathed more freely. The room seemed to settle into place around me, it became familiar again, but I felt exhausted by the evening's events. I wanted the warm cocoon of my bed. In reality it would be cold, unless I filled myself a hot water bottle, and I felt too tired to do that. It was hard work, being the host. It was all I could do to tidy up the glasses and bottles and ashtrays before going to the bathroom to clean my teeth.

As I pulled the switch-cord, the sudden bright light made my reflection jump out of the mirror at me. The roar of the Xpelair couldn't drown out my gasp of outrage at what I saw. It was there, no matter how often I wiped the condensation from the mirror with my sleeve, a mushroom-like swelling on my neck. The face was not fully formed, but already I could make out the mildly interested eyes and the constant, rather vacant smile.

Conversation Area One

HE'D SPOKEN to her before, this boy who thought he was God. He'd come up to her only the week before last and said he was God and she was an angel. It was the look in his eyes, like he really believed it. Now she saw him sitting there on his own staring into his empty plastic cup, wearing a shirt that looked like it needed a wash and her heart hurt for him. He was just a poor young man who'd lost the place like her own son Michael, and he didn't even have a visitor to talk to.

When she walked up to where he was sitting and stopped, he didn't so much as look up at her, just went on staring into the empty cup.

'Excuse me, son,' she said.

She didn't have time to say anything else, because he stood up from his chair and looked her straight in the eyes. Then he said, 'The Son and the Father and the Holy Ghost. I am the Resurrection and the Light.'

Gertie took a step back from him and asked him if he knew where her boy was. The way he looked right through her made her blood run cold. Then he said, 'Mrs Houliston,' – she had no idea how he knew her name, unless he knew Michael was called Houliston and knew she was Michael's mum – 'I think you will have to look very long and very hard to find your boy.'

There was something far wrong with him, you could tell that, but she had to admit he was very well-spoken.

'Oh,' she said – she was being polite – 'Why is that?'

Then he leaned forward and stared into her eyes like he could see right into her and knew everything that had ever happened to her in her life and he said, 'You'll have to go to hell to find your boy, Mrs Houliston, because that is where your boy is. Your boy is in hell, Mrs Houliston.'

It worried her that he knew her name. Then he started raving at her – bits of the bible all jumbled up with other things like adverts on the t.v. – but luckily a nurse came and led him away. She was going to ask her if she knew where Michael was, but she thought better of it – the poor girl had her hands full enough with that one, so she went into the table-tennis room, but he wasn't there. Nobody was, just the empty tables and, over in the corner, a plant that looked like it needed water. When she came out into the corridor again, another nurse – Sister Nimmo, her badge said – came up and asked her if she could help her.

'I'm looking for my boy,' Gertie told her.

'His name's Michael Houliston.'

'Oh. Yes. . . Michael,' the sister said. She was bonny, with her fair hair and blue eyes, but she was that thin you could've played a tune on her ribs, and as pale as a pint of milk, and she had dark marks under her eyes – one of them was darker than the other one, turning purple. Somebody had done that to her – one of the patients as likely as not. There was that strained look in her eyes as well, like she'd been trying to read something in tiny wee writing, like the phone book or the bible. 'Michael is in Conversation Area One,' she said, 'I've just been talking to him there.'

'Oh, is that right?' said Gertie. 'Conversation what?'

'Conversation Area One.' Then she gave her the directions. Up the corridor, through a double set of doors, up the stairs, turn left, along another corridor and through another door.

She was out of breath by the time she got there. He didn't notice her, sitting with his eyes shut and his earphones in his ears. She didn't think a personal stereo was a very good idea for somebody with mental problems. It was just a way of cutting himself off from the world around him and hiding behind whatever he was listening to. She took a look at the room. It was just a room with a few chairs in it and a coffee table. It didn't have a window, and all that there was on the wall was a noticeboard with nothing on it except a sign somebody had printed in big letters saying 'This is Thursday'. Michael sat there with his arm thrown over the back of the chair, shaking his head and moving his feet in time to the music he was listening to on his wee black earphones. It was that loud she could hear it when she sat down beside him and put down her bag. He opened his eyes and saw her and took the earphones off his ears.

'Hi, Ma,' he said.

'Hello, son. How are you this week?'

'Okay.'

She fished her hanky out of her sleeve. It wrung her heart to see him again and she just wanted to greet. She always wanted to greet when she saw him because he wasn't happy and because it was terrible to think he might be mad. There had never been any madness in her family, at least none that she'd heard about, but she'd seen it before, when she'd worked as a cleaner in the Infirmary. Some of the cases that came in there were mental, and not just the suicides either.

'How are you, Ma?'

He'd taken the earphones off his head, making the noise coming out of them louder, and now he was looking at her like he didn't even recognise her. She sniffled and blew her nose.

'Ye didnae hear me there, did ye? Wi they things in your ears. I don't know how you can listen to that damned rammy. It would drive me batchie. Switch it off son, eh? It gies me the willies.'

He switched it off and leaned back in his chair. His mouth hung open and it was like he was looking at nothing. He didn't say anything else and he didn't look at her. He was on something, she could tell that by the way his movements were slow and tired, like he was in slow motion. He looked like he was trying to remember something, then he said,

'Me as well. It gives me the willies as well, Ma.'

'Well why d'ye listen to it then? What is it anyway?'

'It's just some jazz, Ma.'

'Is that what ye cry it? Well it gies me the willies.'

'If it didn't give you the willies, it wouldn't be jazz, Ma.'

'Sounds like the monkey-hoose in the zoo at feeding time, if ye ask me.'

She was trying to make him laugh, or at least give her a smile, but he just looked at the wall as if he couldn't see anything there and said, 'They're happy, then.'

'What, son?'

'The monkeys. At feeding time. I expect they're happy then.'

She had no idea what on earth he meant by that, but she agreed with him anyway. At least he was talking again. A few weeks ago she had come to visit him and he hadn't said a word. Since then, most weeks he'd not said much. It had been like trying to get blood from a stone to get him to answer a question, but tonight he was talking, at least that was something.

'Have they stopped yer medication, Michael?'

'They changed the tablets, Ma.'

'So what is it they're gi'en ye now?'

He didn't seem to hear the question. He just stared into space and fiddled with the wires on his earphones, winding them round and round his fingers then unwinding them again. When he didn't speak it always made her talk too much. She knew she was doing it but she couldn't help herself.

'Sorry I'm late the night, son. My watch is stopped. It's never done that before. What a job I had finding ye the night, Michael. I went into the television lounge, but there was naebody in there. The t.v. was on though. A waste of electricity. Not only that, it's public money they're frittering away. Anyway, ye werenae in there. I thought ye might be watching the film. I saw the start of it before I came out the night. It was about somebody just like you, who goes to the university. . . and he cannae get on wi his studying. It was philosophy he was studying as well and not only that, it was the very same philosophy you were studying – would ye credit that, Michael? What d'ye cry it again?

'What, Ma?'

He was miles away.

'You know. Thon philosopher wi the funny name.'

'A lot of them had funny names, Ma.'

'Tell me some.'

She was trying to get him talking as much as anything else, but he took so long thinking about it before he said, 'Kant. Heidegger. Schopenhauer. Nietzsche.'

'That's it. They were studyin that Neechie. They were studyin one of his books. . . what was it called again? What books did he write, Michael?'

If she could get him talking about the books he read at the university, she might find out what it was that had turned his mind and changed him into somebody you couldn't have a normal conversation with. But he just yawned and said, 'He wrote a lot of books, Ma.'

'Tell me some, then.'

You had to keep at him to get anything out of him, that was the thing.

'The Anti-Christ. Thus Spake Zarathustra. Beyond Good and Evil.'

'That's it. Be and Good and Evil. An this boy, a student, him an his pal read this Be and Good and Evil an it goes to their heids, Michael, it drives the both of them yon way. An they turn intae right bad buggers the pair of them. They murder a bairn. A wee lassie. Oh, the very thought. . . It made me feel ill. I didnae see the end. I hope they hung them. I was thinkin it was earlier ye see, because my watch stopped. Then I nodded off in my chair and when I woke up I looked at the clock. Quarter past six, it was. I says tae masel, God almighty – is that the time? I'll be late for Michael.'

She knew she was talking too much but what else could you do when the other person just sat there not even nodding their head at what you were saying, not even looking at you. She shut up and waited for him to say something, but he didn't. If she waited much longer it was going to make her want to greet again. She could feel the tears like needles jabbing at the backs of her eyes.

'I wasn't expecting you, Ma.'

'Well ye should've been. Ye know I come on Thursdays. Did ye forget I was coming?'

'No, Ma. I forgot it was Thursday.'

It was a bad sign if he was forgetting things, forgetting things like the day of the week – mind you, she did it herself sometimes – him that used to be able to remember so much, whole pages of things he had to remember for his exams at school, and he'd been that good at it as well. A lot of good it had done him by the looks of it.

'How could ye forget it was Thursday? Look, up there. They've even written it's Thursday up there on the noticeboard.'

'That always says that, Ma.'

But he didn't look up at the noticeboard. He just went on fidgeting with the wires of his earphones and licking his lips like he was thirsty. He didn't look at things any more, his eyes were like windows with the blinds down. He looked like he was always looking at something away in the distance, but like it was somewhere inside him, away in the distance inside himself.

'Well then, ye shouldnae have forgotten then, should ye?'

He didn't have anything to answer to that. She looked up at the sign on the noticeboard. This is Thursday. Of course, if it always said that. . .

'Oh. . . ye mean it always says it's Thursday? Ye mean it's wrong?'

'Not always, Ma.'

'That's a relief. Ye mean it says it's Thursday when it's Thursday.'

He stopped fidgeting with the wires for a minute and frowned, like he was trying to work out something really difficult in his head, then he said,

'It says it's Thursday when it's Thursday, Ma. But it isn't always Thursday. But since it always says it's Thursday, it's not always wrong. It's right once a week, Ma – when it's Thursday.'

'Oh Michael, you've lost me there. Either it's right or it's wrong. I had to look for ye high and low the night. I went intae the canteen and I met that boy that thinks he's God. He knew I was lookin for you like, he's no that daft. He knew my name – how did he know that, Michael?'

'God is omnipotent, Ma.'

'Is that what's wrong wi him? You wouldnae think it, to look at him. Anyway, I looked everywhere. I looked in the table-tennis room, but ye werenae in there.'

'No?'

She looked at him – was he being cheeky? It would be good if he was. It might mean he was getting back to his normal self, the boy who used to play practical jokes on her, putting things in her slippers and tying the legs of her tights in a knot.

'No, ye werenae. Because ye dinnae play table-tennis.

Mibbe ye should take it up. It's a sport.'

'I know it's a sport, Ma.'

'I had to look for ye somewhere, Michael. Then I met sister what's-her-name, ye know, that yin wi the fair hair.'

'Sister Nimmo.'

'Aye, her. She's a very bonny lassie, d'ye no think, Michael? Only she had a nasty black eye. And she said she thought ye were in Conversation Area One. I felt that stupid. I had no idea what she was talking about, Michael. Ye never told me about these conversation areas. So I said, oh, Conversation Area One? Where is that, again? I didnae want to let on I'd never seen it. Then she sent me up here. So is this it?'

'What, Ma?'

He was miles away again.

'Conversation Area One. Is this it?'

'Yes. This is Conversation Area One.'

'Fancy that. How many are there then?'

He had to think about that one for a long time, then he said, 'Two.'

So there were two of them. She wondered what the other one was like. This one was all right, except it didn't have a window. She liked a view, even when it was dark. She cleared her throat. It was her turn to speak.

'What's the other yin like?'

'What?'

'Michael, try to pay attention, son. I'm no here for long. I'm sayin, the other Conversation Area, Number Two – what's it like?

'I don't know, Ma.'

'Ye don't know? Have ye never seen it then?'

'No, I've never been in it.'

'Well – mibbe we should try it. Next Thursday.'

He didn't say anything to that, didn't look interested one way or the other. He just went on winding the wires round his fingers and then unwinding them. She had to bite her tongue to stop herself telling him off for it.

'It's nice to see ye talking, son. Have ye been out this week?'

'No, I've been in.'

'Ye should get out in the grounds. Lovely Hydrangeas. And the Rhododendrons need to be seen to be believed. I'm always telling ye to get out, but ye dinnae listen to yer mother.'

'I can't go out, Ma.'

'Why no, son?'

He looked down at his feet then, like when he was a wee laddie and he'd done something wrong. It was terrible to see your own son, twenty-five years old, with all his education and everything, looking like a wee boy who's done something wrong.

'I lost my privileges.'

'What privileges, Michael?'

'My walking privileges.'

It was the first she'd heard of 'walking privileges'.

'What, you mean they won't let you go out? Not even in the hospital grounds? Why not, Michael?'

'I argued with Sister Nimmo.'

'Oh, Michael, ye shouldnae argue wi the staff. Ye'll only make it worse for yersel. I hope it wasnae you gave her the black eye.'

No answer one way or another.

'Michael, ye shouldnae sit all on your own like this, ye should be a bit sociable wi the others. They're all in the same boat as you, after all. Ye were miles away when I came along.'

'I was thinking, Ma.'

'I don't know how ye can think wi they things on yer ears, that jazz cannae be good for yer brain. Ye think too much anyway, Michael, ye always did.

'I was thinking about Christmas. I was remembering, one Christmas. . . I came downstairs, to get my presents. . . and there weren't any. Mary had hers. . . a nurse's uniform, a doll, games, she had all kinds of presents. And Dad said to me, "Santa must've forgotten to leave yours this year".'

She couldn't remember that at all. Mibbe he was just making it up, or mibbe he really did remember it. It did sound like the kind of thing his dad might've done, mind you, big clown that he was sometimes.

'He said to Mary that I hadn't got any presents and he got her to give me one of hers. She gave me the doll.'

'A doll. Oh, ye wouldnae like that.'

'I smashed its brains out on the fireplace.'

'Oh Michael, ye didnae. That was a bad thing to do.'

'Then Dad told us it was a joke, and he brought out my presents.'

Fancy him remembering all that, if he wasn't making it all up.

'That reminds me, I brought you something.'

She bent down to pick her bag off the floor and unzip it. She'd forgotten about the wee present she'd bought him in Woolies yesterday. She'd been attracted by the picture on the box, then she'd thought it would help him pass the time. When she pulled it out of her bag and saw it was still in the Woolies bag, she thought she should really have wrapped it

'Here ye are. It'll help ye pass the time, son.'

The way he looked at it when she handed it to him, like he was scared to take it off her, like she'd put a bomb in his hands.

'What is it, Ma?'

'A wee surprise.'

'I thought it was. Thanks, Ma.'

Then he took it off her and just laid it in his lap quite the thing as if that was that.

'Are ye no gonnae open it, at least?'

He picked it up again. He looked worried by it, as if a wee present was something he didn't know what to do with.

'I bet ye cannae guess what it is.'

He shook the box and heard the pieces moving about inside.

'It's a jigsaw, Ma.'

He was still a clever laddie even if his mind had turned.

'Ye always liked the jigsaws. Used to spend hours doing them when ye were wee.'

'Did I?'

'Oh aye. Ye must remember that. Ye were jigsaw daft. Ye always liked to fit the last piece, to finish the picture.

'Thanks, Ma.'

He was just going to put it down again and leave it at that.

'Take it out the bag at least, Michael. See what the picture is.'

When he took it out and saw the picture on the front, he looked like he was reading his own death sentence.

'What's the matter, Michael – d'ye no like it? It's called "Sunflowers". It's by Van Gogh.'

'Thanks, Ma.'

'That's all right son. There's nothing like flowers to brighten up yer life. Ye should get out in the grounds.'

He leaned over and put the jigsaw down on the floor. She saw the back of his head, with the hair tapering into the nape of his neck, and it made her heart hurt.

'I will when I get my walking privileges back.'

'What were ye arguing wi her about anyway?'

'Who, Ma?'

'Nurse what's-her-name.'

'Sister Nimmo. We had a disagreement about the nature of the human condition, Ma.'

'Oh ye didnae, did ye? Ye should leave the human condition well alone, Michael, if ye want to get on in life. Ye see, there's no the demand for philosophers like what there used to be. See that Neechie? When ye studied him. It didnae make ye want to. . . do somethin like they boys in the film, did it?

'What, Ma?'

'To kill a bairn, like that.'

He looked like the question had got through to him but he didn't know how to answer it. She explained the story to him.

'They didnae even know her. Ye could mibbe understand it if it was somebody ye knew, somebody at yer work, somebody ye'd fell oot wi – but a complete stranger, and a bairn. . . the very thought makes me feel ill. All the same, if you ask me, that Neechy's got a lot to answer for. What did he think anyway? What did he say in his books that made they boys want to do something like that?'

'God is dead.'

'Eh?'

'He said "God is dead".'

'He did not, did he? That's a terrible thing to say. It should be banned, if ye ask me. Anyway – how can God die? He's eternal and everlasting, everybody knows that. Even I know that. So how could he die?'

'I don't know, Ma.'

'Well he was wrong, wasn't he? I mean. . . I just met God. In the television lounge!'

She tried to laugh, but when she did laugh a bit it hurt so much she had to stop. She looked at her watch. Her stopped watch.

'I keep forgetting the damn thing's wrong.'

Michael moved around in his chair and looked at her, as if he'd just noticed she was there. He rubbed his eyes, as if he was waking up.

'Not always, Ma. Your watch. It's right twice a day, Ma.'

'That's not much guid tae me, is it? Anyway, it must be time I was away. I've never been in one of these Conversation Areas before. They're nice though, aren't they? Nicely. . . set out. And they're very quiet, aren't they, Michael? Michael?' He had settled back down in his chair. He was miles away again. 'I'm saying they're quiet, aren't they? These Conversation Areas. Very quiet.'

'Yes, Ma. Very quiet.'

'I dare say the other yin's quiet as well. I dare say it's much the same as this yin.'

He took a long time to answer, then all he said was, 'Yes, I expect it is.'

An Invisible Man

SOMETIMES on dark winter mornings he watched them before the doors were opened, pressing their hands and faces against the glass, a plague of moths wanting in to the light. But you couldn't look at them like that, as an invading swarm. To do the job, you had to get in among them, make yourself invisible. You had to blend in, pretend to be one of them, but you also had to observe them, you had to see the hand slipping the 'Game Boy' into the sleeve. Kids wore such loose clothes nowadays, baggy jeans and jogging tops two sizes too big for them. It was the fashion, but it meant they could hide their plunder easily. You had to watch the well-dressed gentlemen as well – the Crombie and the briefcase could conceal a fortune in luxury items. When it came down to it, you were a spy.

He was in the Food Hall and they were rushing around him. He picked up a wire basket and strolled through the vegetables, doing his best to look interested in a packet of

Continental Salad, washed and ready to use. It was easy to stop taking anything in and let the shopping and the shoplifting happen around you, a blur, an organism, an animal called The Public. The Public was all over the shop: poking its nose into everything; trying on the clean new underwear; squirting the testers on its chin, on its wrists, behind its ears; wriggling its fingers into the gloves; squeezing its warm, damp feet into stiff, new shoes; tinkering with the computers; thumbing the avocados.

He was watching a grey-haired lady dressed in a sagging blue raincoat, probably in her sixties, doing exactly that. The clear blue eyes, magnified by thick lenses, looked permanently shocked. A disappointed mouth, darkened by a plum-coloured lipstick, floundered in a tight net of wrinkles. There was something in her movements that was very tense, yet she moved slowly, as if she had been stunned by some very bad news.

She put down the avocados – three of them, packaged in polythene – as if she'd just realised what they were and that she didn't need them. He followed her as she made her way to the express pay-point and took her place in the queue. He stacked his empty basket and waited on the other side of the cashpoints, impersonating a bewildered husband waiting for the wife he'd lost sight of. He watched her counting her coins from a small black purse. The transaction seemed to fluster her, as if she might not have enough money to pay for the few things she'd bought. A tin of lentil soup. An individual chicken pie. One solitary tomato. Maybe she did need the avocados – or something else.

The pay-point wasn't the obvious place to catch shop-lifters, so they used it. It was like declaring something when you went through customs, in the hope that the real contraband would go unnoticed. Or offering a small sin at confession, hoping that it would distract God from his ferocious omniscience. An amateur tactic. It was easy to catch someone with a conscience, someone who wanted to be caught.

He ambled behind her to the escalator down to Kitchen and Garden. When she came off the escalator, she waited at the bottom, as if not sure where to find what she was looking for. He moved away from her to the saucepans and busied himself opening up a three-tiered vegetable steamer, then he put the lid back on hastily to follow her to the gardening equipment. She moved past the lawn-mowers and the sprinklers until she came to a display of seed packets.

It wasn't often that you had this kind of intuition about somebody and it turned out to be right, but as soon as he saw her looking at the seeds, he was certain she was going to steal them. He moved closer to her, picked up a watering can and weighed it in his hand, as if this was somehow a way of testing it, then he saw her dropping packet after packet into the bag. He followed her to the door and outside, then he put his hand on her shoulder. When she turned round he showed her his i.d. Already she was shaking visibly. Her red-veined cheeks had taken on a hectic colour and tears loomed behind her outraged blue eyes.

'Please,' she said, 'arrest me. Before I do something worse.'

He took her back inside and they made the long journey to the top of the store in silence. For the last leg of it he took her through Fabrics – wondering if they might be taken for a couple, a sad old couple shopping together in silence – and up the back staircase so that he wouldn't have to march her through Admin.

It was depressing to unlock the door of his cubbyhole, switch the light on and see the table barely big enough to hold his kettle and his tea things, the one upright chair, the barred window looking out on a fire-escape and the wall-mounted telephone. He asked her to take the packets of seeds out of her bag and put them on the table. She did so, and the sight of the packets, with their gaudy coloured photographs of flowers, made her clench her hand into a fist.

He told her to take a seat while he called security, but when he turned away from her she let out a thin wail that made him recoil from the phone. She had both her temples between her hands, as if afraid her head might explode. She let out another shrill wail. It ripped out of her like something wild kept prisoner for years. It seemed to make the room shrink around them.

'Now now, no noise please,' he said, like a dentist who'd just drilled into a nerve. He cursed himself inwardly for bringing her here alone – he should have collected a security guard on the way. Now he was on his own with her in the cubbyhole and she was wailing. If the people in Admin heard, it might be open to all sorts of interpretation. His job was under threat as it was, what with the security guards and the new surveillance cameras.

She wailed again – a raw outpouring of anger and loss. Christ, he had to get her out of here. He stooped over her and reached out to take one of her hands away from her head, then he thought better of touching her at all. His hand hovered over her as he spoke.

'Look, you don't seem like a habitual shoplifter. . .'

She blurted out that she'd never stolen anything in her life before, but it was hard to make out the words because she was sobbing and coughing at the same time, her meagre body shuddering as if an invisible man had taken her by the shoulders and was shaking her violently.

'I'm sure it was just absent-mindedness. You intended to pay for these. . .' He motioned with a hand to the scattered packets of seeds on the table, but she was having none of it.

'No, I stole them. I don't even like gardening. . .' The words came out in spurts between her coughs and sobs but there was no stopping her now that she'd started. 'It's over-grown, weeds everywhere. It was him who did it. He was mad about his garden. He spent all his time, morning till night, out in all bloody weathers. . .'

He let her talk. Her husband had been obsessed with his garden. It had been his way of getting away – from her, from everyone and everything. He'd withdrawn from the world into his flowering shrubs and geraniums. She hardly saw him, and when he'd died all there was left of him was his garden. Now the weeds were taking over. When she'd seen the seed packets, with their pictures of Dahlias and Pansies and Rhododendrons . . . it made a kind of sense. Why had she stolen them rather than pay for them? He should have known better than to ask. He got the whole story of her financial hardship now that she was on her own, including the cost of the funeral. It was an expensive business, dying.

When she'd finished, she fished a small white handker-chief from her coat pocket to wipe the tears from her eyes. It was the way she did this that reminded him of his mother, the way she had to move her glasses out of the way to get the handkerchief to her eyes. He told her to go home. She looked up at him in surprise, then clutched the handles of her bag, realising she should get out while the going was good. When she stood up her blue eyes were alert with curiosity.

'Why are you doing this?'

'I don't know.'

He had made thieves of so many people. But this one reminded him of his mother. He absolved her with a wave of his hand. Still she made a fuss of thanking him, reaching up to touch his collar. When she'd gone, he noticed the crumpled handkerchief on the floor and bent down to pick it up.

He had stepped into the lift and pressed the button for the ground floor before he realised that the lights weren't working. The doors hissed together and he was alarmed to be shut inside a box of night. He crossed himself without thinking, although he hadn't done so for years. He heard the machinery of the lift working – a slight gasp of the hydraulics he'd never noticed before – then he began to descend slowly through the darkness. He imagined that the lift was his coffin and he was descending into the earth. Then he wondered why they didn't bury people upright, what with cemetery space being at a premium. When his mother had died, hadn't he had to take out a personal loan to cover the funeral and the cost of the plot? As the woman had said, it was an expensive business.

The lift came to a halt, the doors slid apart, but no one was waiting to get in. He looked out at Lingerie. From the crowd of people shambling around the counters rose a line of perfect legs sheathed in stockings and tights, their toes pointing at the roof. Above them the elegant models stood on their plinths, dressed in camisoles and negligees, averting their eyeless faces like disdainful idols.

Some of the creations in there were unbelievable. They were designed to tempt men, so it made sense to put them on the same floor as Menswear. He'd apprehended one man, about his own age, respectable in his choice of casual wear, greying at the sides and balding on top, trying to cram an expensive Gossard scarlet basque into his inside pocket. He'd wanted to buy it – for his wife, he'd said at first, then had admitted later, when he'd got him in the cubbyhole, that it was for his mistress – but he'd felt too embarrassed to take it to a pay-point and hand it over to be wrapped. He'd begged him to let him off – poor man, in his Yves Saint Laurent polo shirt. Maybe not so poor. He'd probably get off with a small fine or an admonishment, and although he was in his fifties, he had a mistress – one who would wear a scarlet basque.

The doors hissed together and he was shut in with the darkness again. She hadn't wanted to be cremated, in case the soul turned out to be located in the Hypothalamus, or some other part of the body. She'd had some funny notions that way. She'd believed in an afterlife, having been brought up a good Catholic, but in her later life – maybe because of him, because he'd turned his back on the priesthood – she'd stopped caring what form the afterlife might take. Heaven or reincarnation – she'd settle for either. In the hospice, she had accepted the services of the priest, the vicar and the visiting humanist, keeping her options open. If there had been a rabbi and a Buddhist coming round, she would have signed up with them too. With more eagerness, maybe, because they would be new to her, and she had always believed in anything she didn't know about, as if the very fact that she hadn't heard of it gave it credence, so complete was her humility.

There was the gasp of the hydraulics as the lift was released and he felt himself sinking again. It all seemed to take much longer in the dark.

He had watched her body shrink into itself like a withering fruit, but she'd gone on smiling, determined to keep up appearances. He remembered the last demented thing she had said to him as she lay there, scandalised by her own condition, about her bedside locker being bugged, about the other patients and their visitors being spies. Then she'd urged him to eat the fruit in the bowl.

'Have a banana, son,' she'd said, then died.

He remembered the moment when the faint pressure of her hand on his had faded away completely, leaving a dead hand there with no touch left in it.

None of it had made any sense to him then, but it did now as he was lowered slowly through the darkness. She'd died in public, in a ward full of strangers. They weren't involved with her death, but they were watching it. She was right – they were spies. And her bedside locker, with its fruit and its flowers and its cards bearing tactfully optimistic messages – in a way it had been bugged.

He hadn't eaten the fruit, but maybe he should have. She had wanted him to, but he'd remembered reading, at the Seminary, about the sin-eaters, the people in ancient times who were hired at funerals to eat beside the corpse and so take upon themselves the sins of the dead.

If they buried people upright the graves would have to be deeper, of course, but they'd take up less horizontal space, which was what you were paying for, in the end. At the same time, the thought of people being buried in a standing position was ridiculous. It made him think of the dead standing in a queue, waiting to be served. They had chosen, and now they

Selected Stories

would have to pay the price. Think of the inscriptions: 'He was, and still is, a fine, upstanding citizen.'

He could hear a tannoyed announcement passing from under his feet to above his head – where was he? Surely he'd reach the ground floor soon. Or maybe he'd gone past the ground floor and he was on his way back down to the Food Hall. The motion of the lift began to make him feel queasy, as if he'd lost control of his own movements and was part of the workings of the store. He felt as if he had been eaten and was now being slowly digested by a huge machine.

The lift came to a halt at last, but the doors didn't open. Where was he? Without the illuminated numbers above the door, it was hard to tell. In a dark lift, you could be anywhere. You could be in the confessional, except that there was no one to confess to. All you had was yourself. He felt the sweat trickle from his scalp and took the crumpled handkerchief from his pocket, but instead of dabbing his brow he brought it to his lips. It tasted faintly of salt. Then he felt himself begin to travel upwards through the darkness, like a slow missile launched into the night, or a soul departing the body.

Other Books
from Argyll Publishing

The Machine Doctor
Peter Burnett

Thirsty Books ISBN:1 902831 33 0 pbk £9.99

Shortlisted **Scottish Book of the Year 2002**

'. . . an exhilarating and anarchic comedy shot through
with a withering social commentary'
Scotland on Sunday

'. . . an ambitious, multi-voiced satire on the soul-
destroying mind-numbing effects of the 21st century. . .
hilarious' **The List**

'. . . ingenious . . . it has energy and commitment, it is
funny and makes a serious point lightly' **The Herald**

The Wind in her Hands
Margaret Gillies Brown

ISBN: 1 902831 41 1 pbk £7.99

'an intriging picture of life early last century' **Caledonia**

'it never flags – the story of a strong woman'
Moray Firth Radio

'inspirational' **Press & Journal**